I0712802

THE MAGI'S APPRENTICE

David Martyn

BLUE FORGE PRESS

Port Orchard ✹ Washington

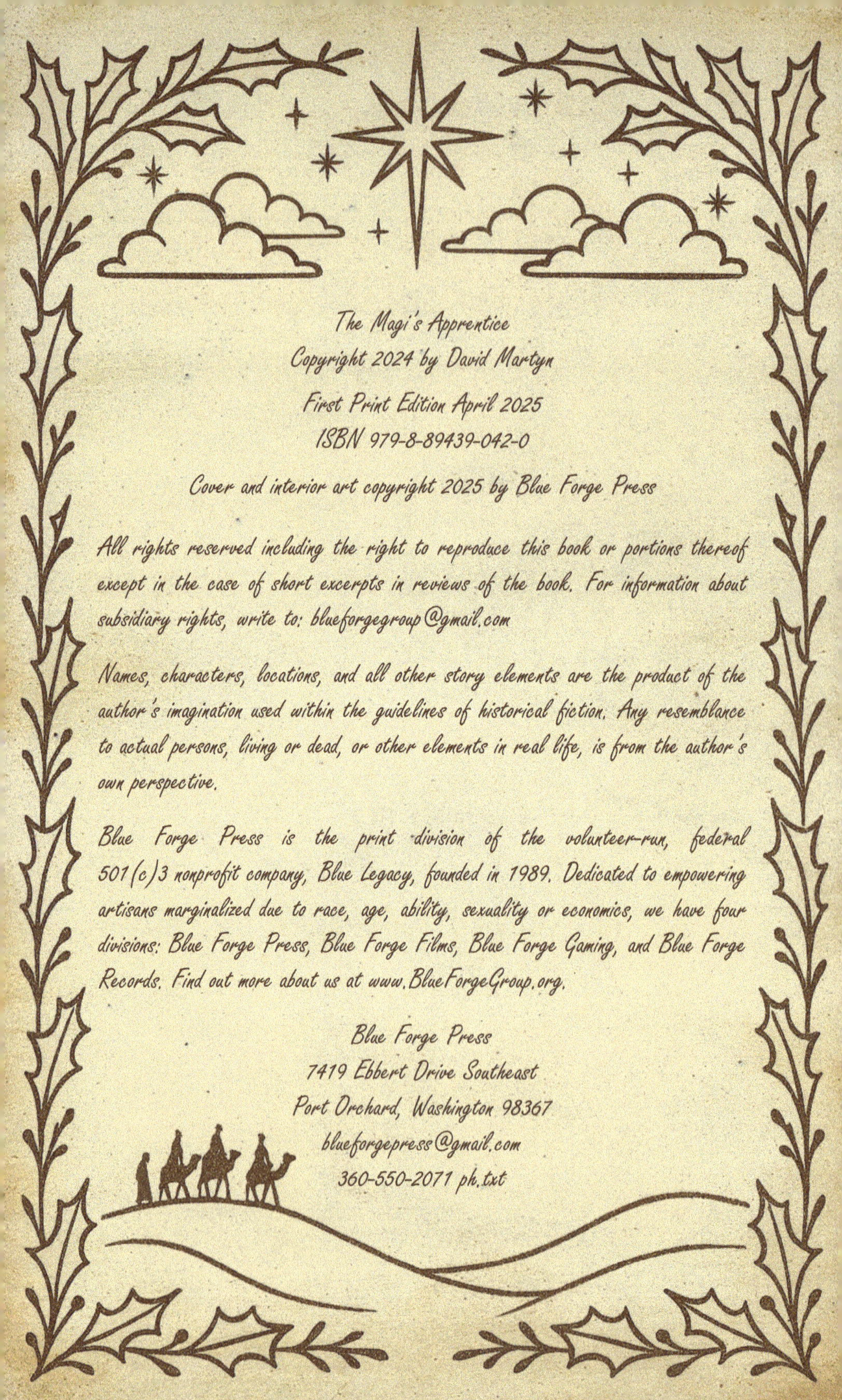

To my grandson, Callum Simonsen—

May you grow in wisdom like my young fictional hero, Salek, a seeker of wisdom.

MORE BY DAVID MARTYN

The Hall of Faith

The Praise Singer:
A Disciple of Melchizedek

The Oak of Weeping:
The Story of Isaac, Rebekah, and Deborah

The Epistle:
A Story of the Early Church

Robert Curtis Mysteries

Called Into Service

Soldiers of the King: The Bramshill Affair

Lords and Ladies: The Banqueting House Plot

For God and King: The Deadly Pamphleteer

Novellas & Short Story Collections

Huldah and the Last Righteous King

A Light in the Darkest Night

www.BlueForgePress.com

THE MAGI'S APPRENTICE

David Martyn

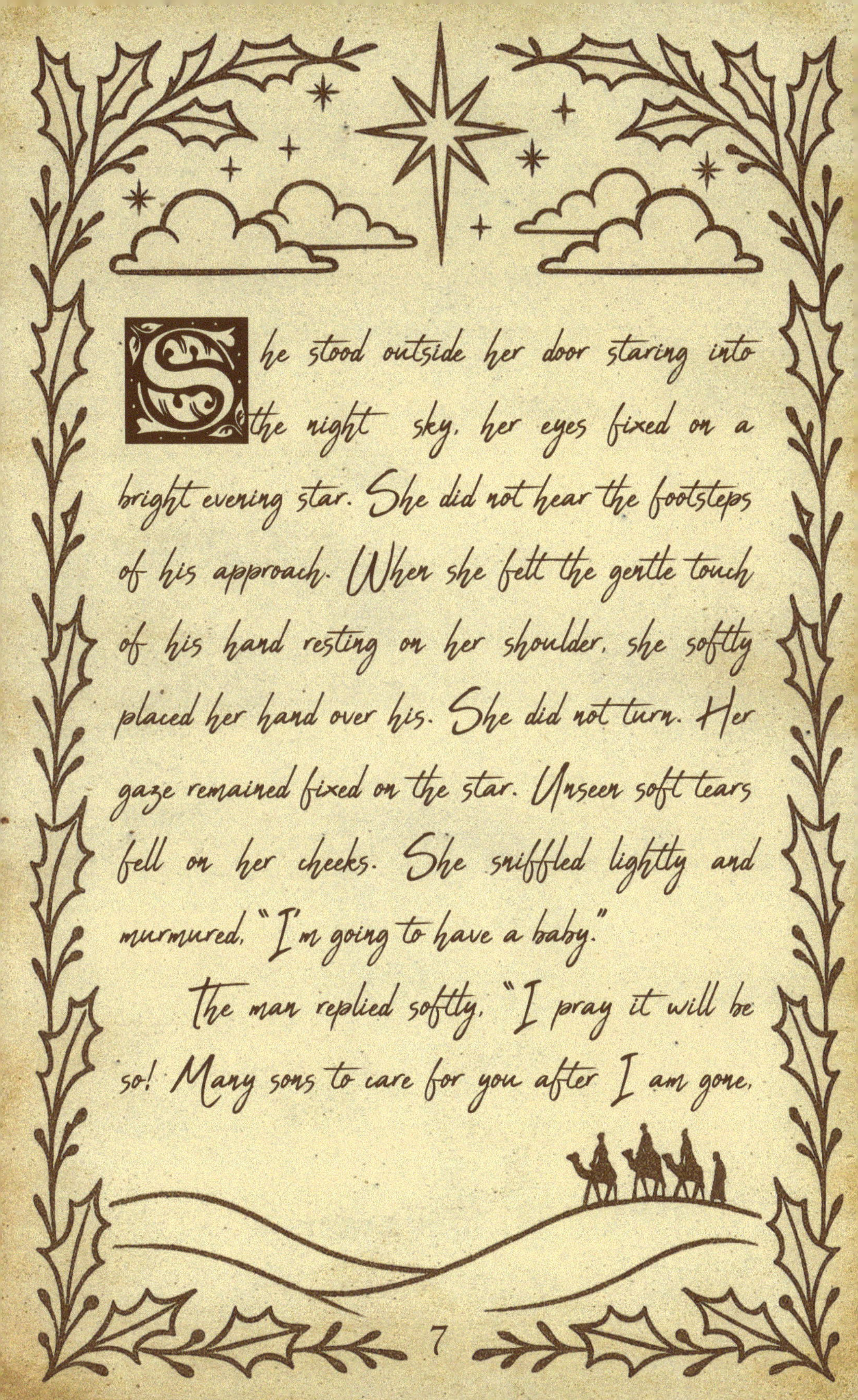

She stood outside her door staring into the night sky, her eyes fixed on a bright evening star. She did not hear the footsteps of his approach. When she felt the gentle touch of his hand resting on her shoulder, she softly placed her hand over his. She did not turn. Her gaze remained fixed on the star. Unseen soft tears fell on her cheeks. She sniffled lightly and murmured, "I'm going to have a baby."

The man replied softly, "I pray it will be so! Many sons to care for you after I am gone,

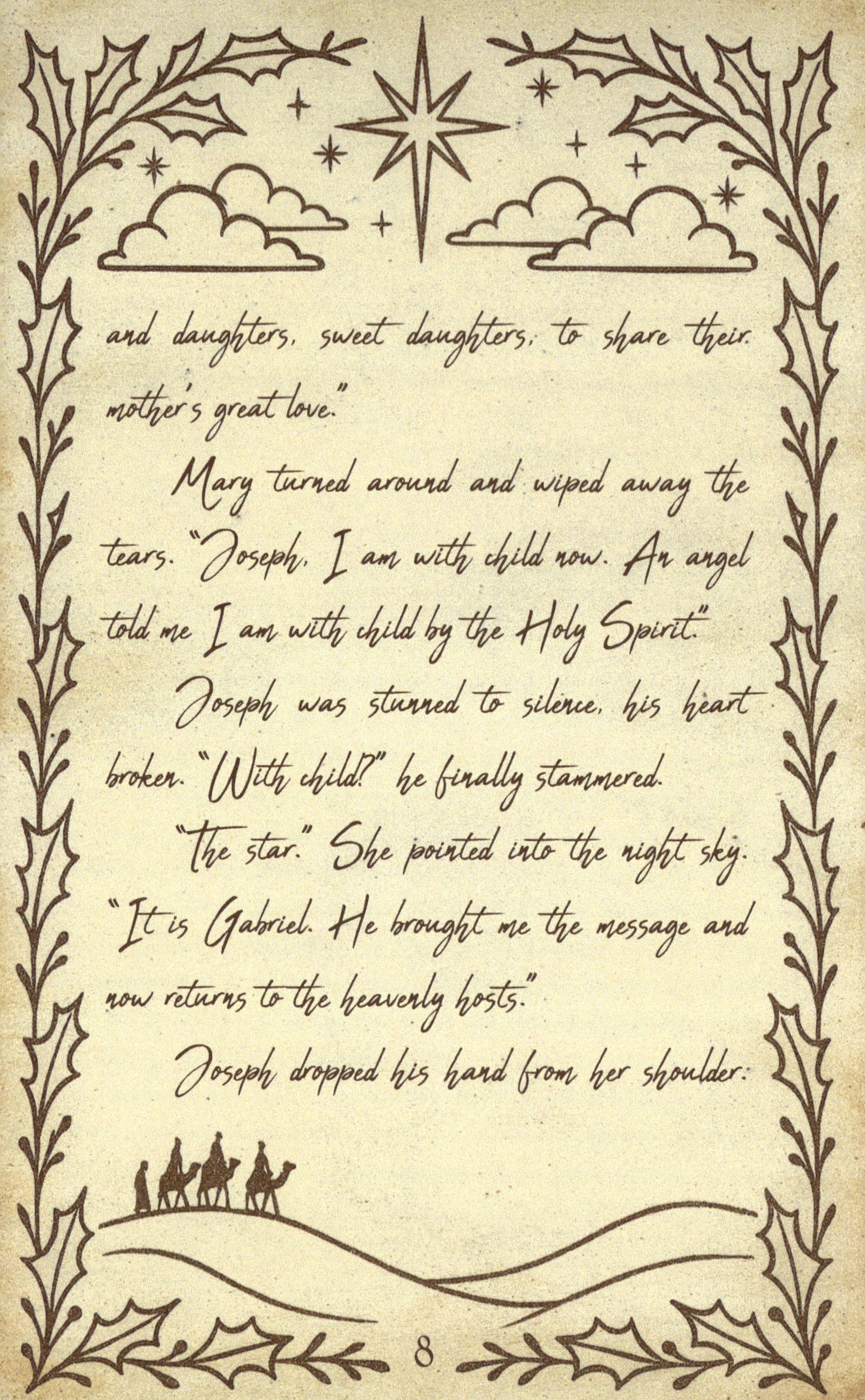

and daughters, sweet daughters, to share their mother's great love."

Mary turned around and wiped away the tears. "Joseph, I am with child now. An angel told me I am with child by the Holy Spirit."

Joseph was stunned to silence, his heart broken. "With child?" he finally stammered.

"The star." She pointed into the night sky. "It is Gabriel. He brought me the message and now returns to the heavenly hosts."

Joseph dropped his hand from her shoulder:

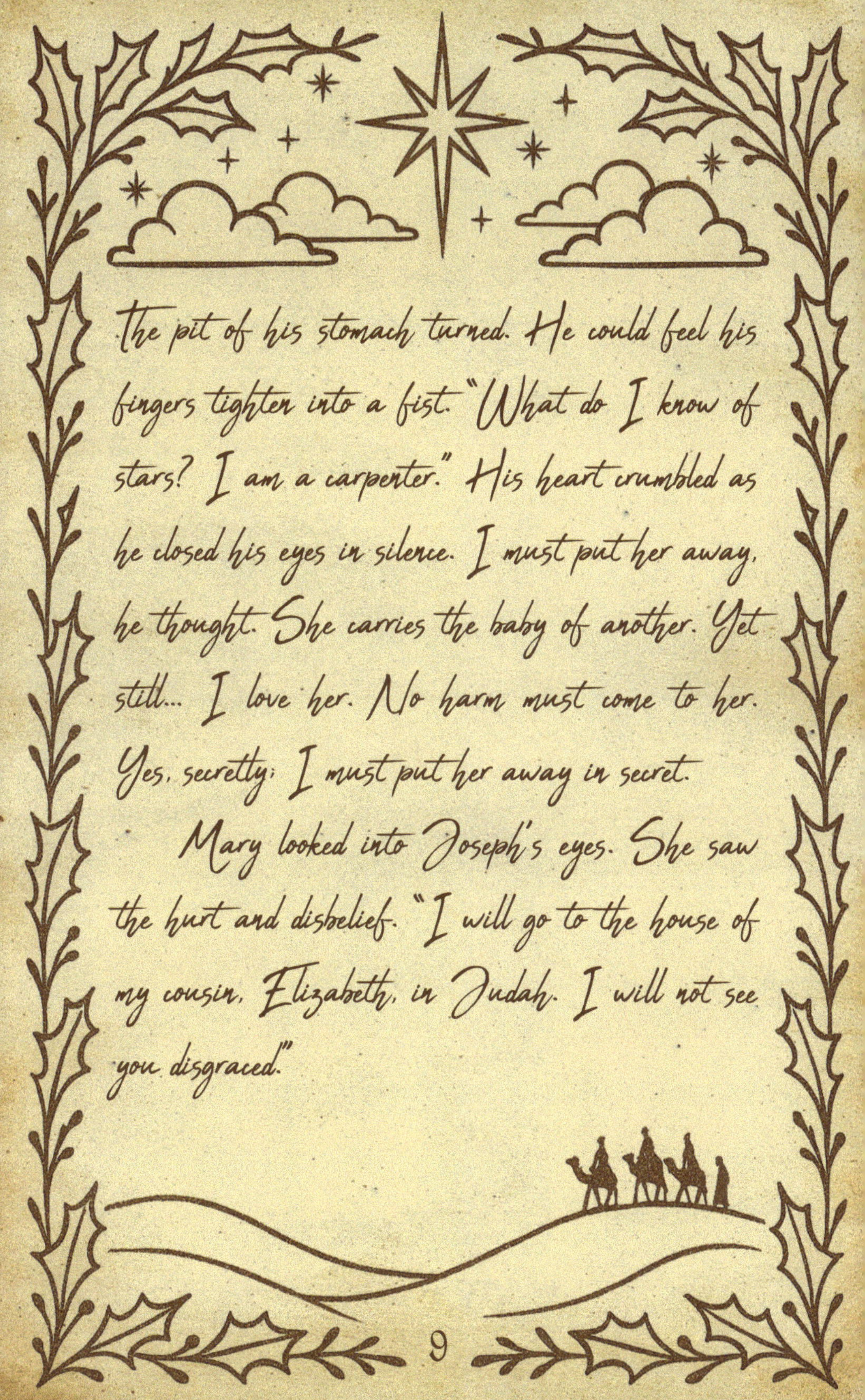

the pit of his stomach turned. He could feel his fingers tighten into a fist. "What do I know of stars? I am a carpenter." His heart crumbled as he closed his eyes in silence. I must put her away, he thought. She carries the baby of another. Yet still... I love her. No harm must come to her. Yes, secretly; I must put her away in secret.

Mary looked into Joseph's eyes. She saw the hurt and disbelief. "I will go to the house of my cousin, Elizabeth, in Judah. I will not see you disgraced."

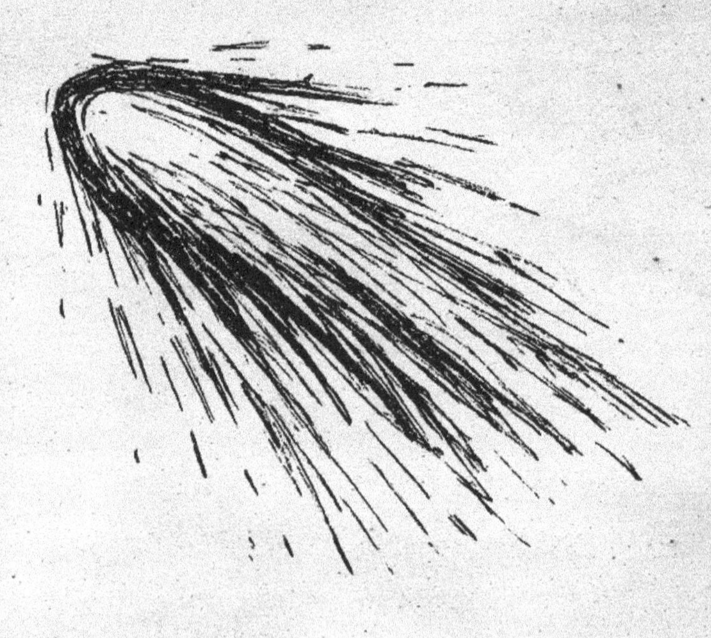

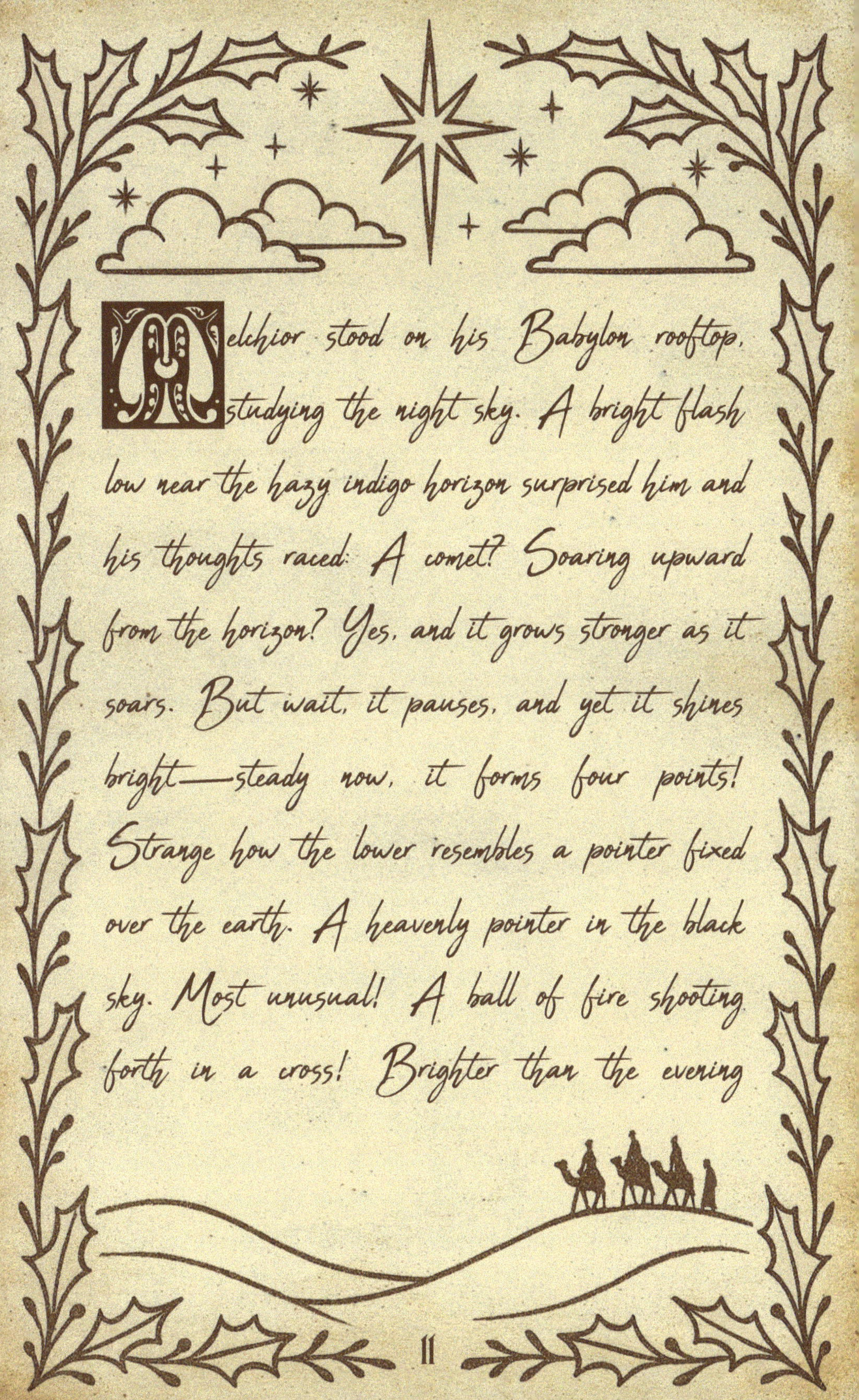

Melchior stood on his Babylon rooftop, studying the night sky. A bright flash low near the hazy indigo horizon surprised him and his thoughts raced: A comet? Soaring upward from the horizon? Yes, and it grows stronger as it soars. But wait, it pauses, and yet it shines bright—steady now, it forms four points! Strange how the lower resembles a pointer fixed over the earth. A heavenly pointer in the black sky. Most unusual! A ball of fire shooting forth in a cross! Brighter than the evening

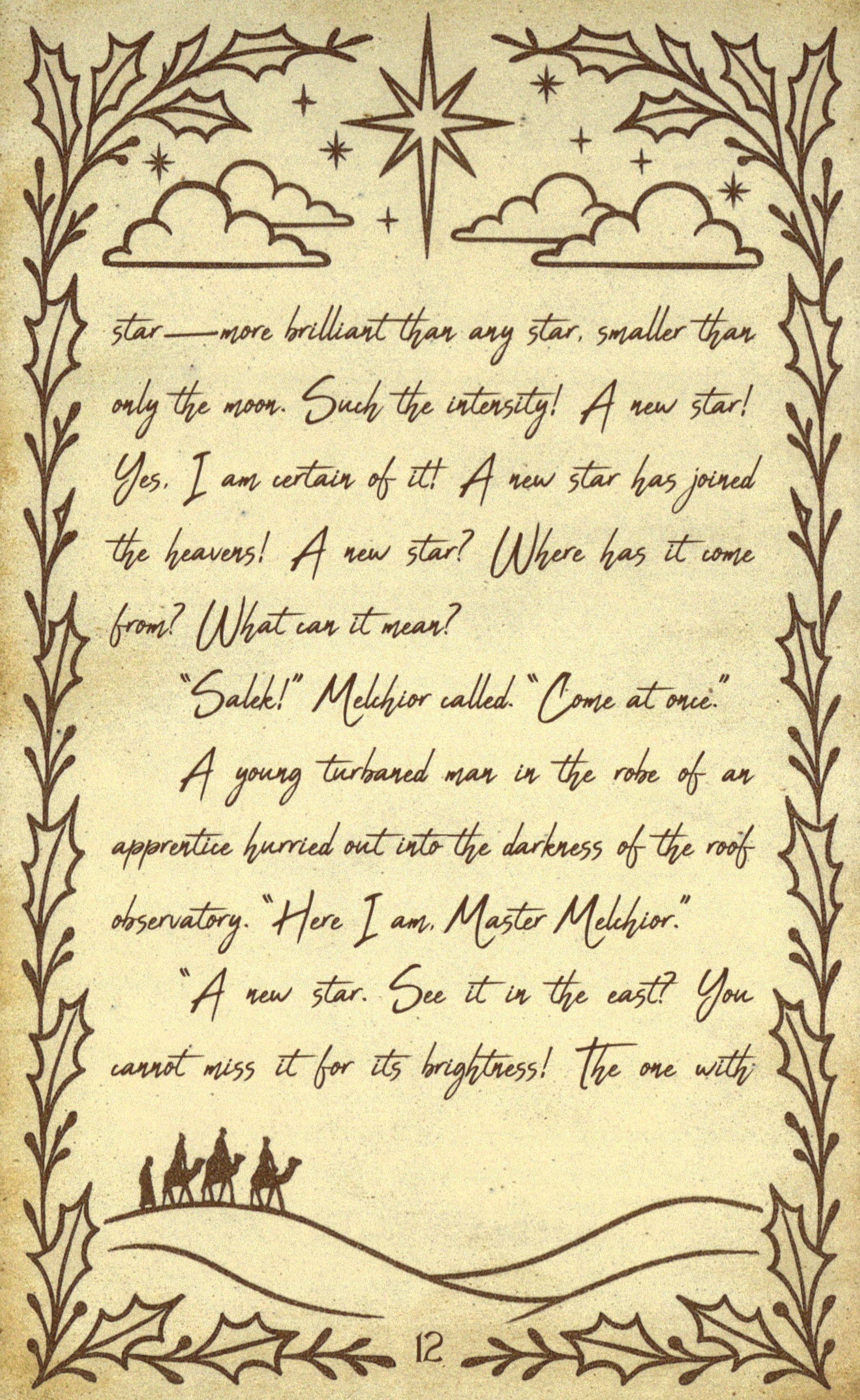

star——more brilliant than any star, smaller than only the moon. Such the intensity! A new star! Yes. I am certain of it! A new star has joined the heavens! A new star? Where has it come from? What can it mean?

"Salek!" Melchior called. "Come at once."

A young turbaned man in the robe of an apprentice hurried out into the darkness of the roof observatory. "Here I am, Master Melchior."

"A new star. See it in the east! You cannot miss it for its brightness! The one with

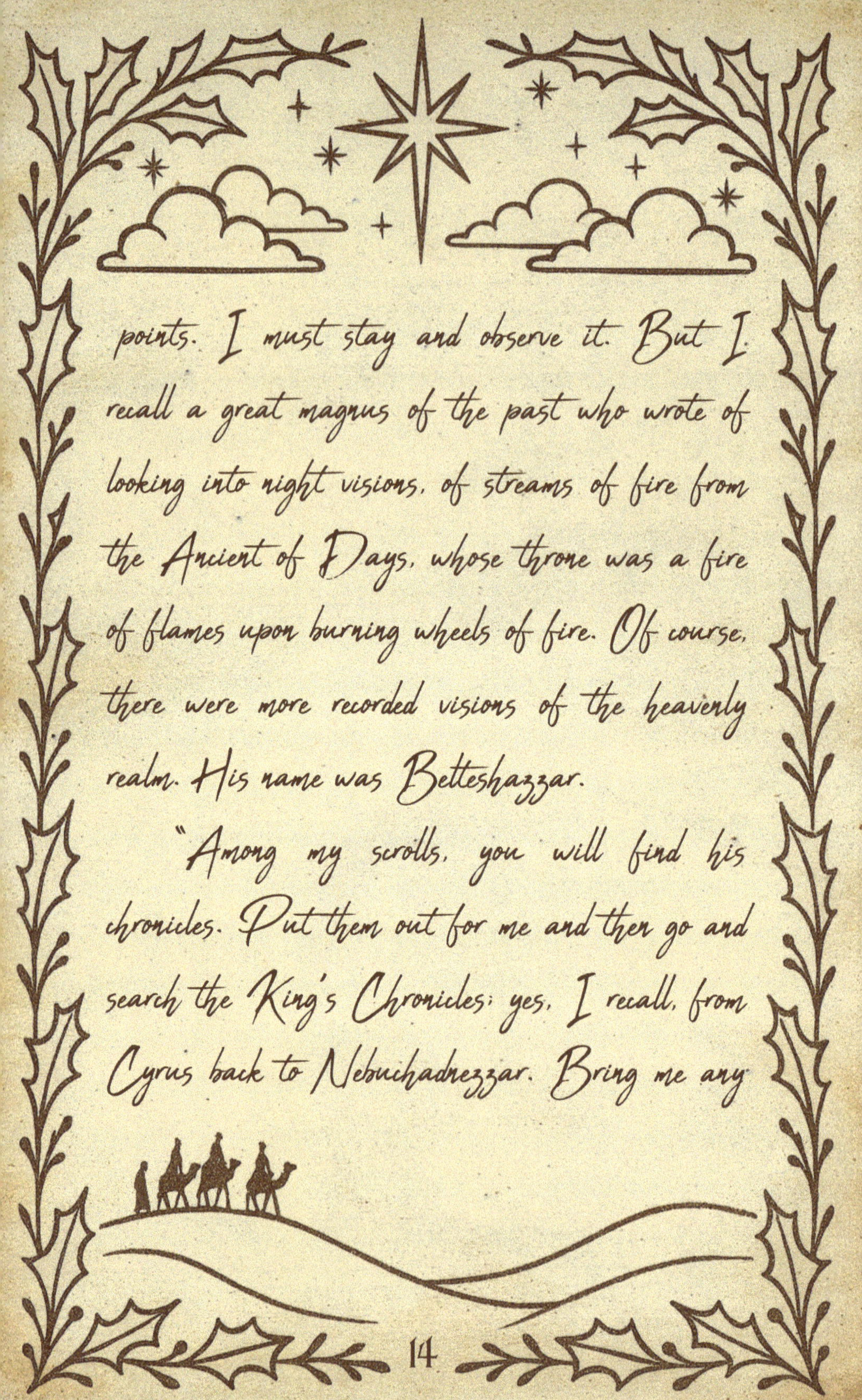

points. I must stay and observe it. But I recall a great magnus of the past who wrote of looking into night visions, of streams of fire from the Ancient of Days, whose throne was a fire of flames upon burning wheels of fire. Of course, there were more recorded visions of the heavenly realm. His name was Belteshazzar.

"Among my scrolls, you will find his chronicles. Put them out for me and then go and search the King's Chronicles; yes, I recall, from Cyrus back to Nebuchadrezzar. Bring me any

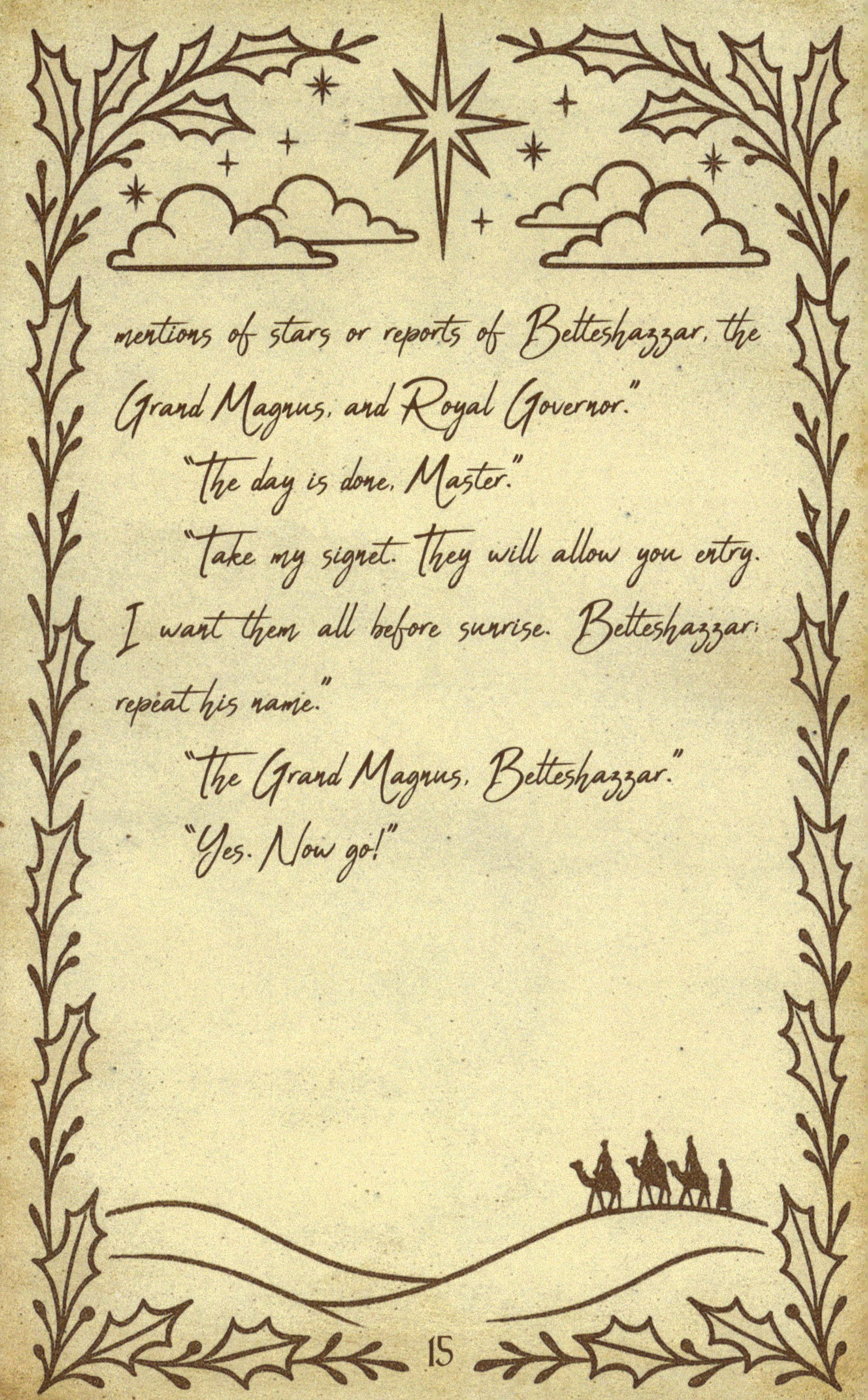

mentions of stars or reports of Betteshazzar, the Grand Magnus, and Royal Governor."

"The day is done, Master."

"Take my signet. They will allow you entry. I want them all before sunrise. Betteshazzar; repeat his name."

"The Grand Magnus, Betteshazzar."

"Yes. Now go!"

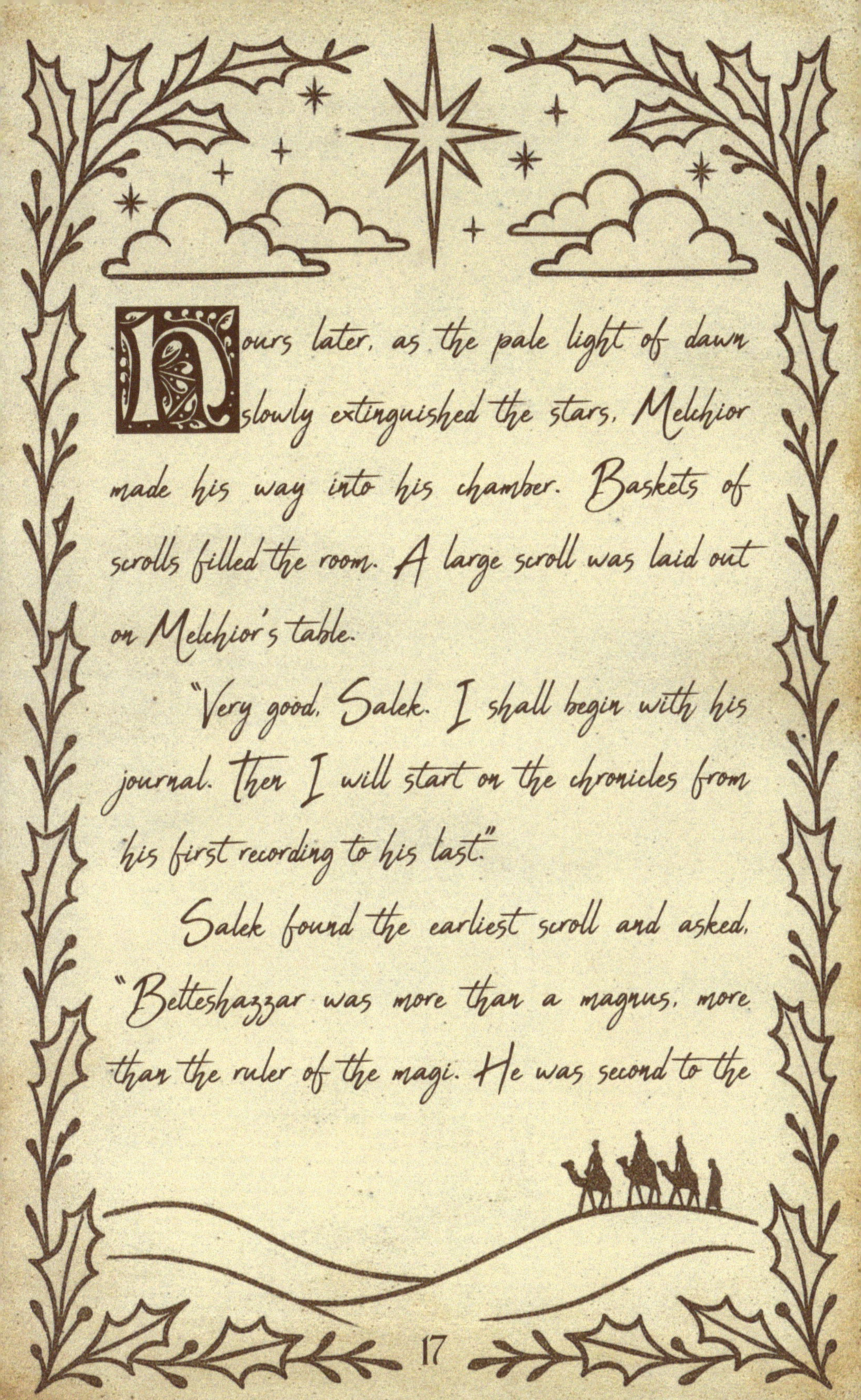

ours later, as the pale light of dawn slowly extinguished the stars, Melchior made his way into his chamber. Baskets of scrolls filled the room. A large scroll was laid out on Melchior's table.

"Very good, Salek. I shall begin with his journal. Then I will start on the chronicles from his first recording to his last."

Salek found the earliest scroll and asked, "Belteshazzar was more than a magnus, more than the ruler of the magi. He was second to the

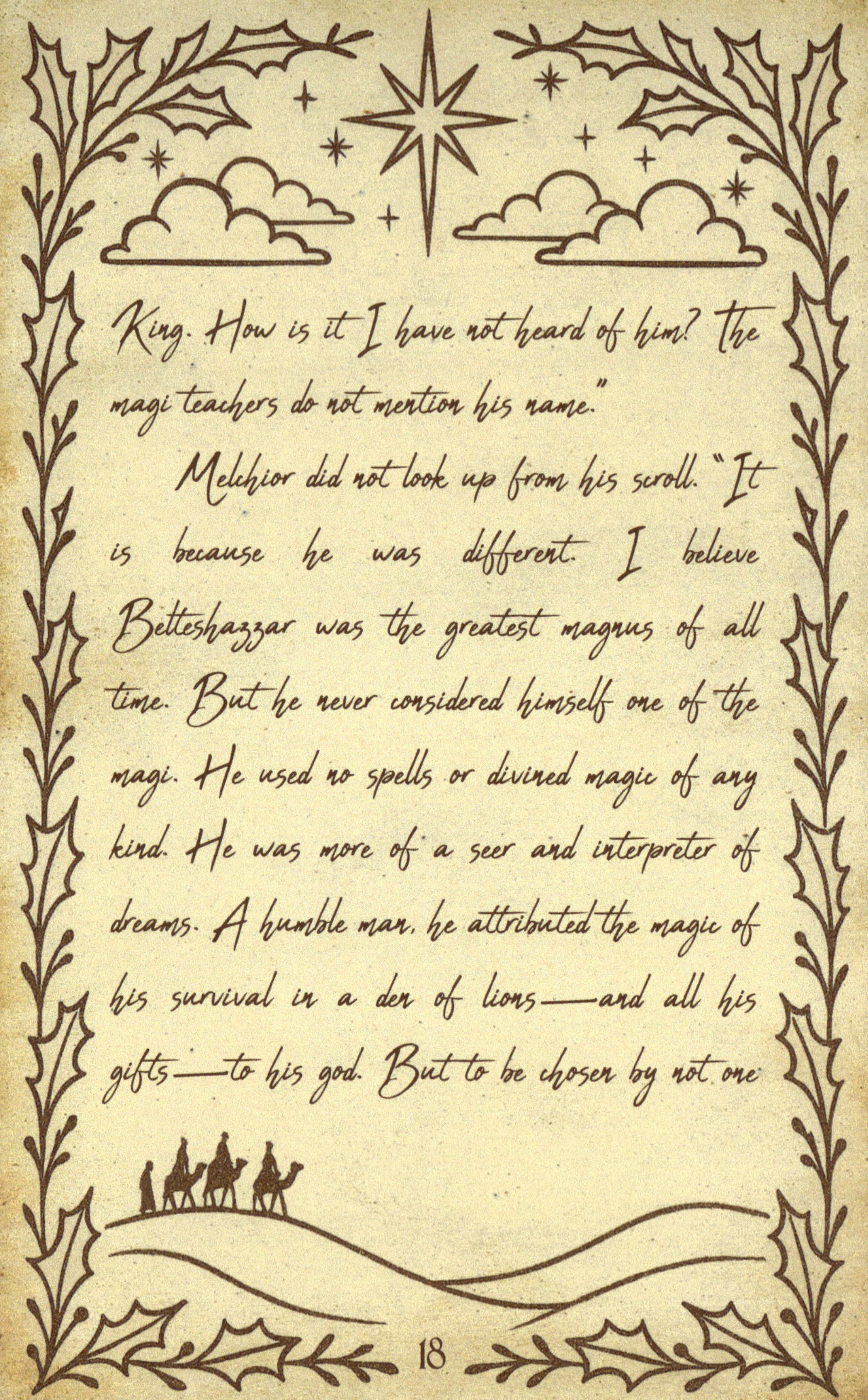

King. How is it I have not heard of him? The magi teachers do not mention his name."

Melchior did not look up from his scroll. "It is because he was different. I believe Belteshazzar was the greatest magnus of all time. But he never considered himself one of the magi. He used no spells or divined magic of any kind. He was more of a seer and interpreter of dreams. A humble man, he attributed the magic of his survival in a den of lions——and all his gifts——to his god. But to be chosen by not one

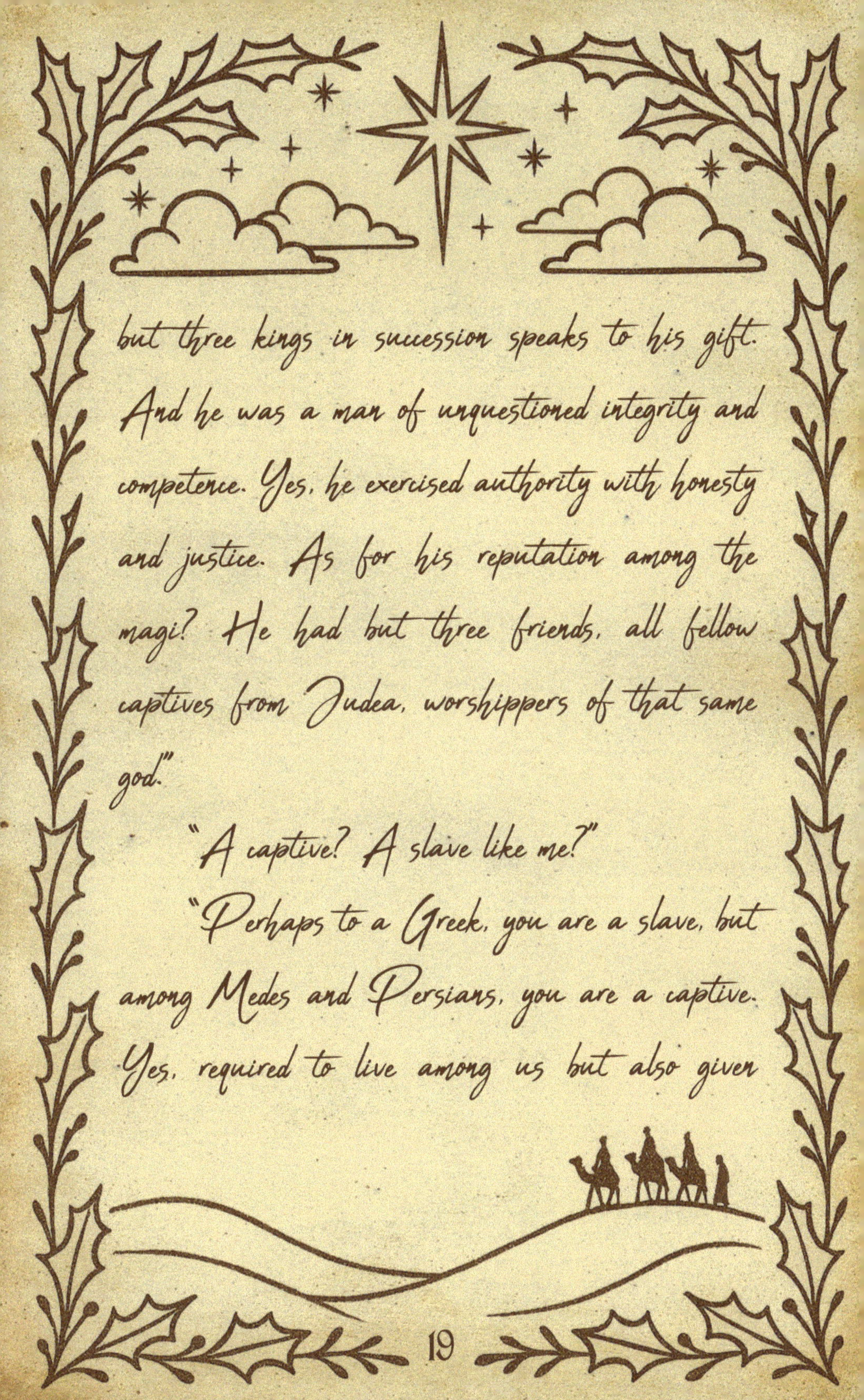

but three kings in succession speaks to his gift.
And he was a man of unquestioned integrity and
competence. Yes, he exercised authority with honesty
and justice. As for his reputation among the
magi? He had but three friends, all fellow
captives from Judea, worshippers of that same
god."

"A captive? A slave like me?"

"Perhaps to a Greek, you are a slave, but
among Medes and Persians, you are a captive.
Yes, required to live among us but also given

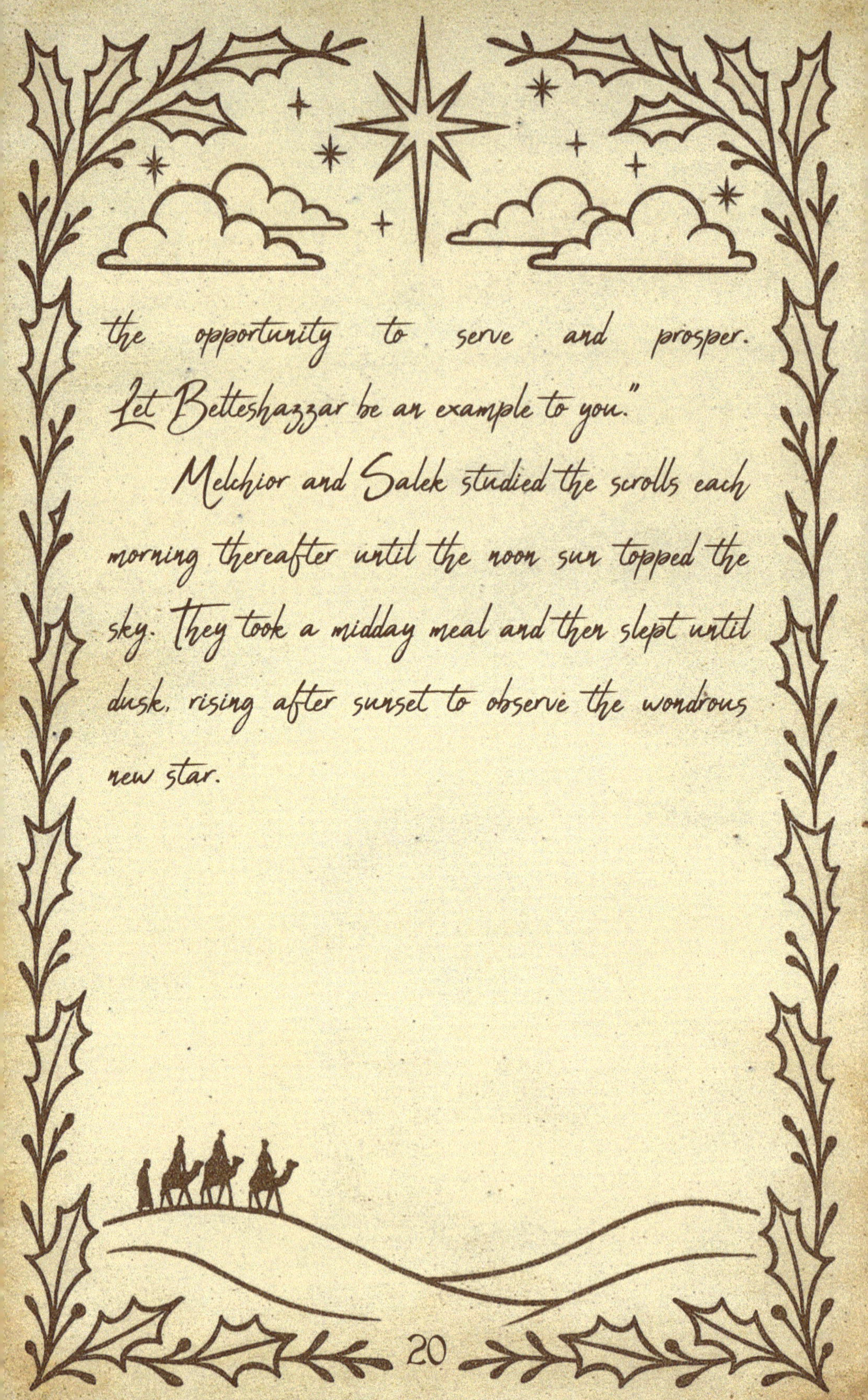

the opportunity to serve and prosper. Let Belteshazzar be an example to you."

Melchior and Salek studied the scrolls each morning thereafter until the noon sun topped the sky. They took a midday meal and then slept until dusk, rising after sunset to observe the wondrous new star.

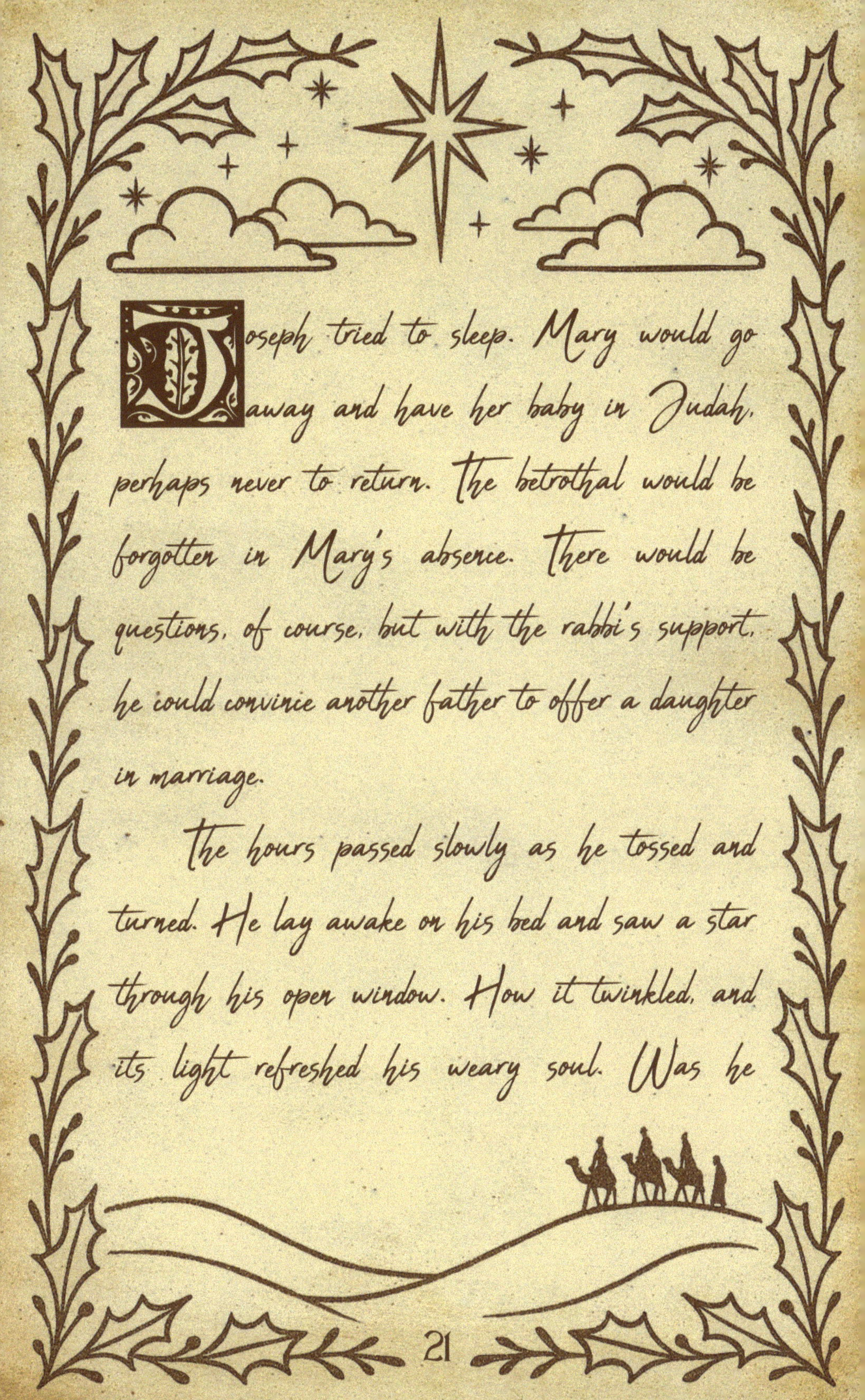

Joseph tried to sleep. Mary would go away and have her baby in Judah, perhaps never to return. The betrothal would be forgotten in Mary's absence. There would be questions, of course, but with the rabbi's support, he could convince another father to offer a daughter in marriage.

The hours passed slowly as he tossed and turned. He lay awake on his bed and saw a star through his open window. How it twinkled, and its light refreshed his weary soul. Was he

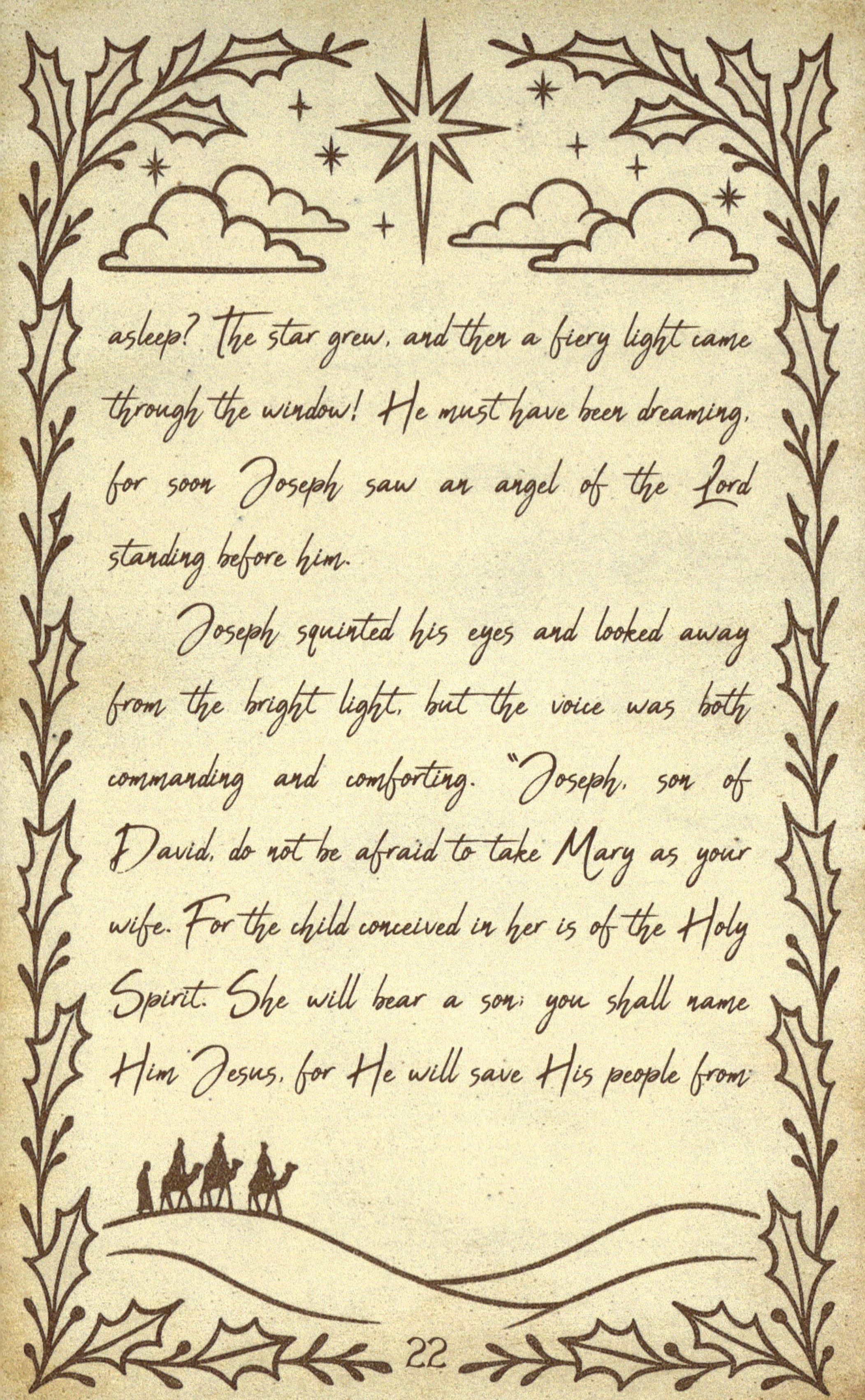

asleep? The star grew, and then a fiery light came through the window! He must have been dreaming, for soon Joseph saw an angel of the Lord standing before him.

Joseph squinted his eyes and looked away from the bright light, but the voice was both commanding and comforting. "Joseph, son of David, do not be afraid to take Mary as your wife. For the child conceived in her is of the Holy Spirit. She will bear a son; you shall name Him Jesus, for He will save His people from

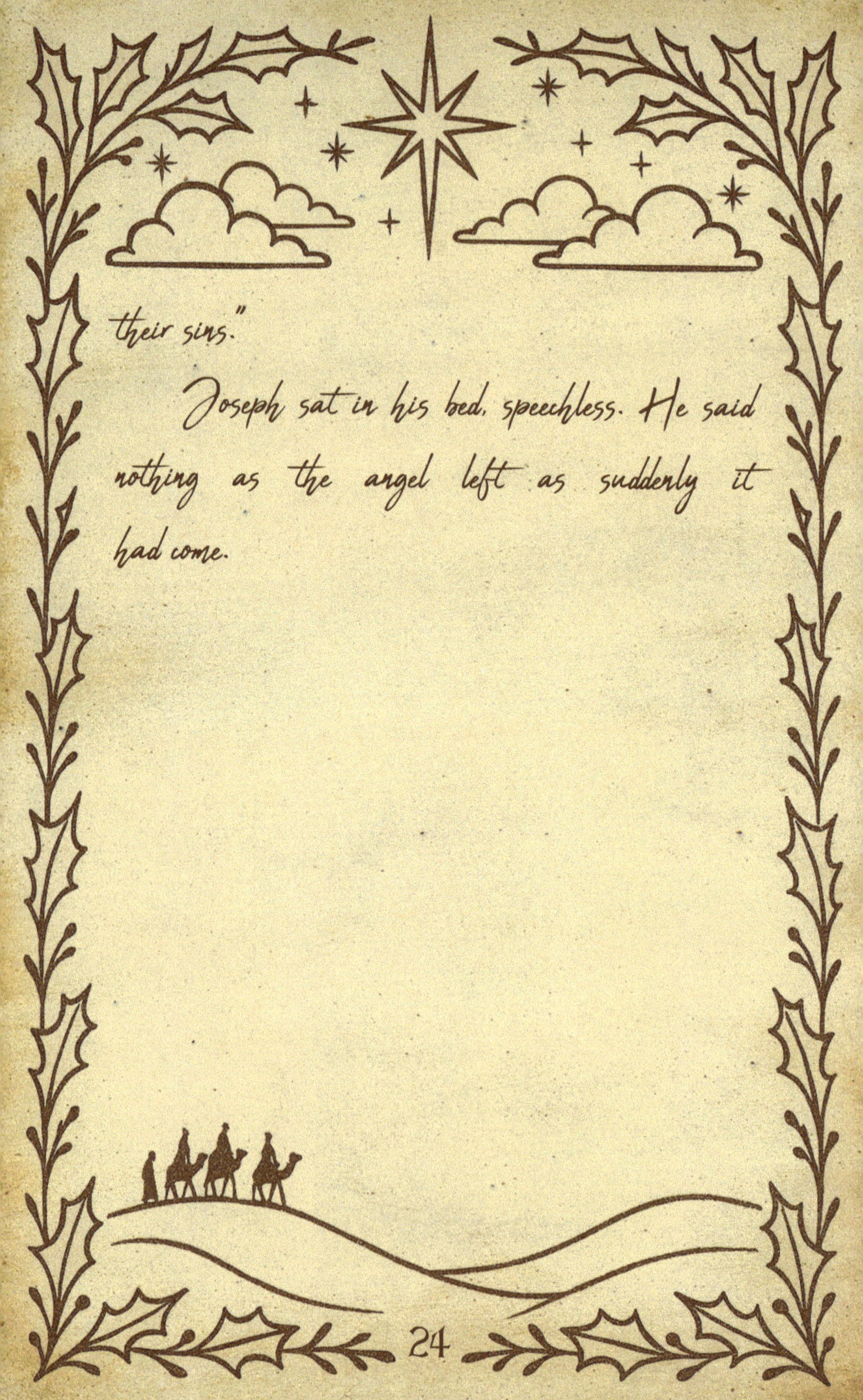

their sins."

Joseph sat in his bed, speechless. He said nothing as the angel left as suddenly it had come.

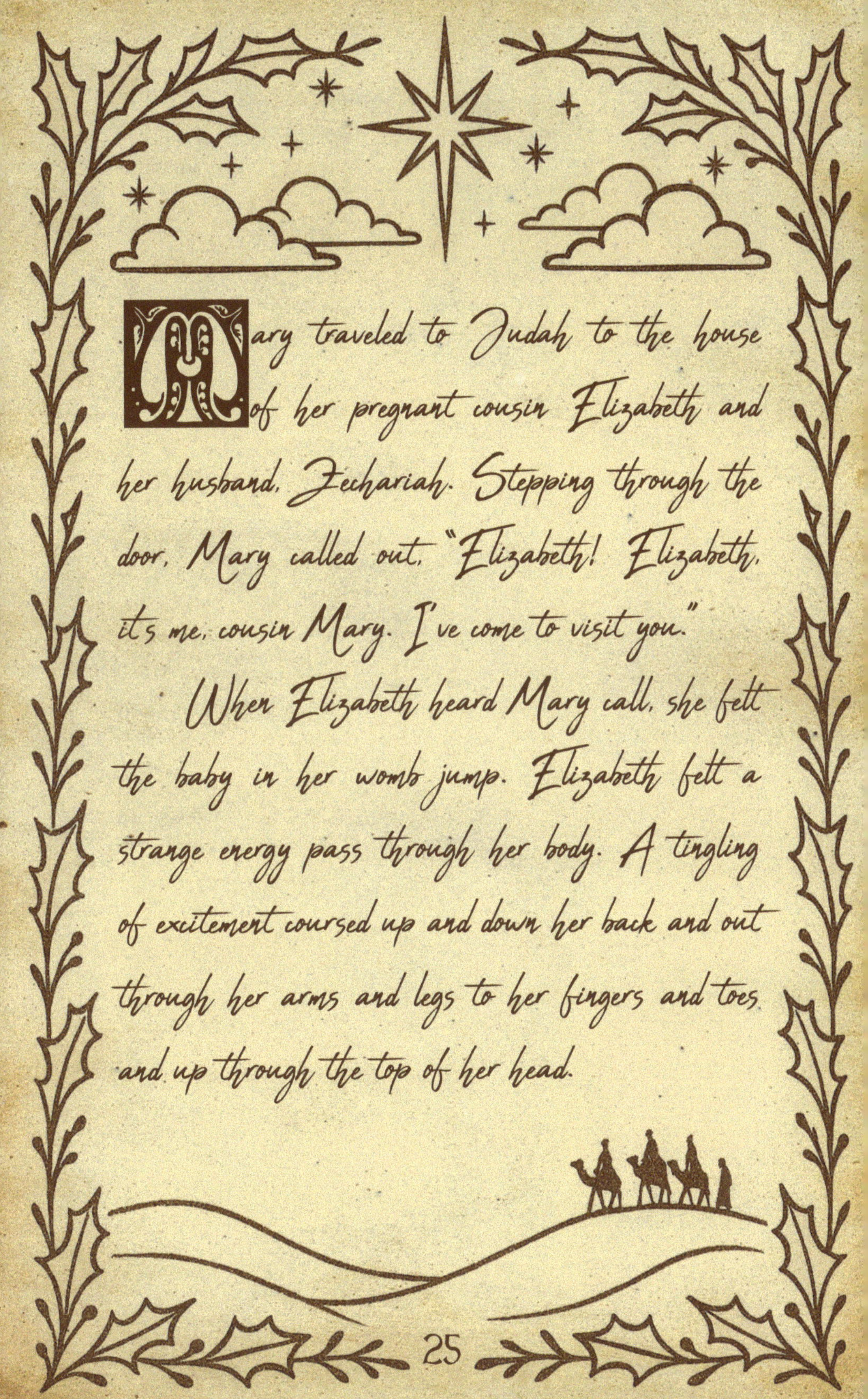

ary traveled to Judah to the house of her pregnant cousin Elizabeth and her husband, Zechariah. Stepping through the door, Mary called out, "Elizabeth! Elizabeth, it's me, cousin Mary. I've come to visit you."

When Elizabeth heard Mary call, she felt the baby in her womb jump. Elizabeth felt a strange energy pass through her body. A tingling of excitement coursed up and down her back and out through her arms and legs to her fingers and toes, and up through the top of her head.

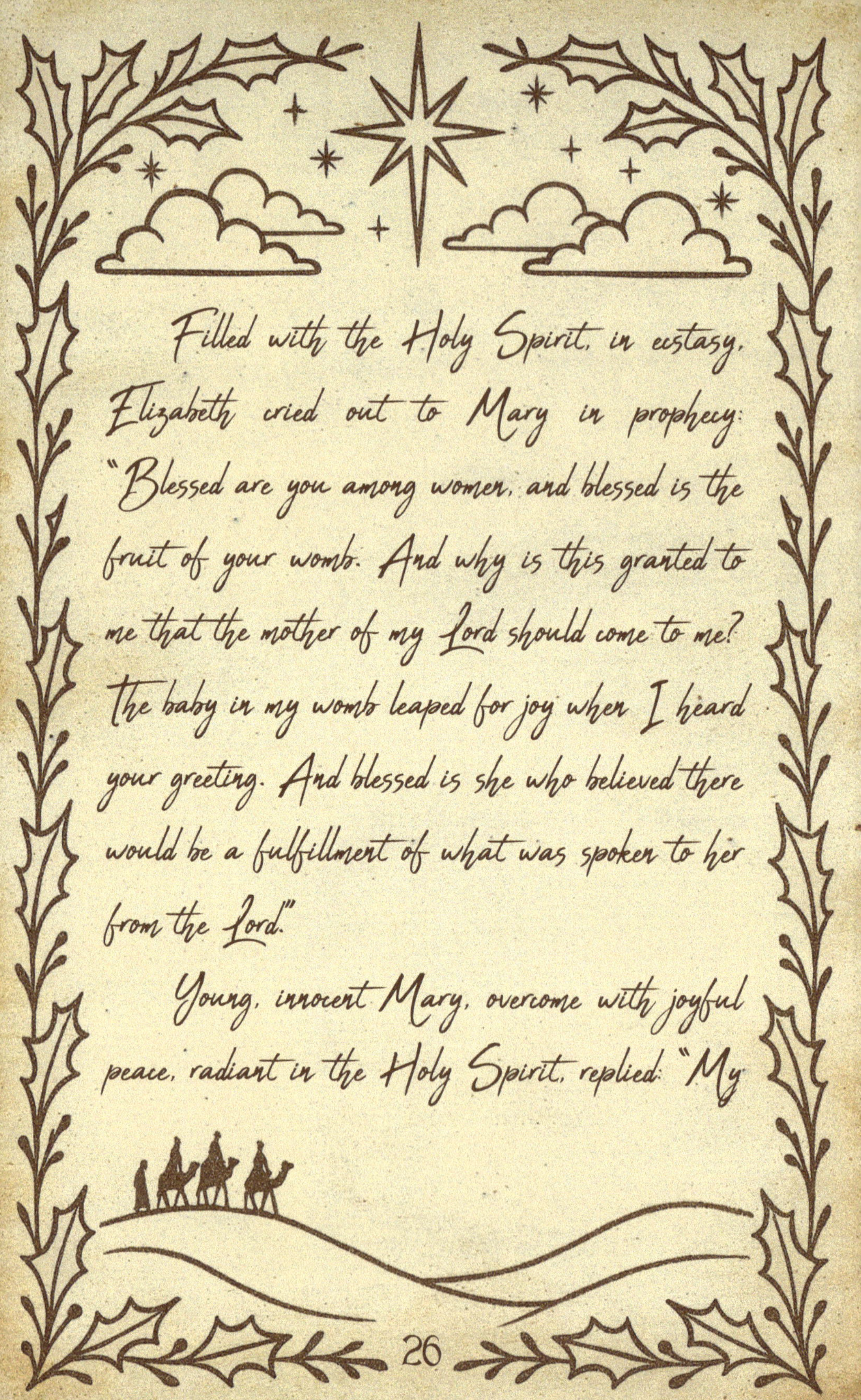

Filled with the Holy Spirit, in ecstasy, Elizabeth cried out to Mary in prophecy: "Blessed are you among women, and blessed is the fruit of your womb. And why is this granted to me that the mother of my Lord should come to me? The baby in my womb leaped for joy when I heard your greeting. And blessed is she who believed there would be a fulfillment of what was spoken to her from the Lord."

Young, innocent Mary, overcome with joyful peace, radiant in the Holy Spirit, replied: "My

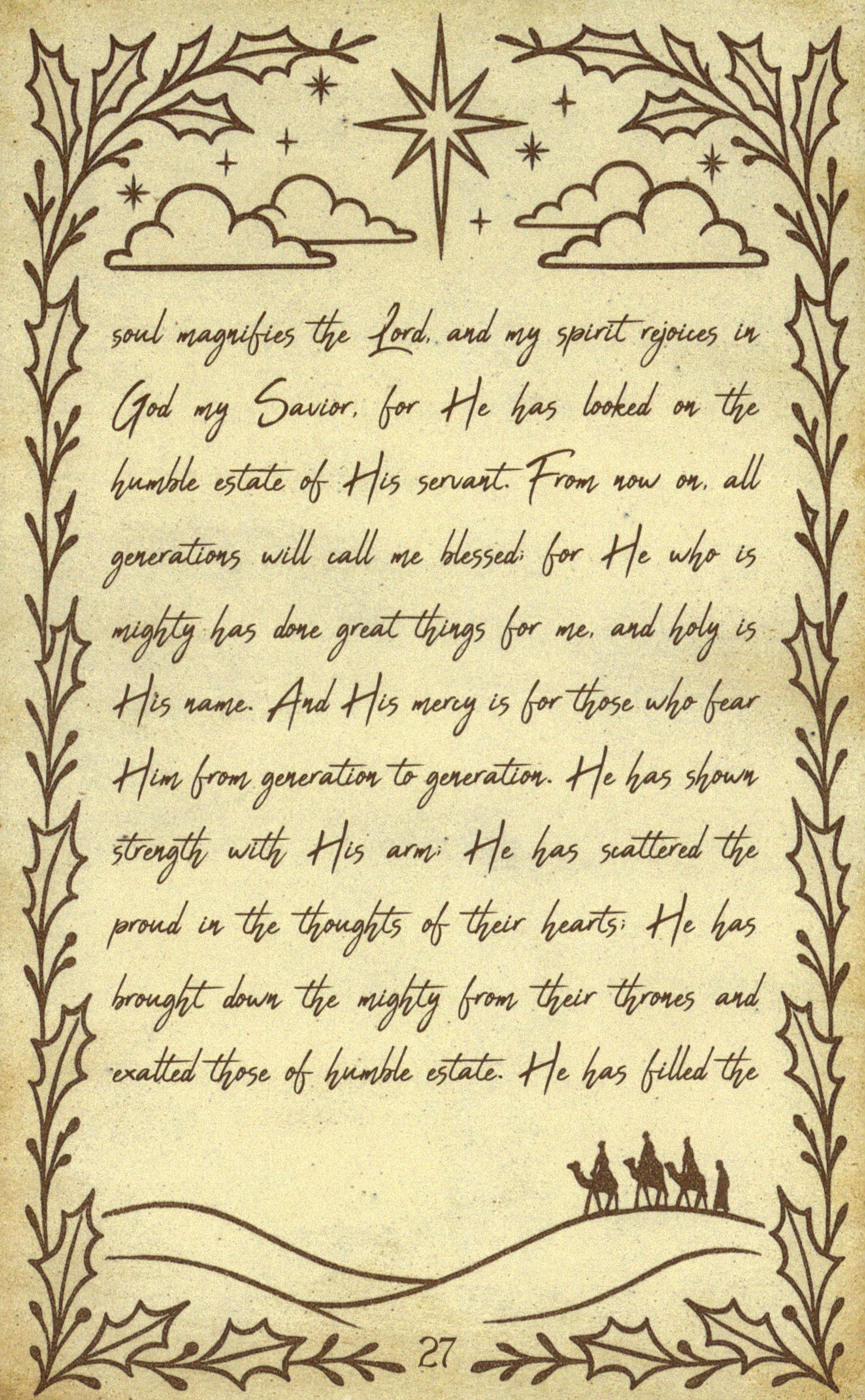
soul magnifies the Lord, and my spirit rejoices in
God my Savior, for He has looked on the
humble estate of His servant. From now on, all
generations will call me blessed; for He who is
mighty has done great things for me, and holy is
His name. And His mercy is for those who fear
Him from generation to generation. He has shown
strength with His arm; He has scattered the
proud in the thoughts of their hearts; He has
brought down the mighty from their thrones and
exalted those of humble estate. He has filled the

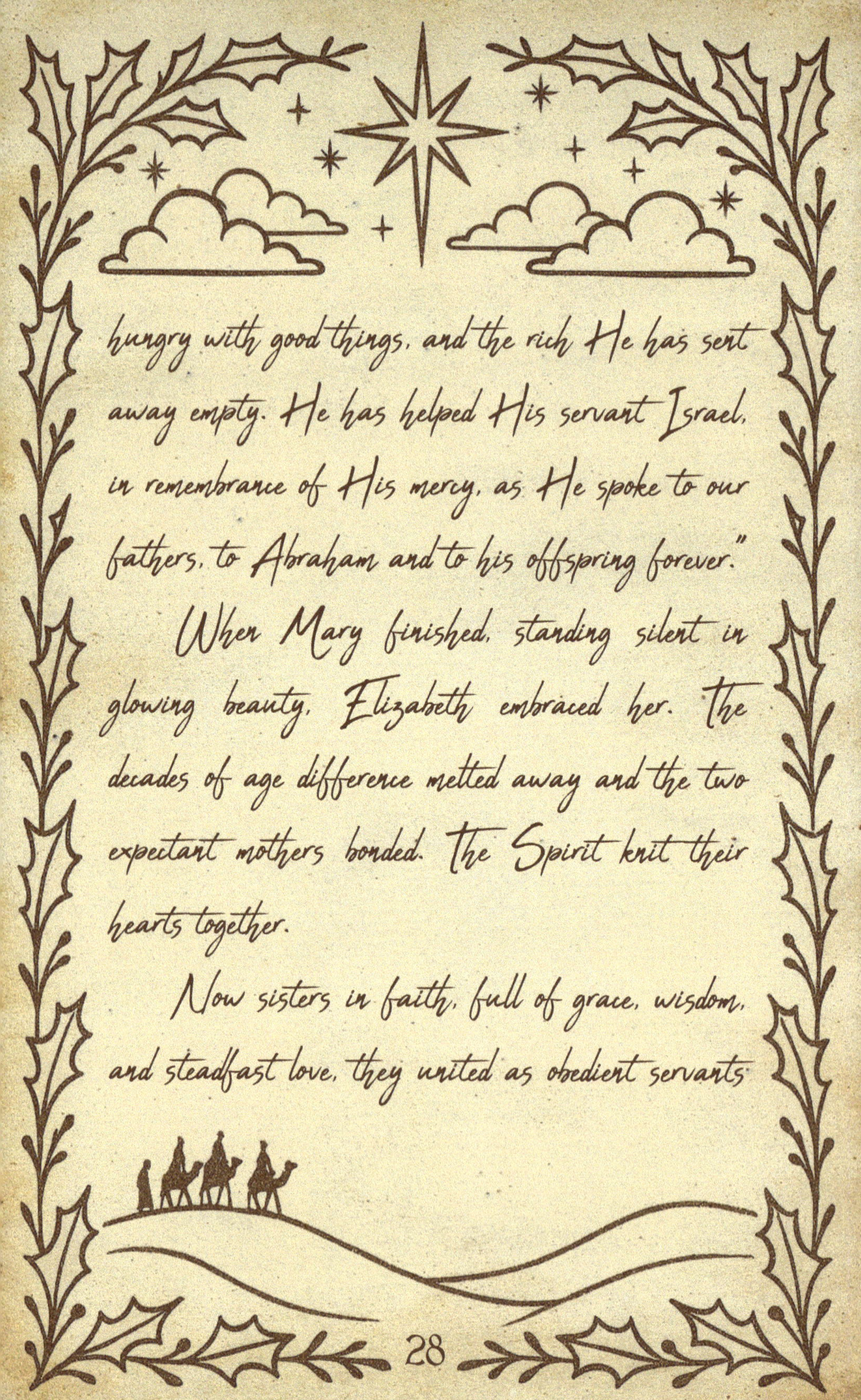

hungry with good things, and the rich He has sent away empty. He has helped His servant Israel, in remembrance of His mercy, as He spoke to our fathers, to Abraham and to his offspring forever."

When Mary finished, standing silent in glowing beauty, Elizabeth embraced her. The decades of age difference melted away and the two expectant mothers bonded. The Spirit knit their hearts together.

Now sisters in faith, full of grace, wisdom, and steadfast love, they united as obedient servants

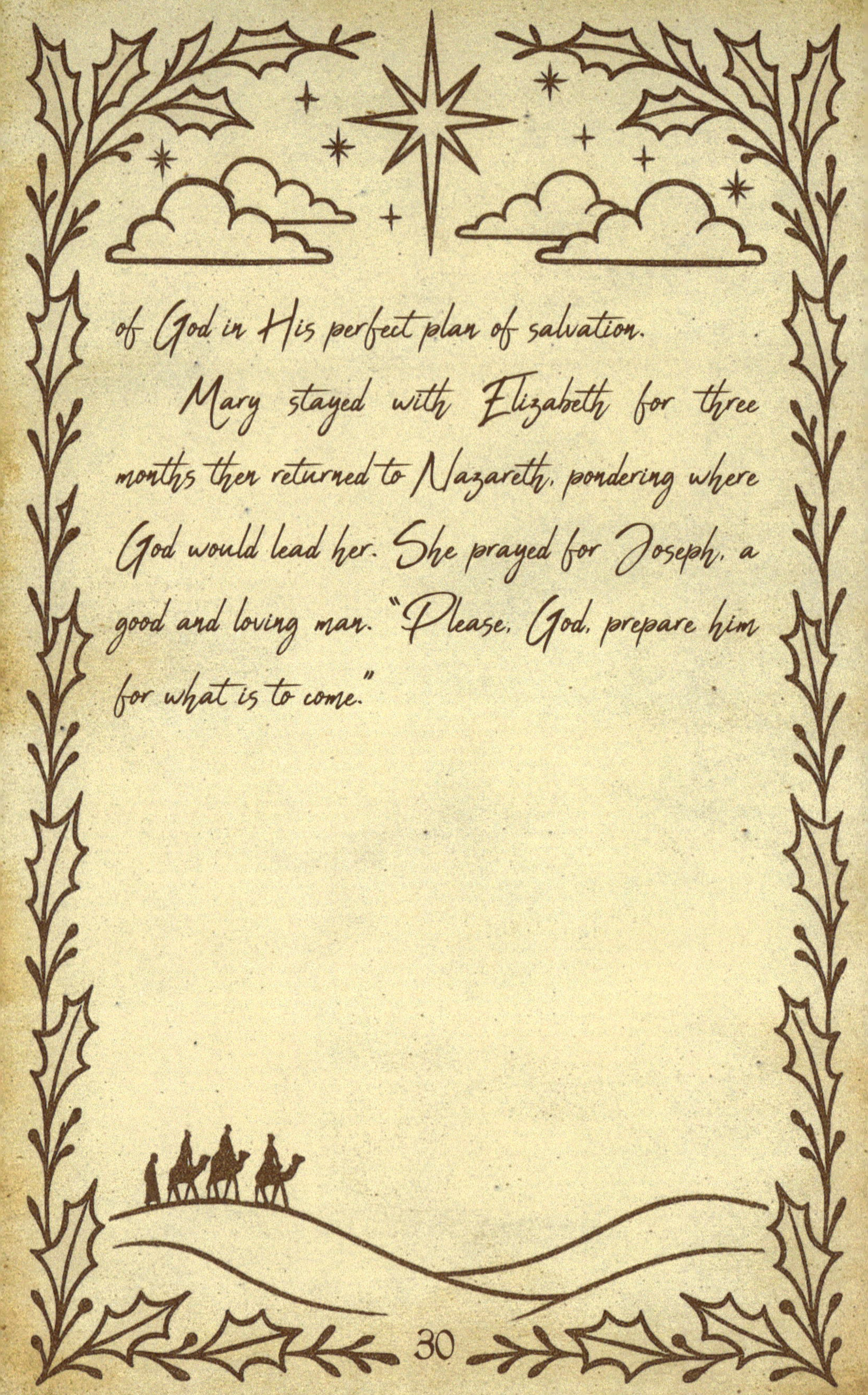

of God in His perfect plan of salvation.

Mary stayed with Elizabeth for three months then returned to Nazareth, pondering where God would lead her. She prayed for Joseph, a good and loving man. "Please, God, prepare him for what is to come."

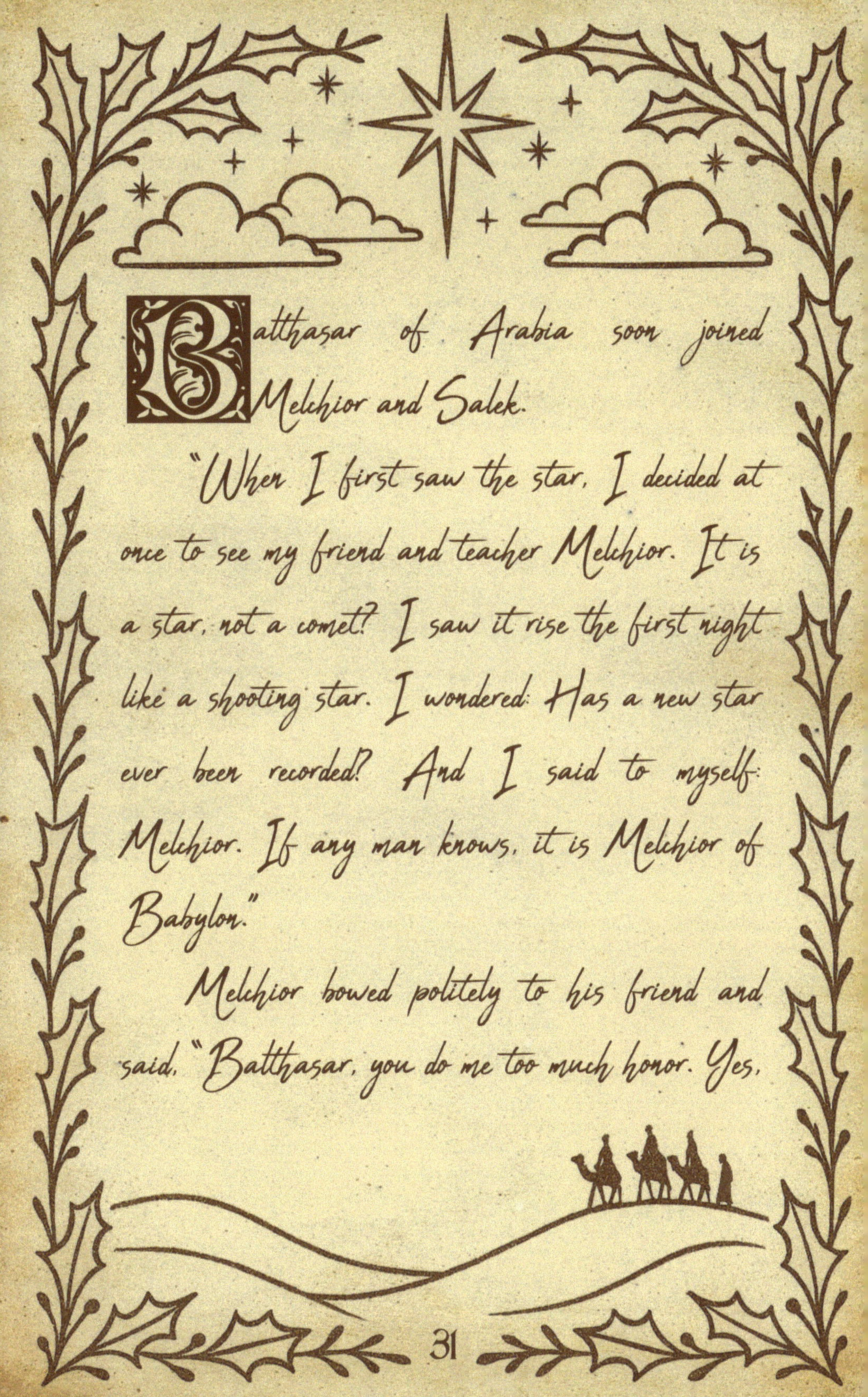

Balthasar of Arabia soon joined Melchior and Salek.

"When I first saw the star, I decided at once to see my friend and teacher Melchior. It is a star, not a comet! I saw it rise the first night like a shooting star. I wondered: Has a new star ever been recorded? And I said to myself: Melchior. If any man knows, it is Melchior of Babylon."

Melchior bowed politely to his friend and said, "Balthasar, you do me too much honor. Yes,

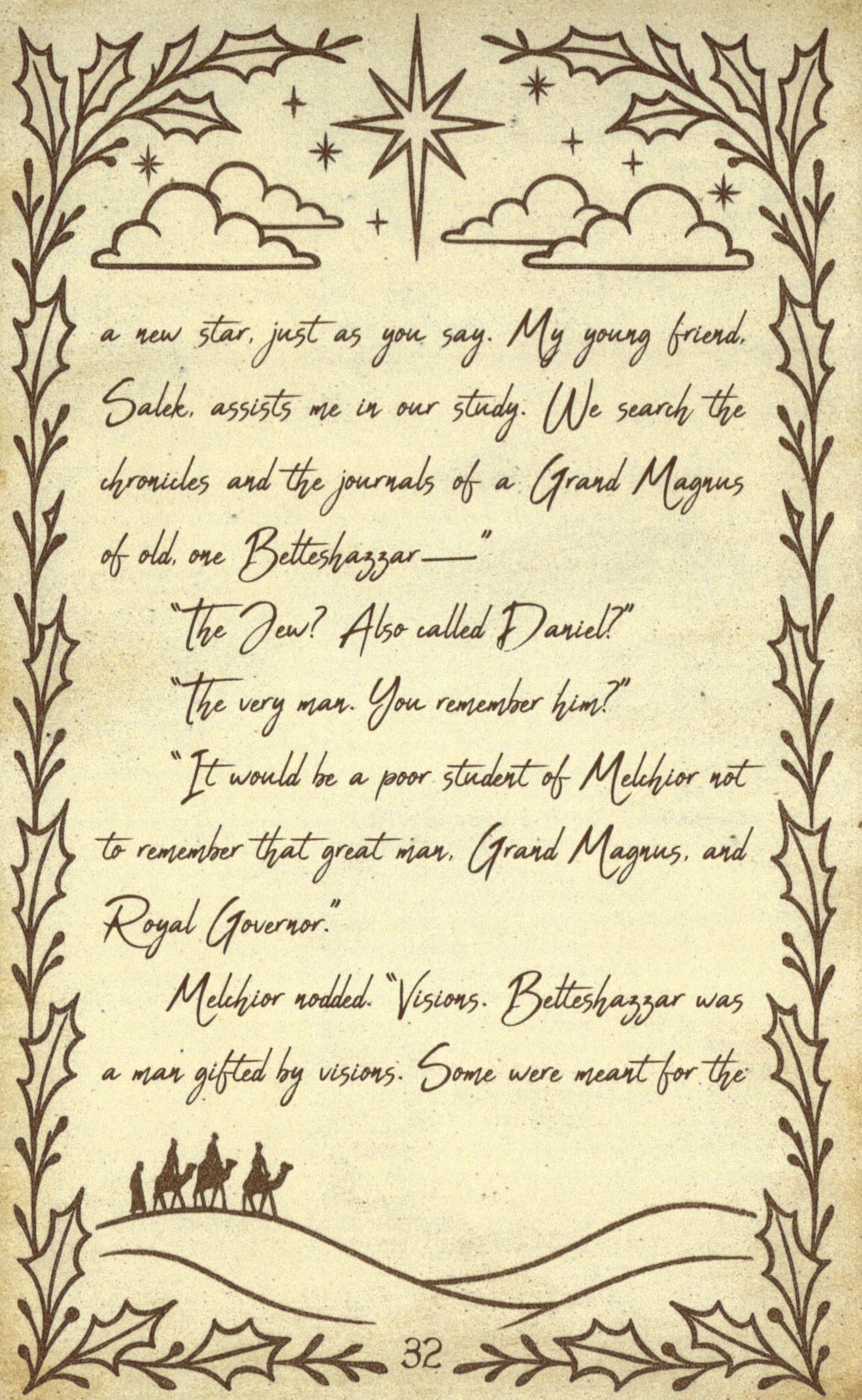

a new star, just as you say. My young friend, Salek, assists me in our study. We search the chronicles and the journals of a Grand Magnus of old, one Betteshazzar—"

"The Jew? Also called Daniel?"

"The very man. You remember him?"

"It would be a poor student of Melchior not to remember that great man, Grand Magnus, and Royal Governor."

Melchior nodded. "Visions. Betteshazzar was a man gifted by visions. Some were meant for the

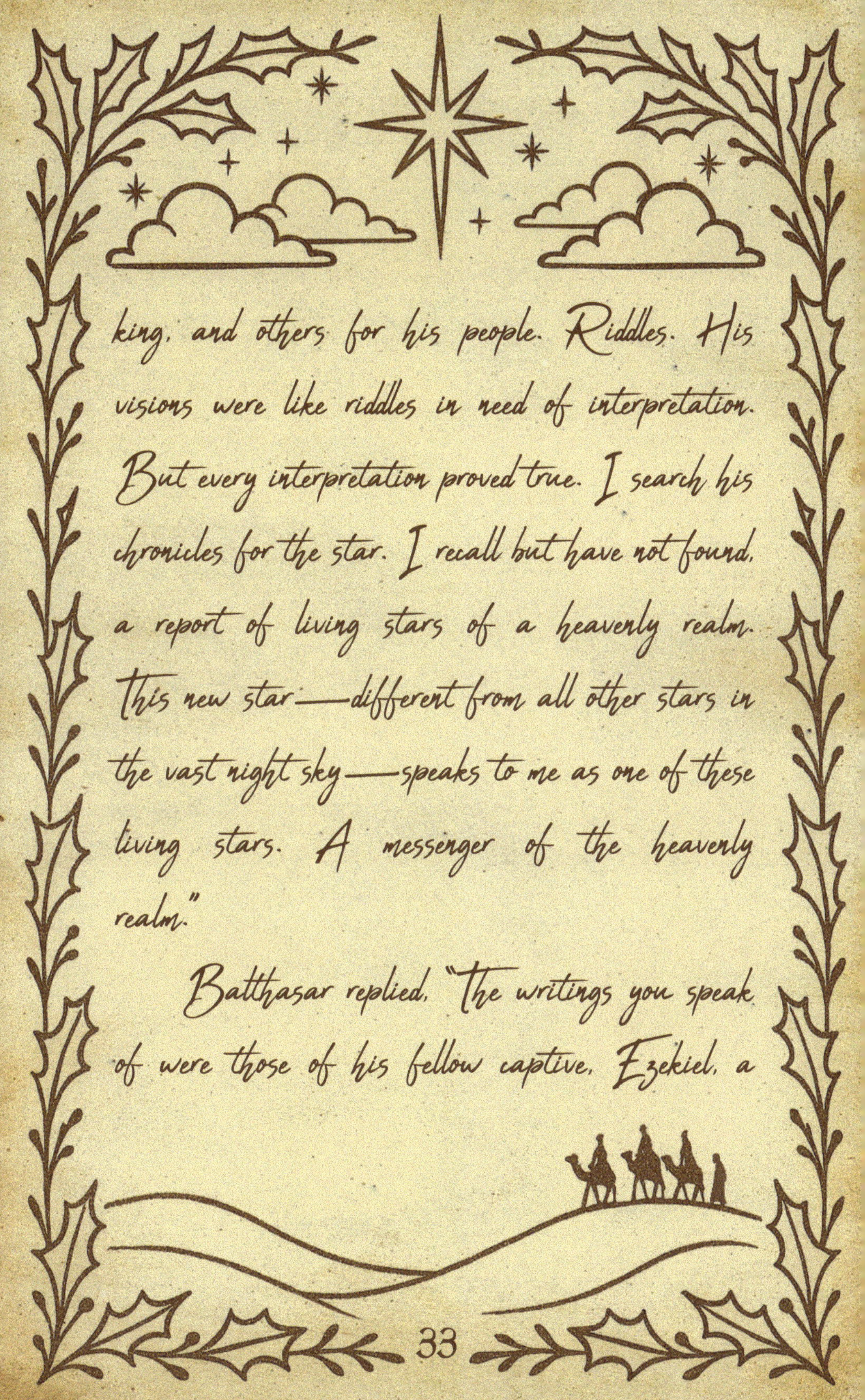

king, and others for his people. Riddles. His visions were like riddles in need of interpretation. But every interpretation proved true. I search his chronicles for the star. I recall but have not found, a report of living stars of a heavenly realm. This new star—different from all other stars in the vast night sky—speaks to me as one of these living stars. A messenger of the heavenly realm."

Balthasar replied, "The writings you speak of were those of his fellow captive, Ezekiel, a

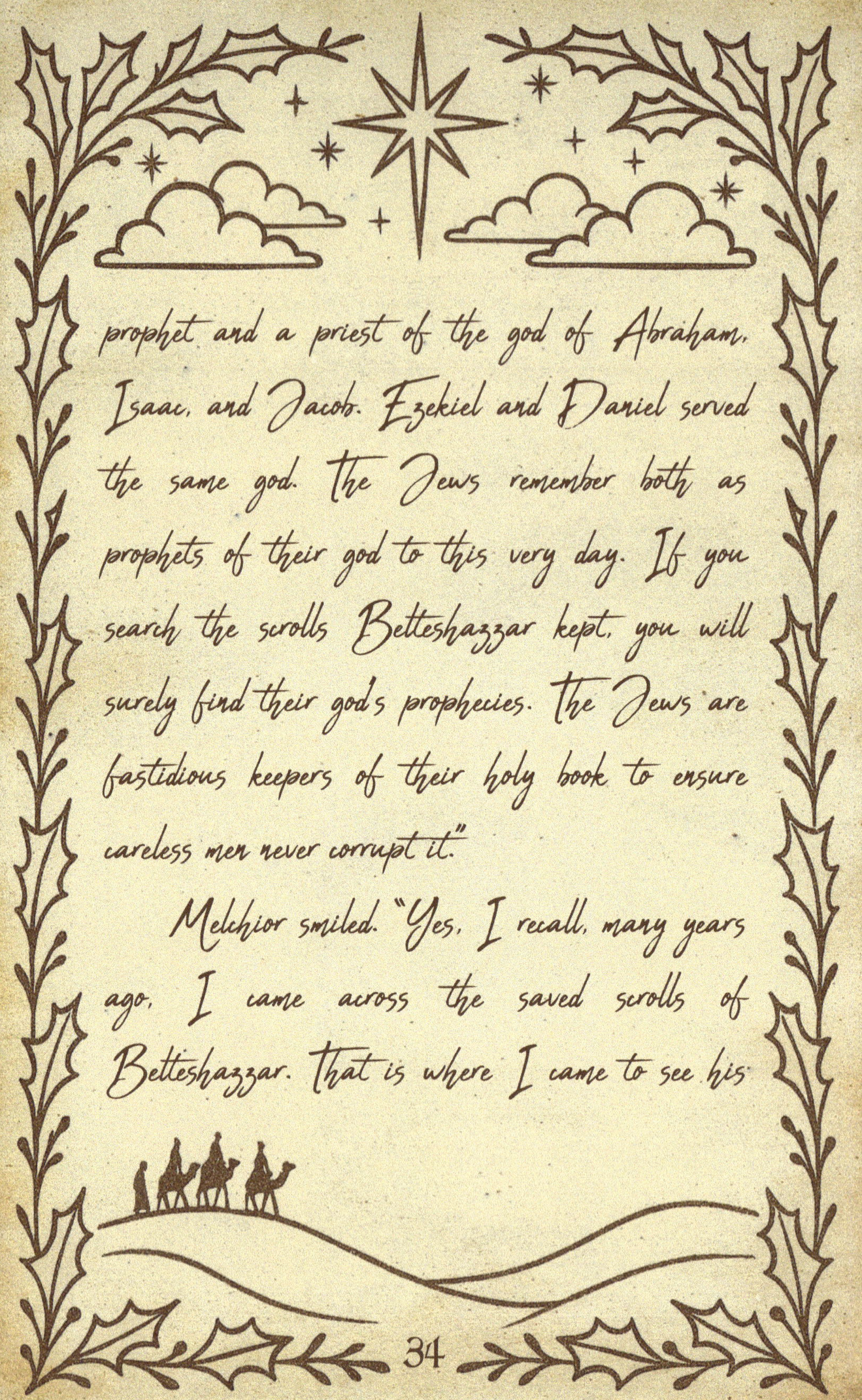

prophet and a priest of the god of Abraham, Isaac, and Jacob. Ezekiel and Daniel served the same god. The Jews remember both as prophets of their god to this very day. If you search the scrolls Belteshazzar kept, you will surely find their god's prophecies. The Jews are fastidious keepers of their holy book to ensure careless men never corrupt it."

Melchior smiled. "Yes, I recall, many years ago, I came across the saved scrolls of Belteshazzar. That is where I came to see his

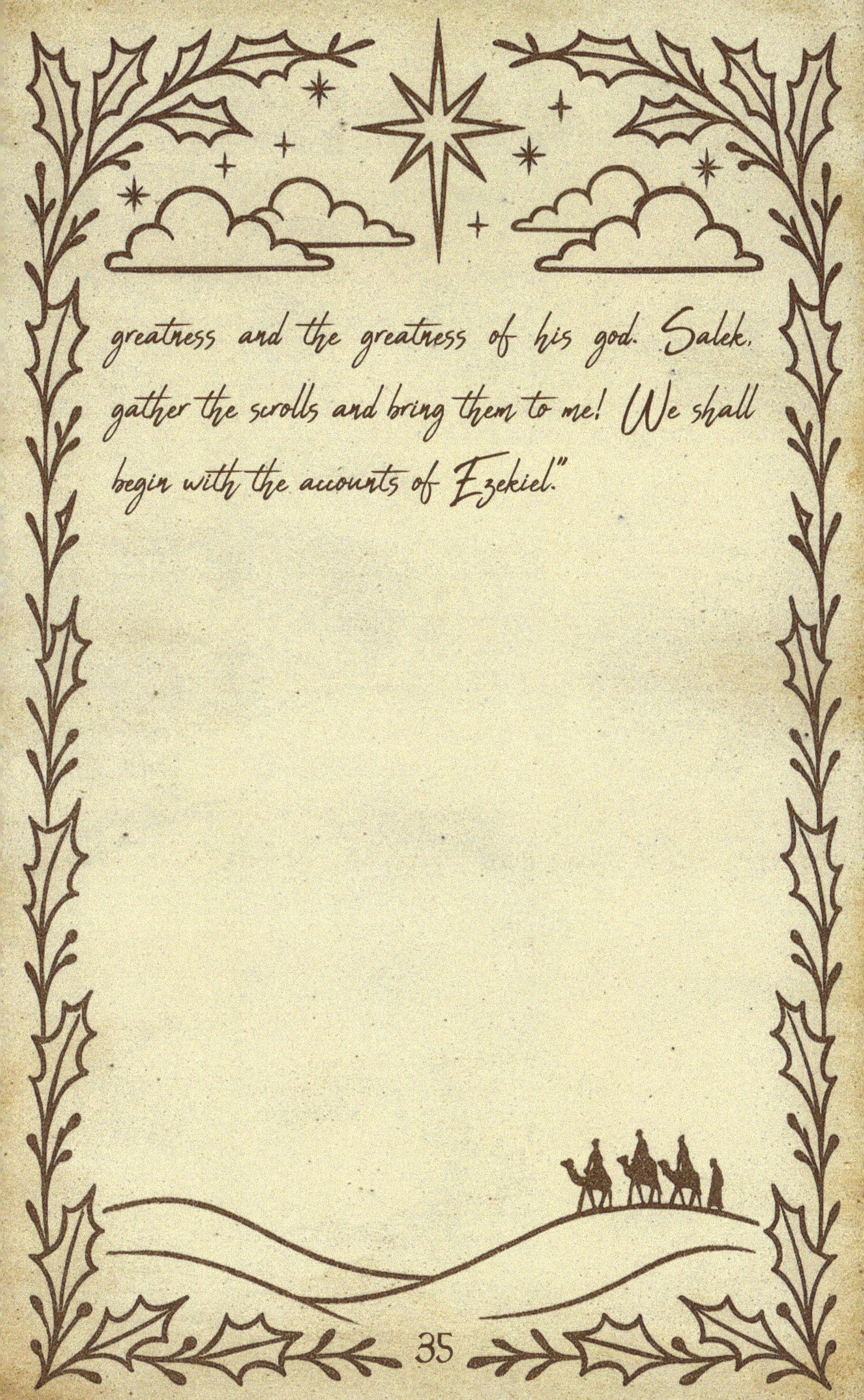

greatness and the greatness of his god. Salek, gather the scrolls and bring them to me! We shall begin with the accounts of Ezekiel."

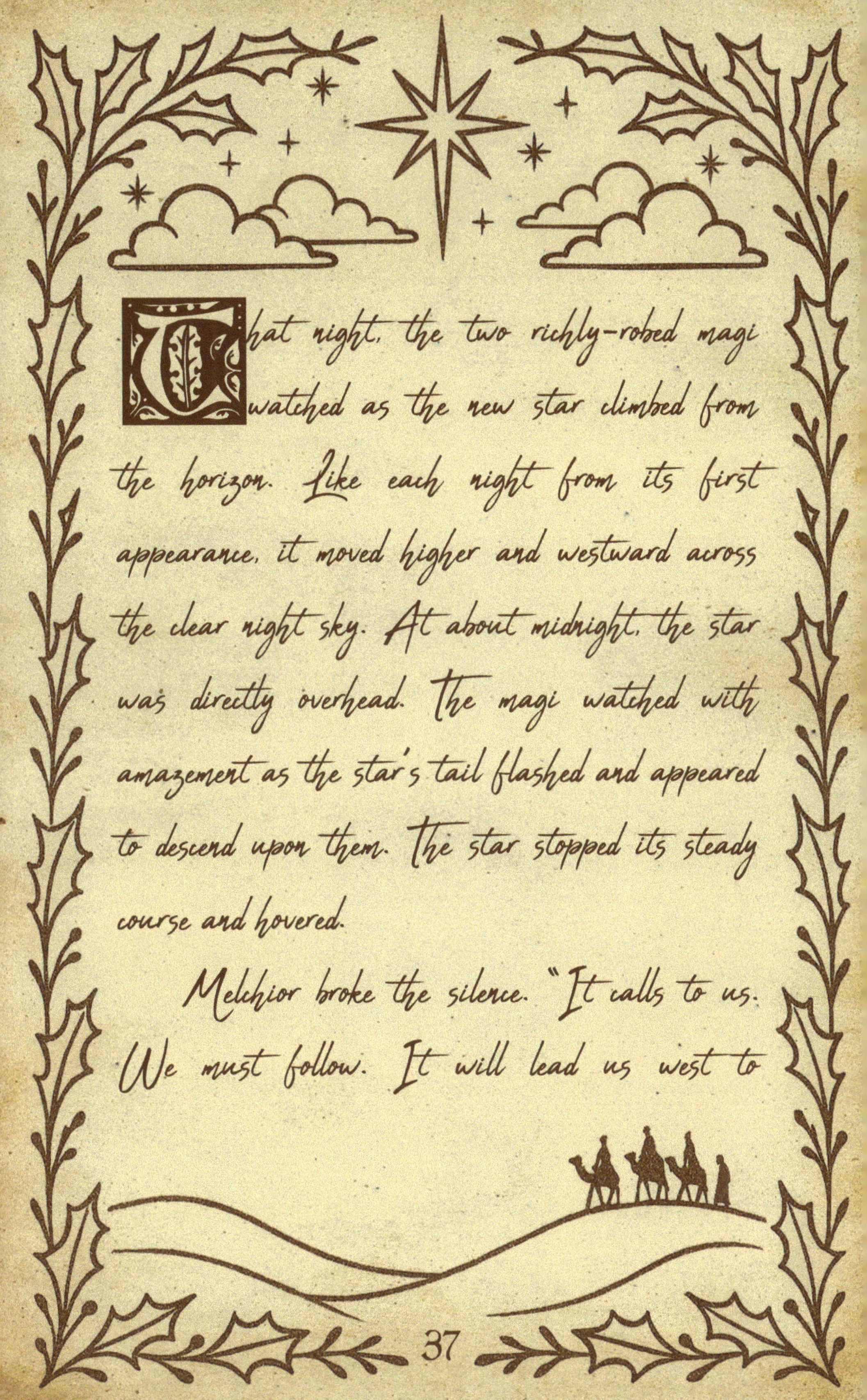

That night, the two richly-robed magi watched as the new star climbed from the horizon. Like each night from its first appearance, it moved higher and westward across the clear night sky. At about midnight, the star was directly overhead. The magi watched with amazement as the star's tail flashed and appeared to descend upon them. The star stopped its steady course and hovered.

Melchior broke the silence. "It calls to us. We must follow. It will lead us west to

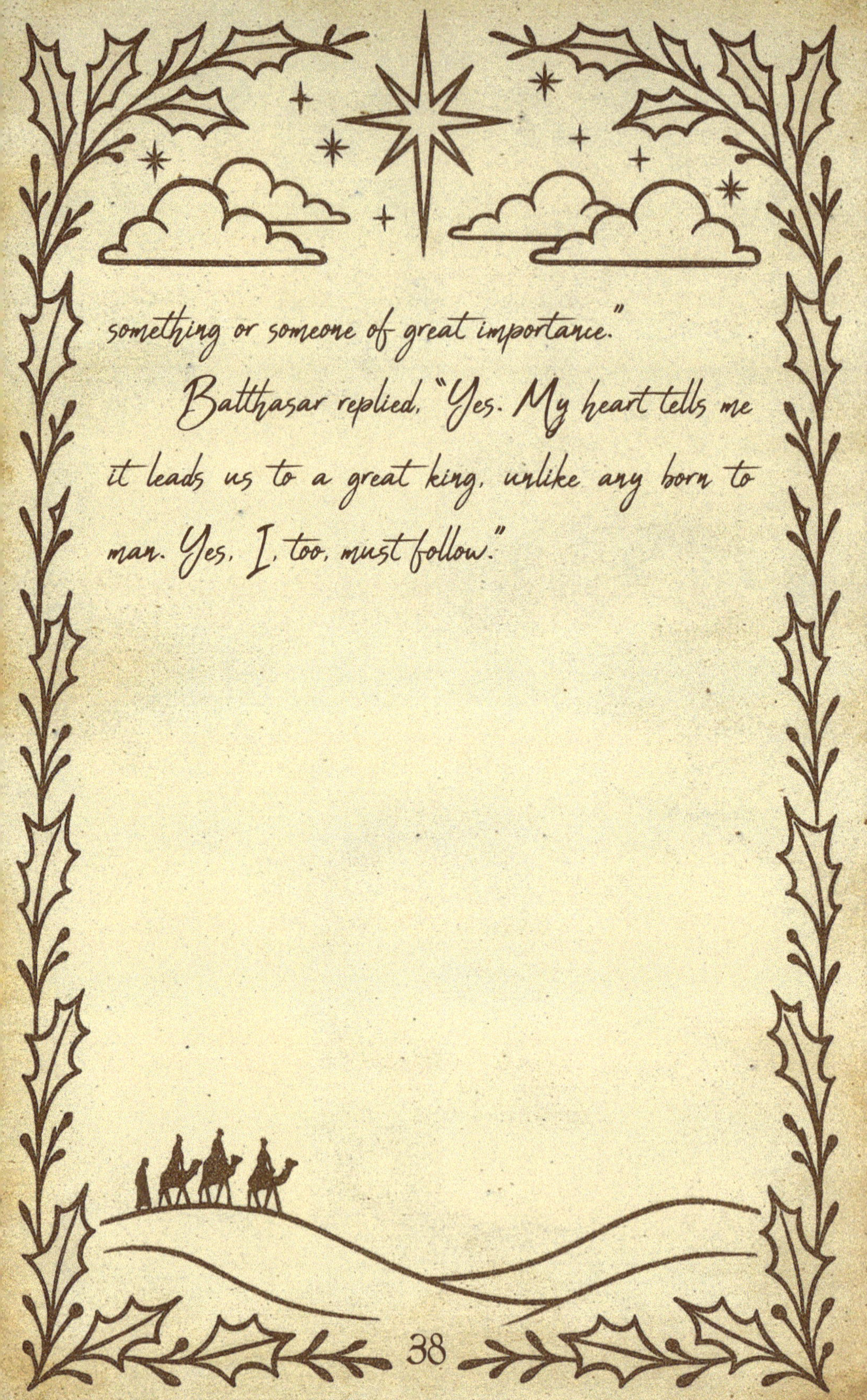

something or someone of great importance."

Balthasar replied, "Yes. My heart tells me it leads us to a great king, unlike any born to man. Yes, I, too, must follow."

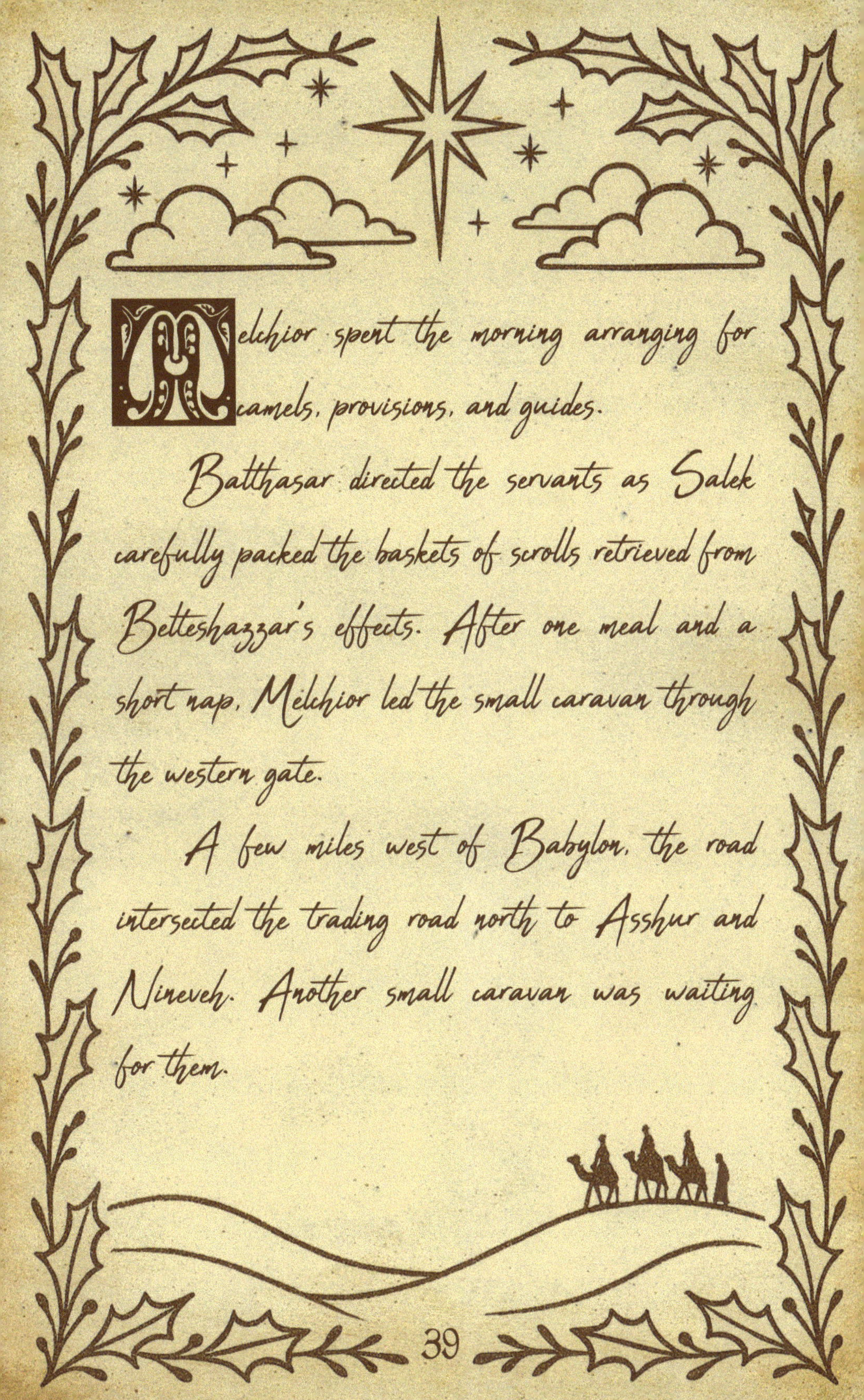

Melchior spent the morning arranging for camels, provisions, and guides.

Balthasar directed the servants as Salek carefully packed the baskets of scrolls retrieved from Belteshazzar's effects. After one meal and a short nap, Melchior led the small caravan through the western gate.

A few miles west of Babylon, the road intersected the trading road north to Asshur and Nineveh. Another small caravan was waiting for them.

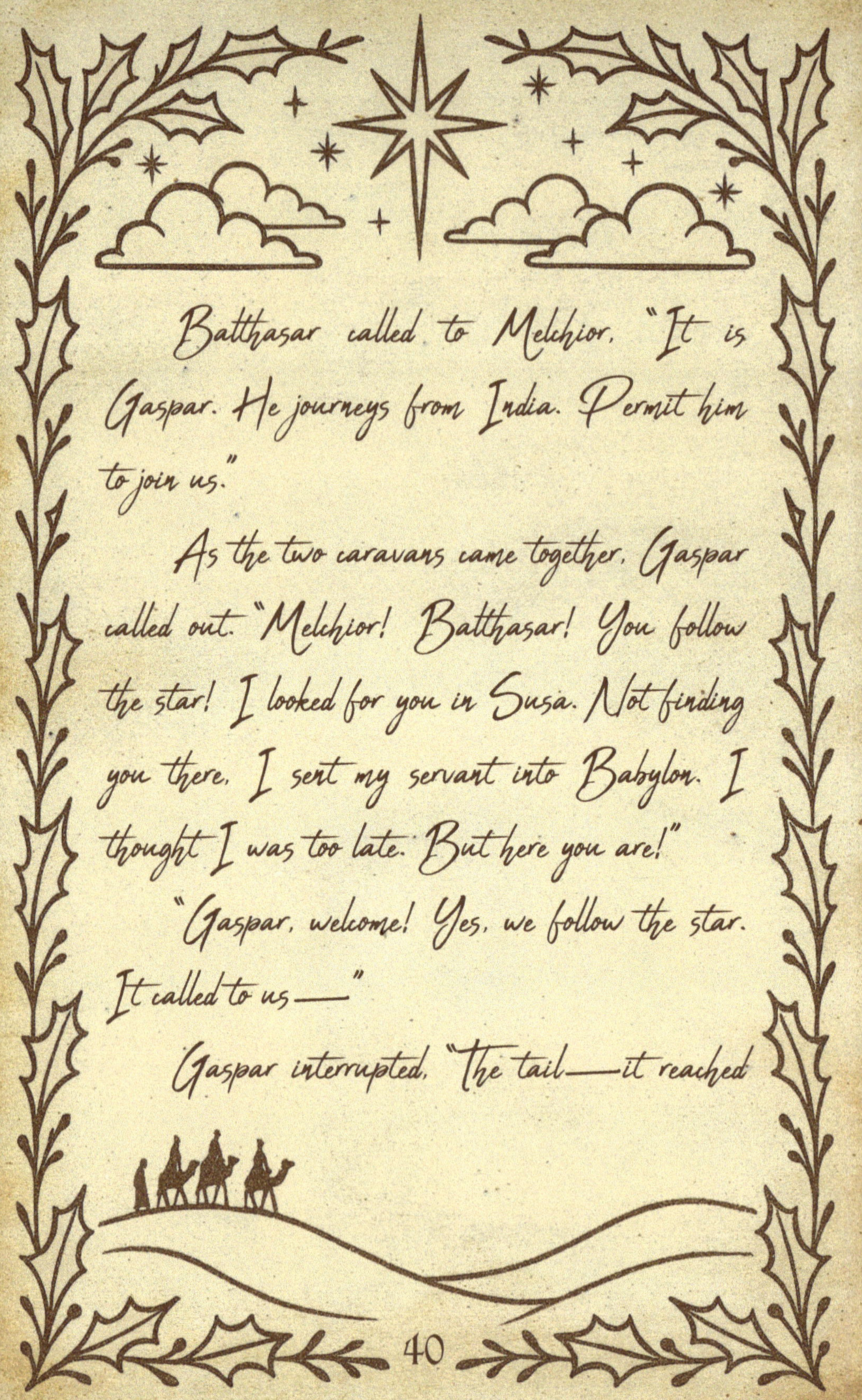

Balthasar called to Melchior, "It is Gaspar. He journeys from India. Permit him to join us."

As the two caravans came together, Gaspar called out. "Melchior! Balthasar! You follow the star! I looked for you in Susa. Not finding you there, I sent my servant into Babylon. I thought I was too late. But here you are!"

"Gaspar, welcome! Yes, we follow the star. It called to us——"

Gaspar interrupted, "The tail——it reached

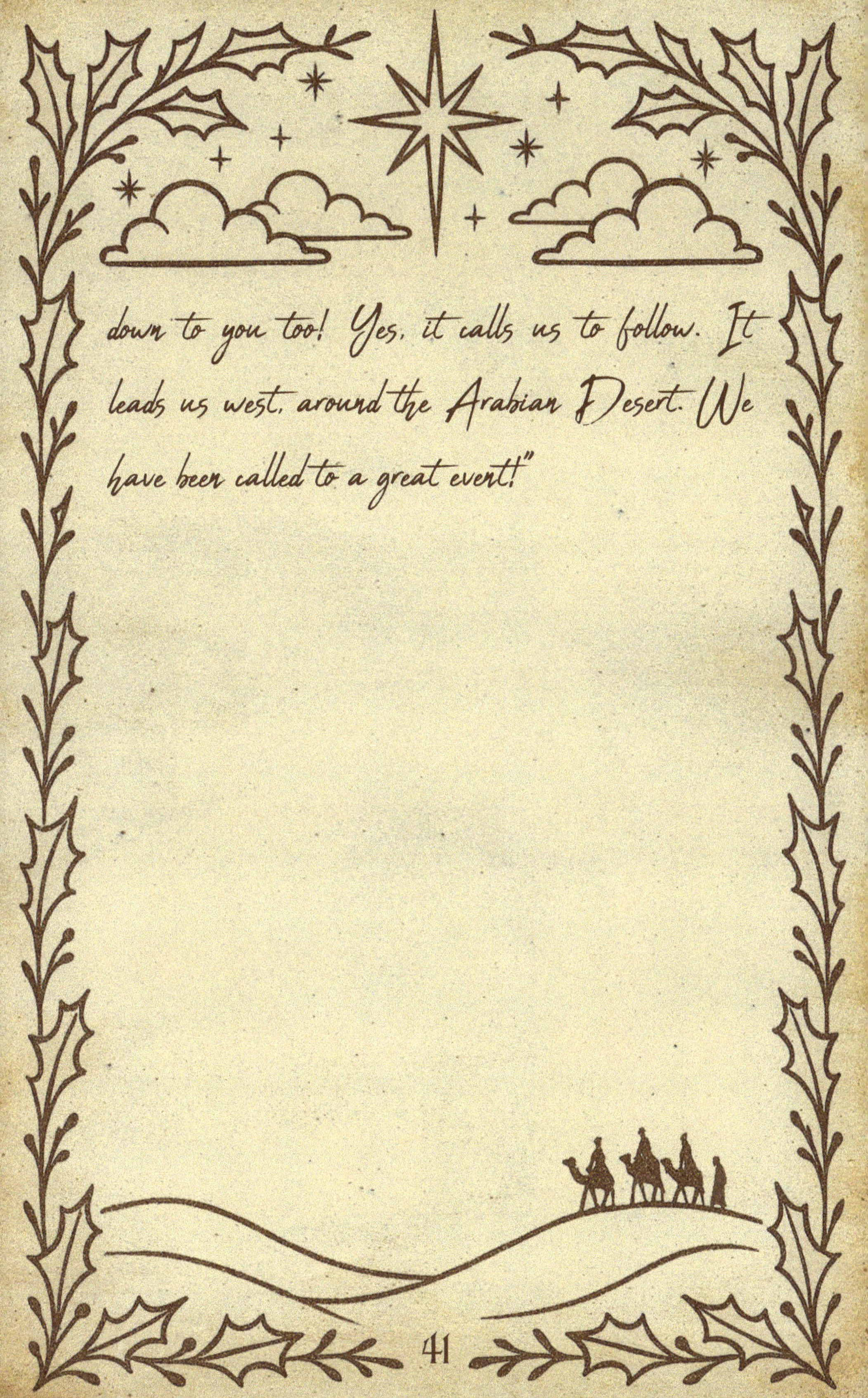

down to you too! Yes, it calls us to follow. It leads us west, around the Arabian Desert. We have been called to a great event!"

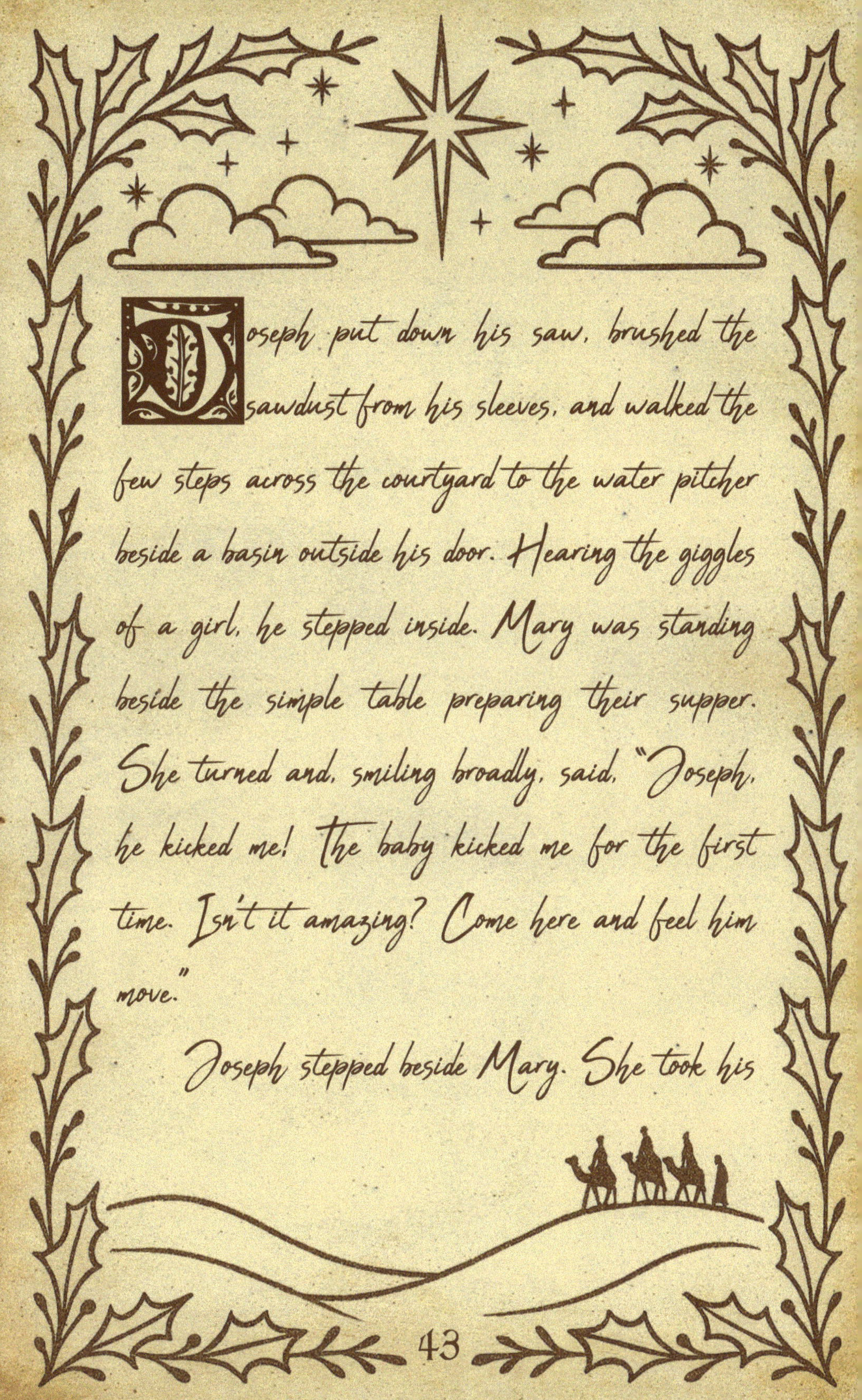

oseph put down his saw, brushed the sawdust from his sleeves, and walked the few steps across the courtyard to the water pitcher beside a basin outside his door. Hearing the giggles of a girl, he stepped inside. Mary was standing beside the simple table preparing their supper. She turned and, smiling broadly, said, "Joseph, he kicked me! The baby kicked me for the first time. Isn't it amazing? Come here and feel him move."

Joseph stepped beside Mary. She took his

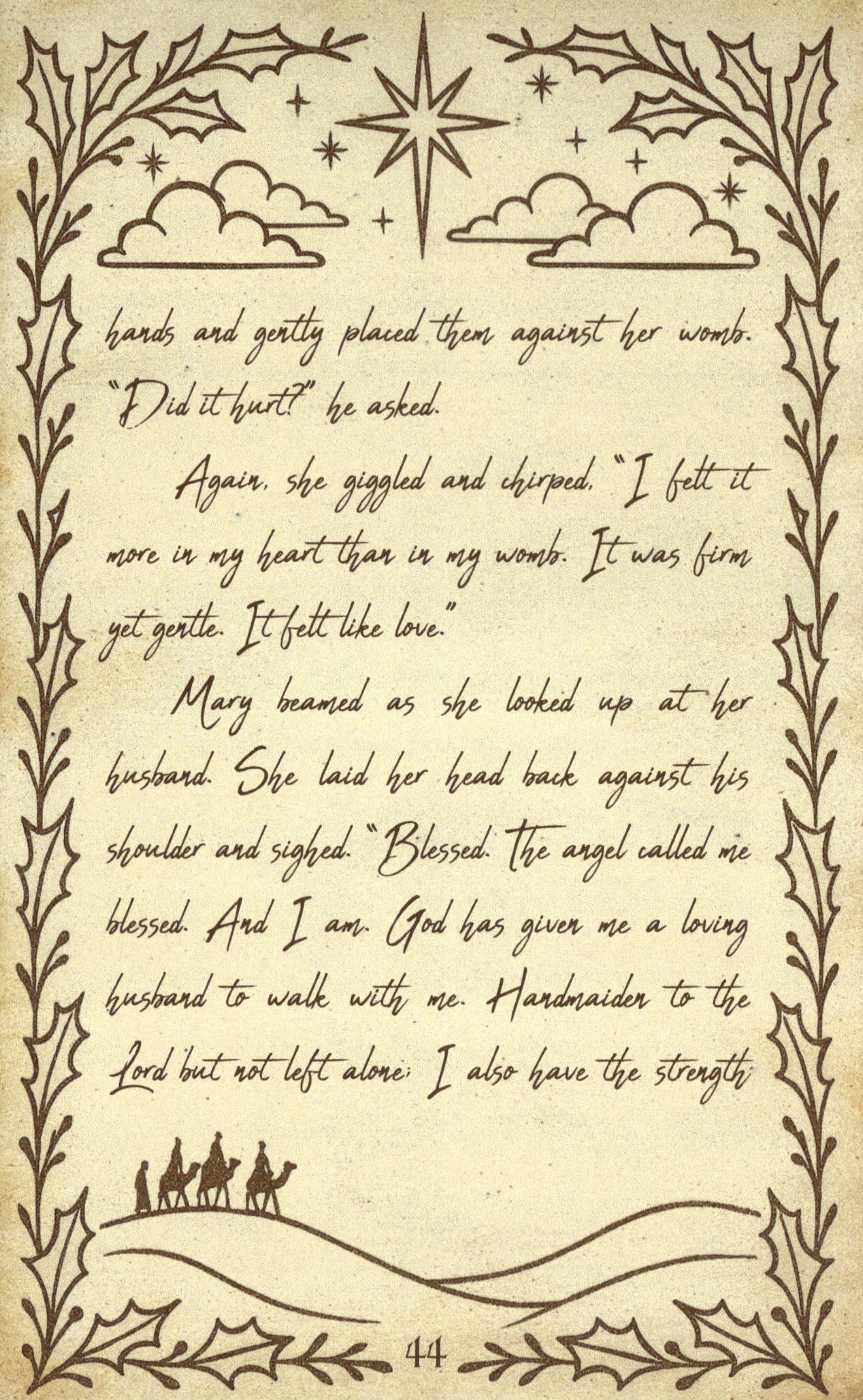

hands and gently placed them against her womb. "Did it hurt?" he asked.

Again, she giggled and chirped, "I felt it more in my heart than in my womb. It was firm yet gentle. It felt like love."

Mary beamed as she looked up at her husband. She laid her head back against his shoulder and sighed. "Blessed. The angel called me blessed. And I am. God has given me a loving husband to walk with me. Handmaiden to the Lord but not left alone; I also have the strength

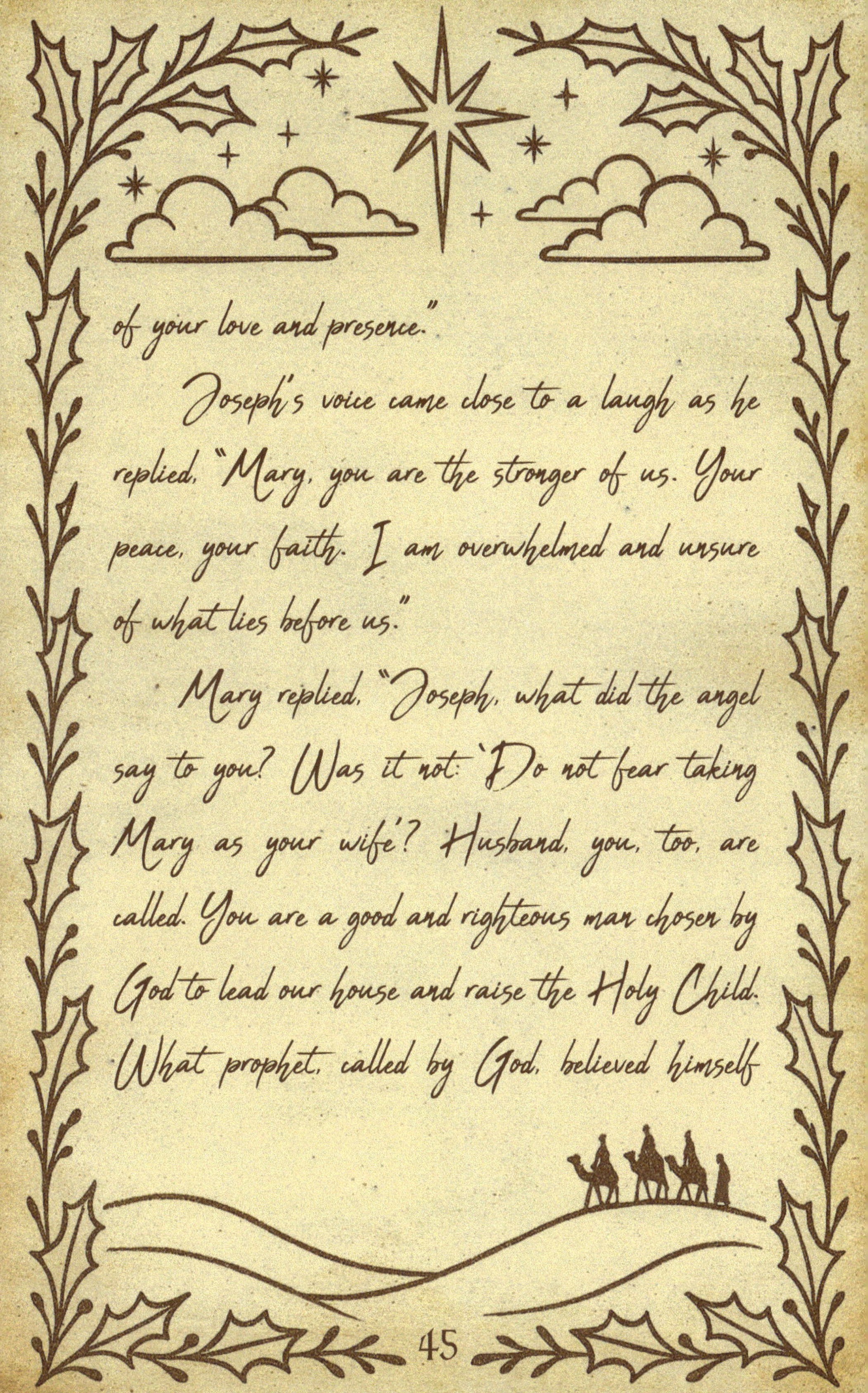

of your love and presence."

Joseph's voice came close to a laugh as he replied, "Mary, you are the stronger of us. Your peace, your faith. I am overwhelmed and unsure of what lies before us."

Mary replied, "Joseph, what did the angel say to you? Was it not: 'Do not fear taking Mary as your wife'? Husband, you, too, are called. You are a good and righteous man chosen by God to lead our house and raise the Holy Child. What prophet, called by God, believed himself

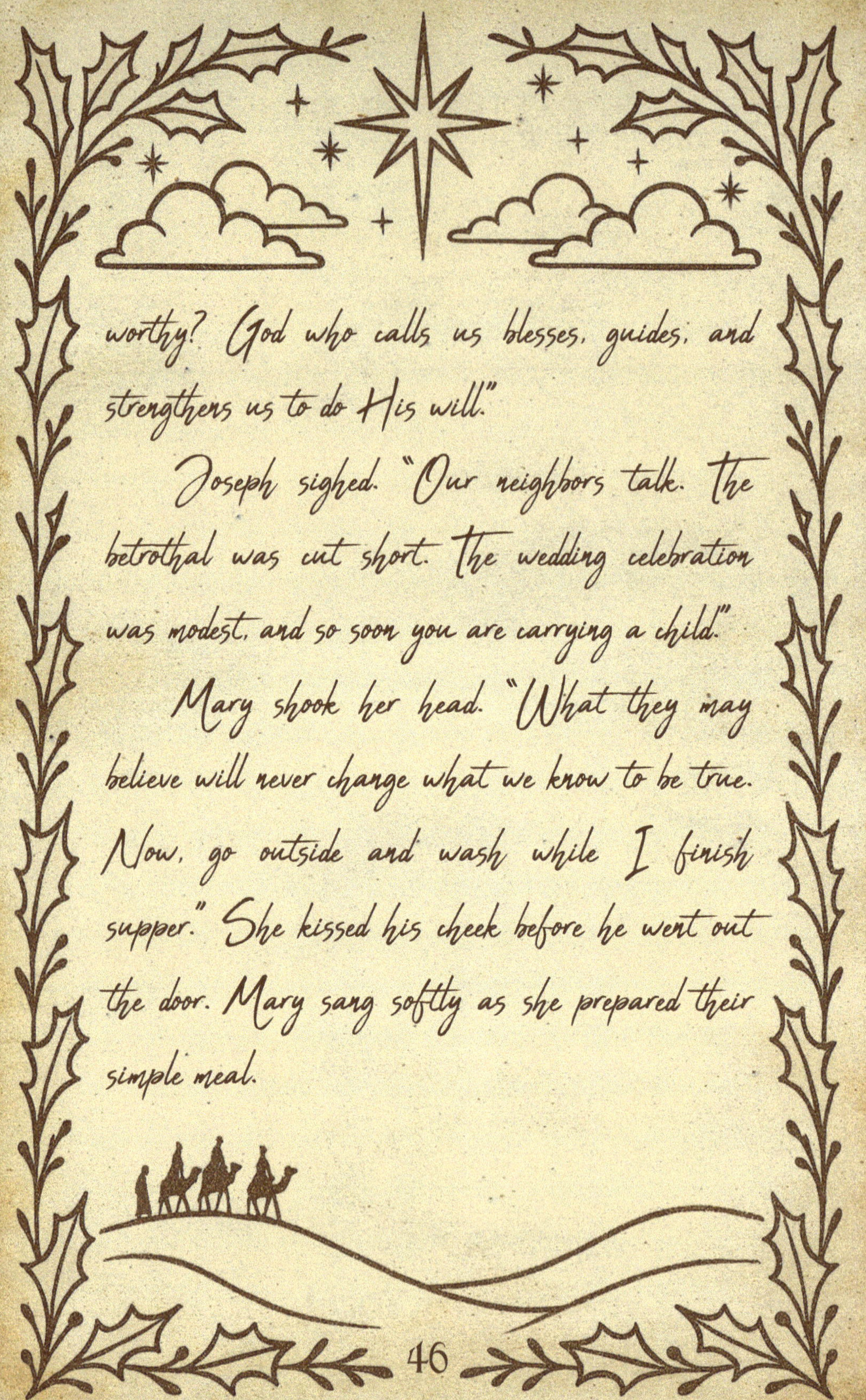

worthy? God who calls us blesses, guides, and strengthens us to do His will."

Joseph sighed. "Our neighbors talk. The betrothal was cut short. The wedding celebration was modest, and so soon you are carrying a child."

Mary shook her head. "What they may believe will never change what we know to be true. Now, go outside and wash while I finish supper." She kissed his cheek before he went out the door. Mary sang softly as she prepared their simple meal.

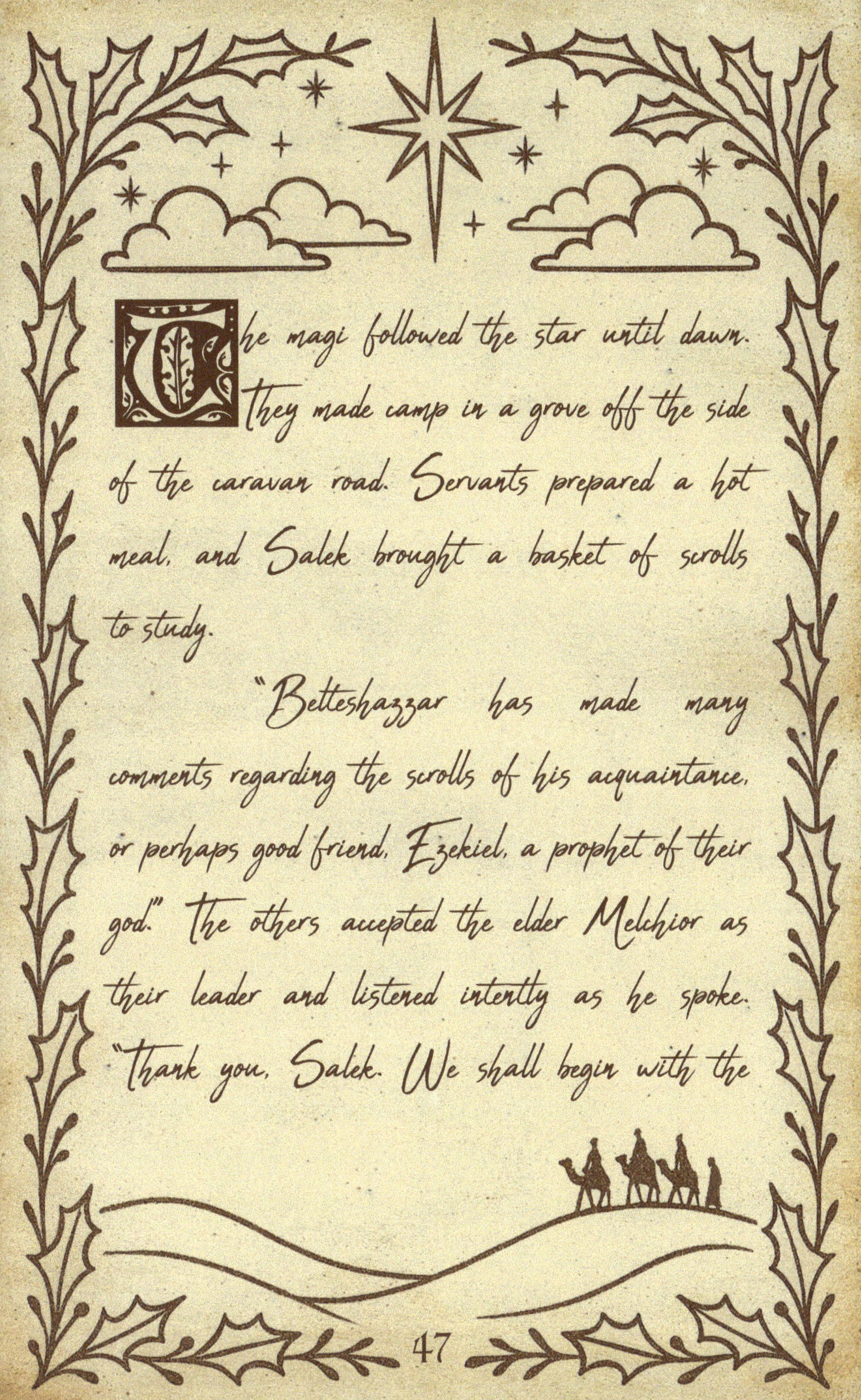

The magi followed the star until dawn. They made camp in a grove off the side of the caravan road. Servants prepared a hot meal, and Salek brought a basket of scrolls to study.

"Betteshazzar has made many comments regarding the scrolls of his acquaintance, or perhaps good friend, Ezekiel, a prophet of their god." The others accepted the elder Melchior as their leader and listened intently as he spoke. "Thank you, Salek. We shall begin with the

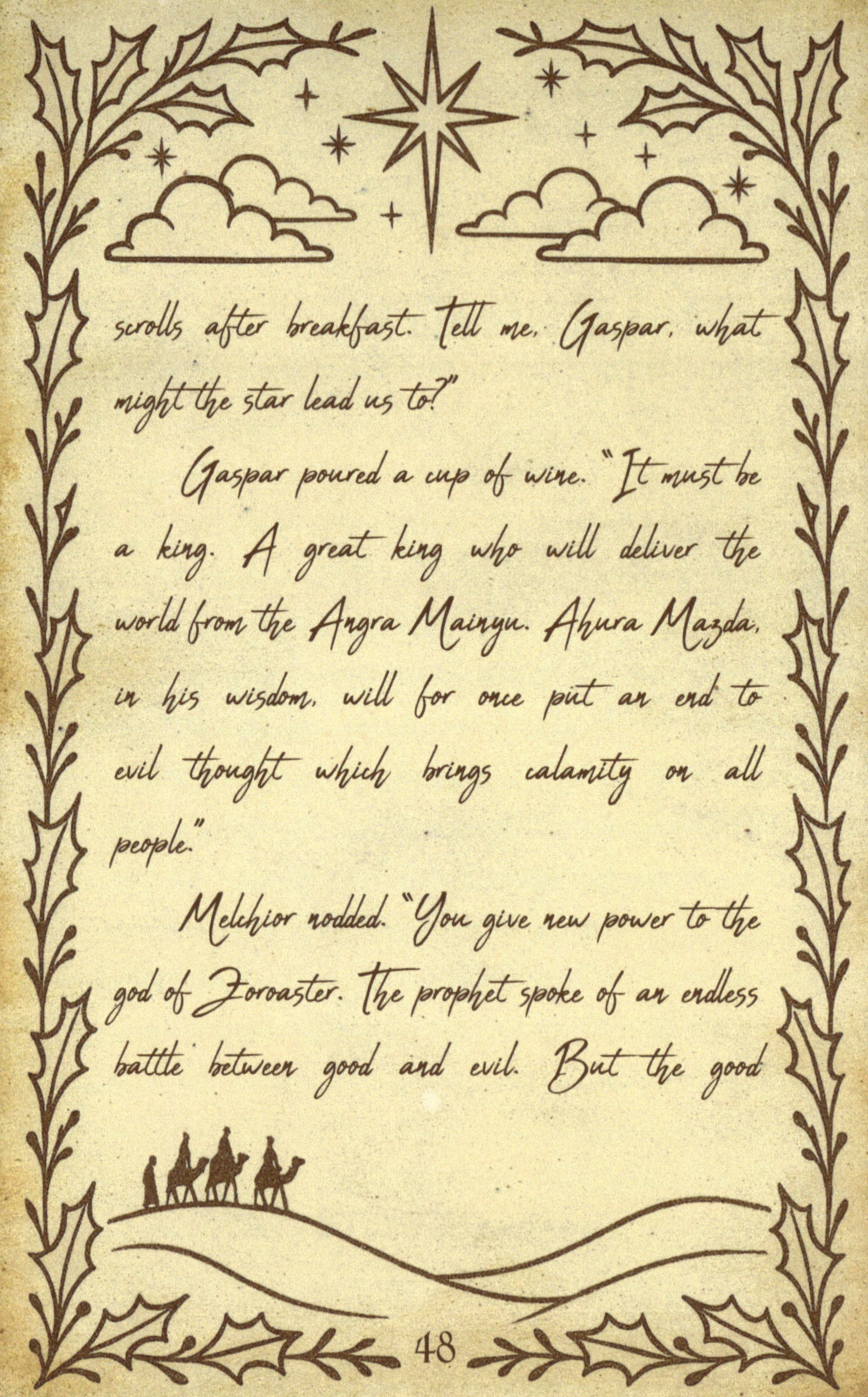

scrolls after breakfast. Tell me, Gaspar, what might the star lead us to?"

Gaspar poured a cup of wine. "It must be a king. A great king who will deliver the world from the Angra Mainyu. Ahura Mazda, in his wisdom, will for once put an end to evil thought which brings calamity on all people."

Melchior nodded. "You give new power to the god of Zoroaster. The prophet spoke of an endless battle between good and evil. But the good

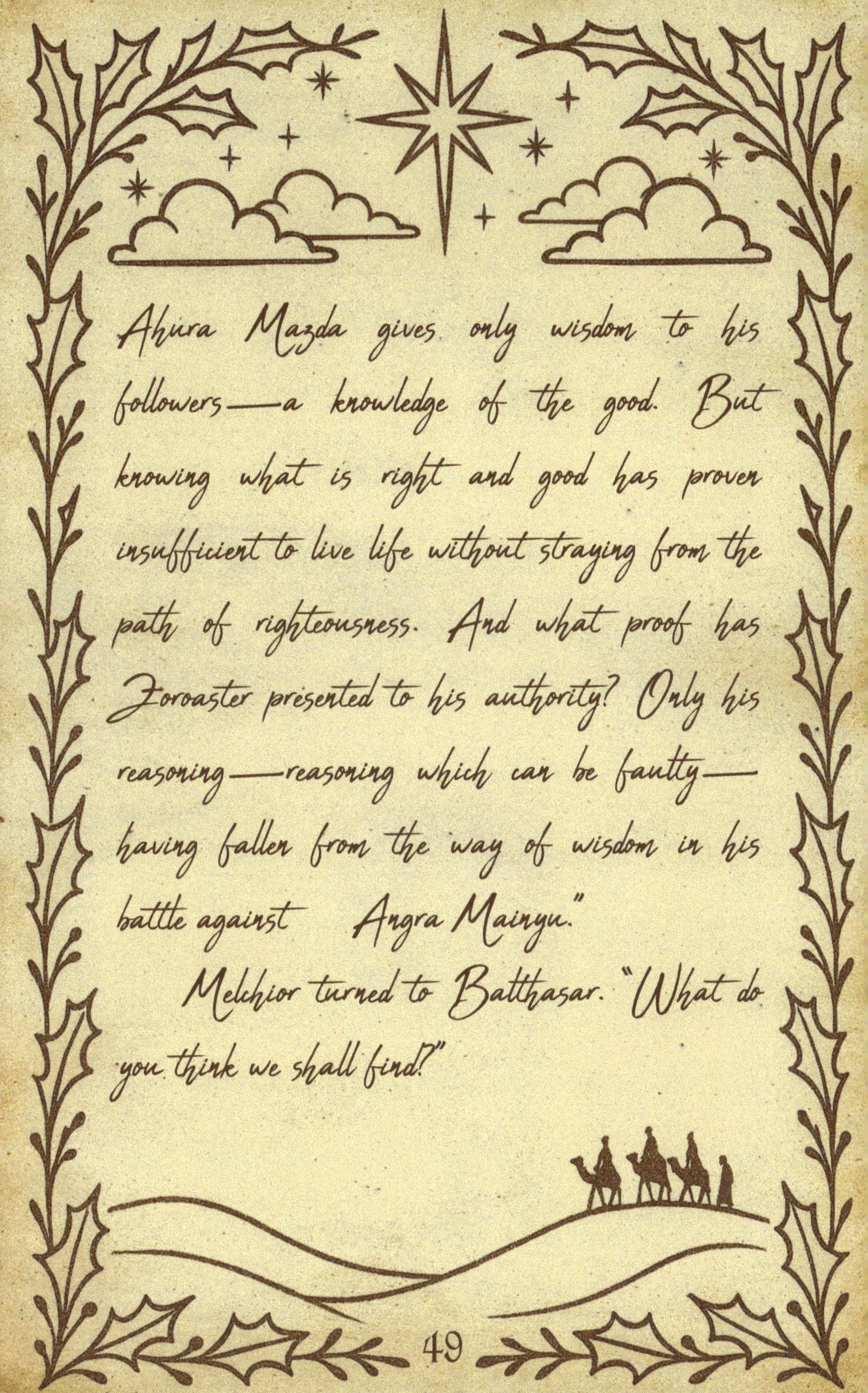

Ahura Mazda gives only wisdom to his followers——a knowledge of the good. But knowing what is right and good has proven insufficient to live life without straying from the path of righteousness. And what proof has Zoroaster presented to his authority? Only his reasoning——reasoning which can be faulty——having fallen from the way of wisdom in his battle against Angra Mainyu."

Melchior turned to Balthasar. "What do you think we shall find?"

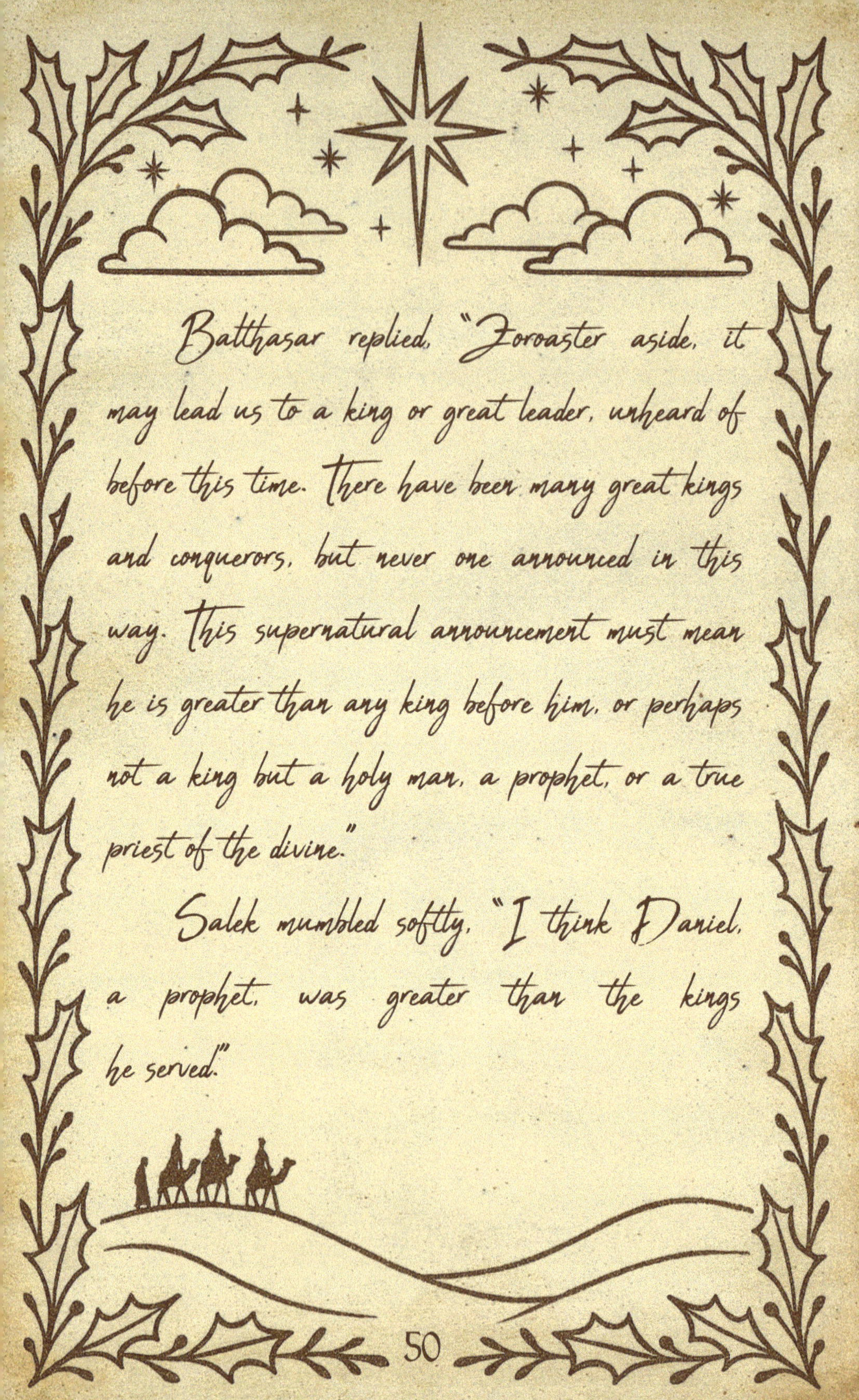

Balthasar replied, "Zoroaster aside, it may lead us to a king or great leader, unheard of before this time. There have been many great kings and conquerors, but never one announced in this way. This supernatural announcement must mean he is greater than any king before him, or perhaps not a king but a holy man, a prophet, or a true priest of the divine."

Salek mumbled softly, "I think Daniel, a prophet, was greater than the kings he served."

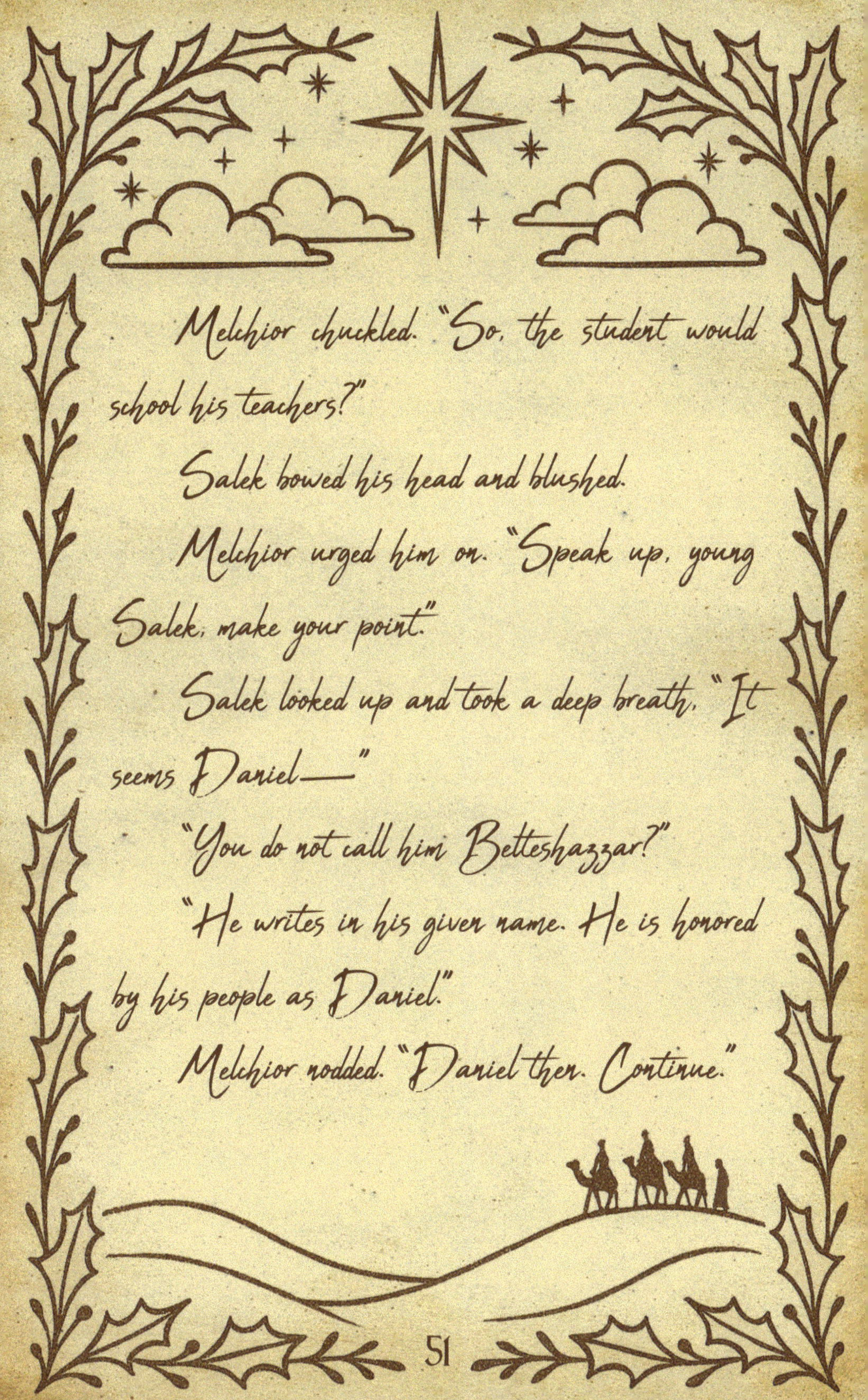

Melchior chuckled. "So, the student would school his teachers?"

Salek bowed his head and blushed.

Melchior urged him on. "Speak up, young Salek, make your point."

Salek looked up and took a deep breath. "It seems Daniel——"

"You do not call him Belteshazzar?"

"He writes in his given name. He is honored by his people as Daniel."

Melchior nodded. "Daniel then. Continue."

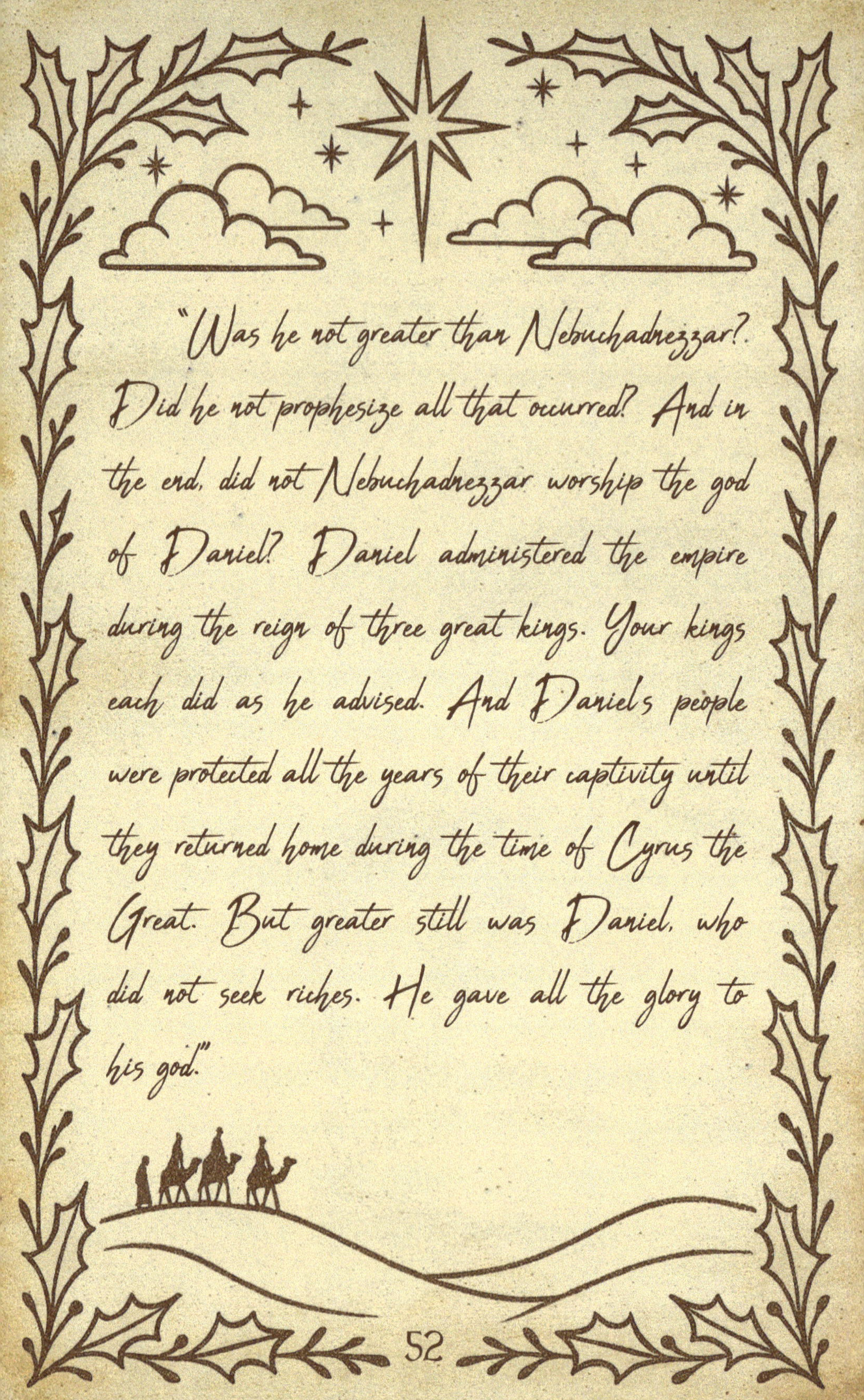

"Was he not greater than Nebuchadnezzar? Did he not prophesize all that occurred? And in the end, did not Nebuchadnezzar worship the god of Daniel? Daniel administered the empire during the reign of three great kings. Your kings each did as he advised. And Daniel's people were protected all the years of their captivity until they returned home during the time of Cyrus the Great. But greater still was Daniel, who did not seek riches. He gave all the glory to his god."

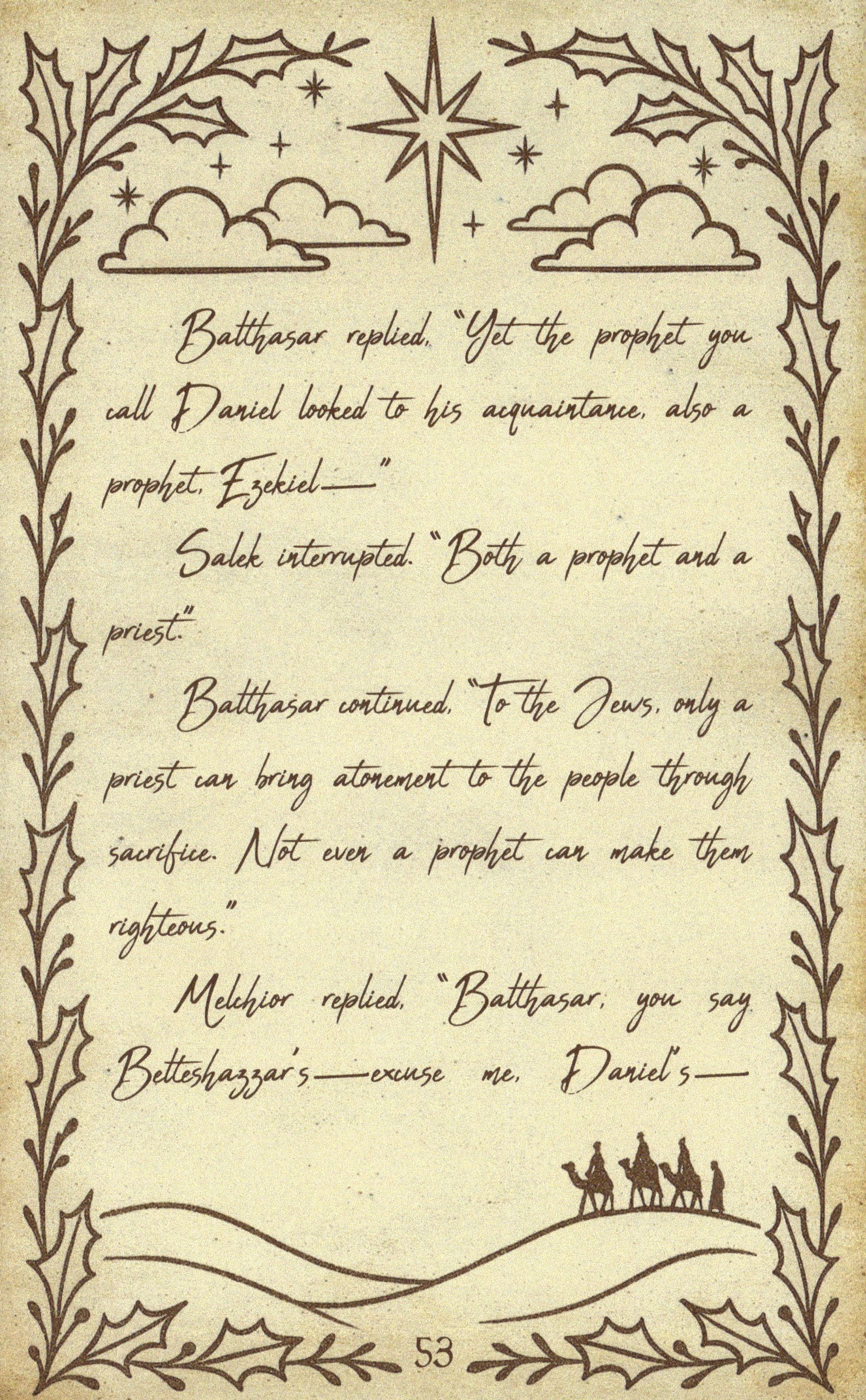

Balthasar replied, "Yet the prophet you call Daniel looked to his acquaintance, also a prophet, Ezekiel——"

Salek interrupted. "Both a prophet and a priest."

Balthasar continued, "To the Jews, only a priest can bring atonement to the people through sacrifice. Not even a prophet can make them righteous."

Melchior replied, "Balthasar, you say Belteshazzar's——excuse me, Daniel's——

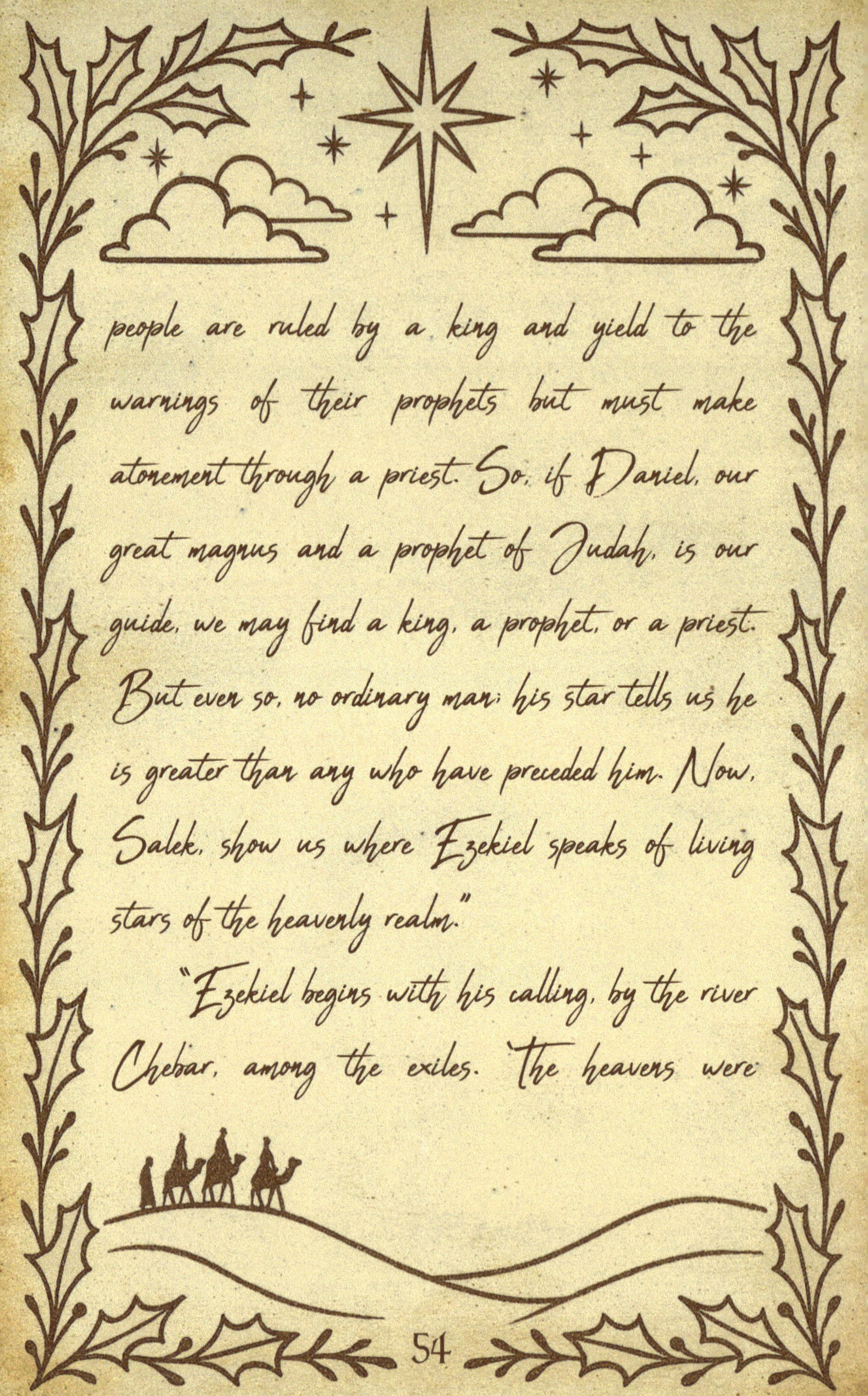

people are ruled by a king and yield to the warnings of their prophets but must make atonement through a priest. So, if Daniel, our great magnus and a prophet of Judah, is our guide, we may find a king, a prophet, or a priest. But even so, no ordinary man; his star tells us he is greater than any who have preceded him. Now, Salek, show us where Ezekiel speaks of living stars of the heavenly realm."

"Ezekiel begins with his calling, by the river Chebar, among the exiles. The heavens were

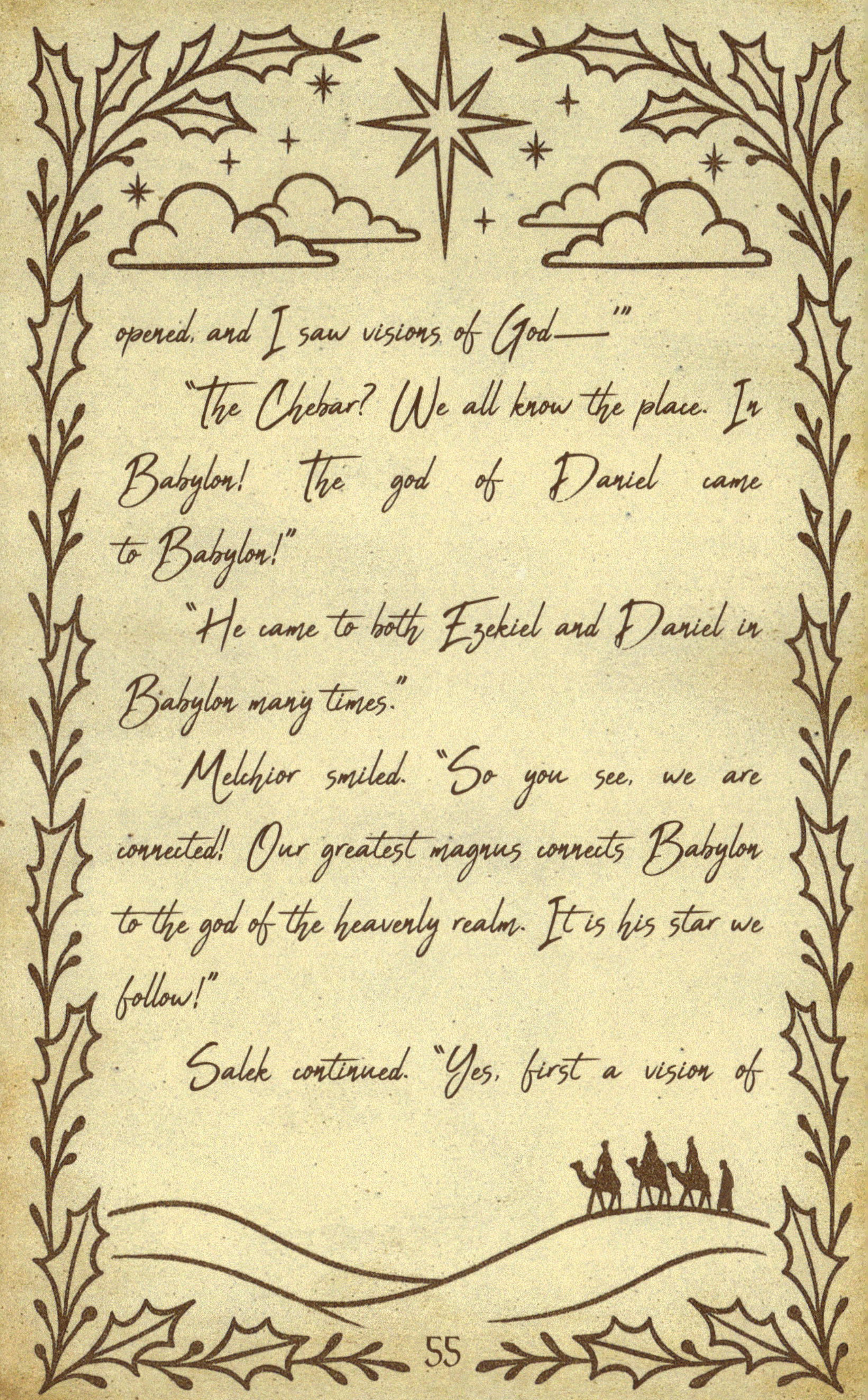

opened, and I saw visions of God——'"

"the Chebar? We all know the place. In Babylon! The god of Daniel came to Babylon!"

"He came to both Ezekiel and Daniel in Babylon many times."

Melchior smiled. "So you see, we are connected! Our greatest magnus connects Babylon to the god of the heavenly realm. It is his star we follow!"

Salek continued. "Yes, first a vision of

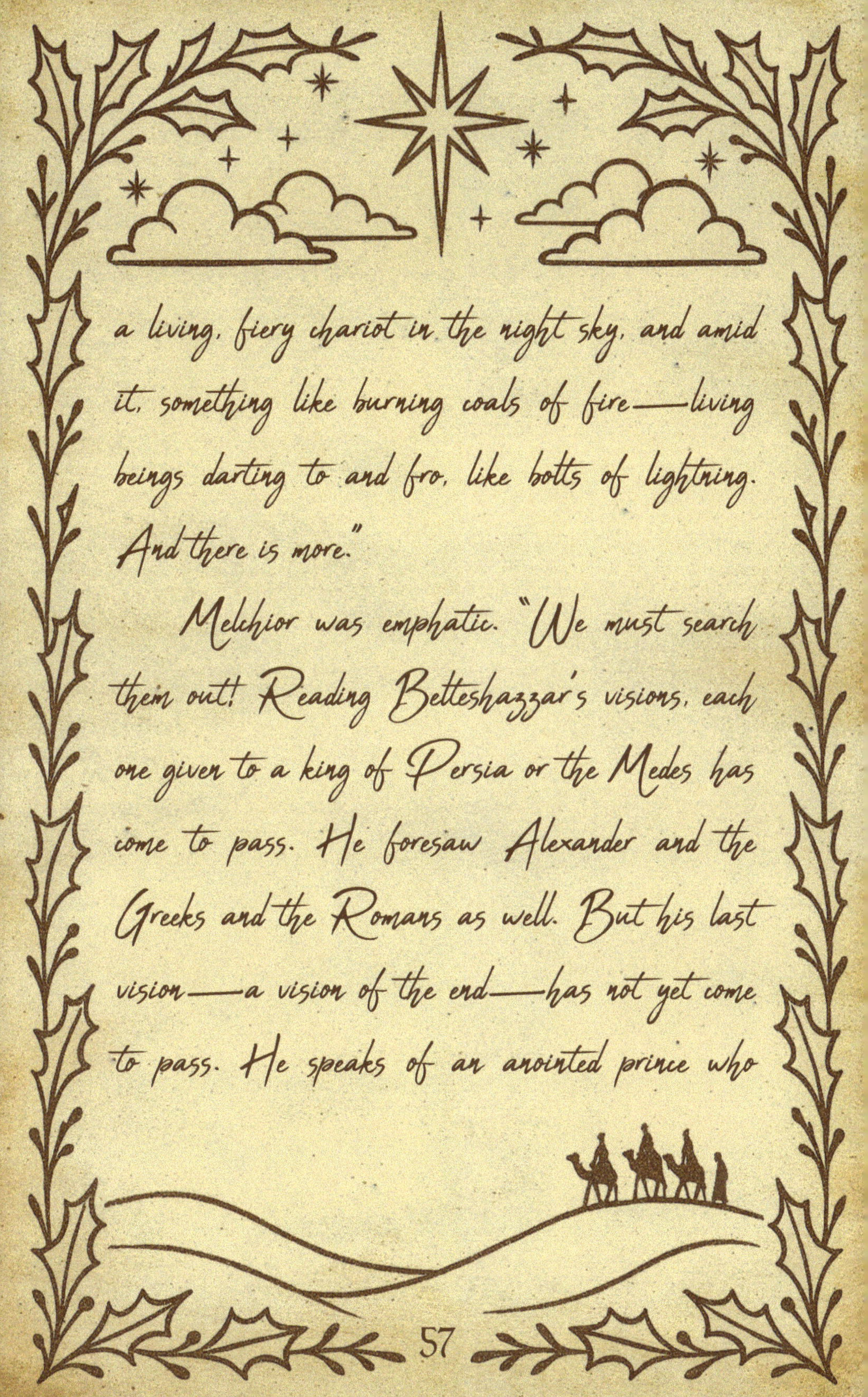

a living, fiery chariot in the night sky, and amid it, something like burning coals of fire—living beings darting to and fro, like bolts of lightning. And there is more."

Melchior was emphatic. "We must search them out! Reading Belteshazzar's visions, each one given to a king of Persia or the Medes has come to pass. He foresaw Alexander and the Greeks and the Romans as well. But his last vision—a vision of the end—has not yet come to pass. He speaks of an anointed prince who

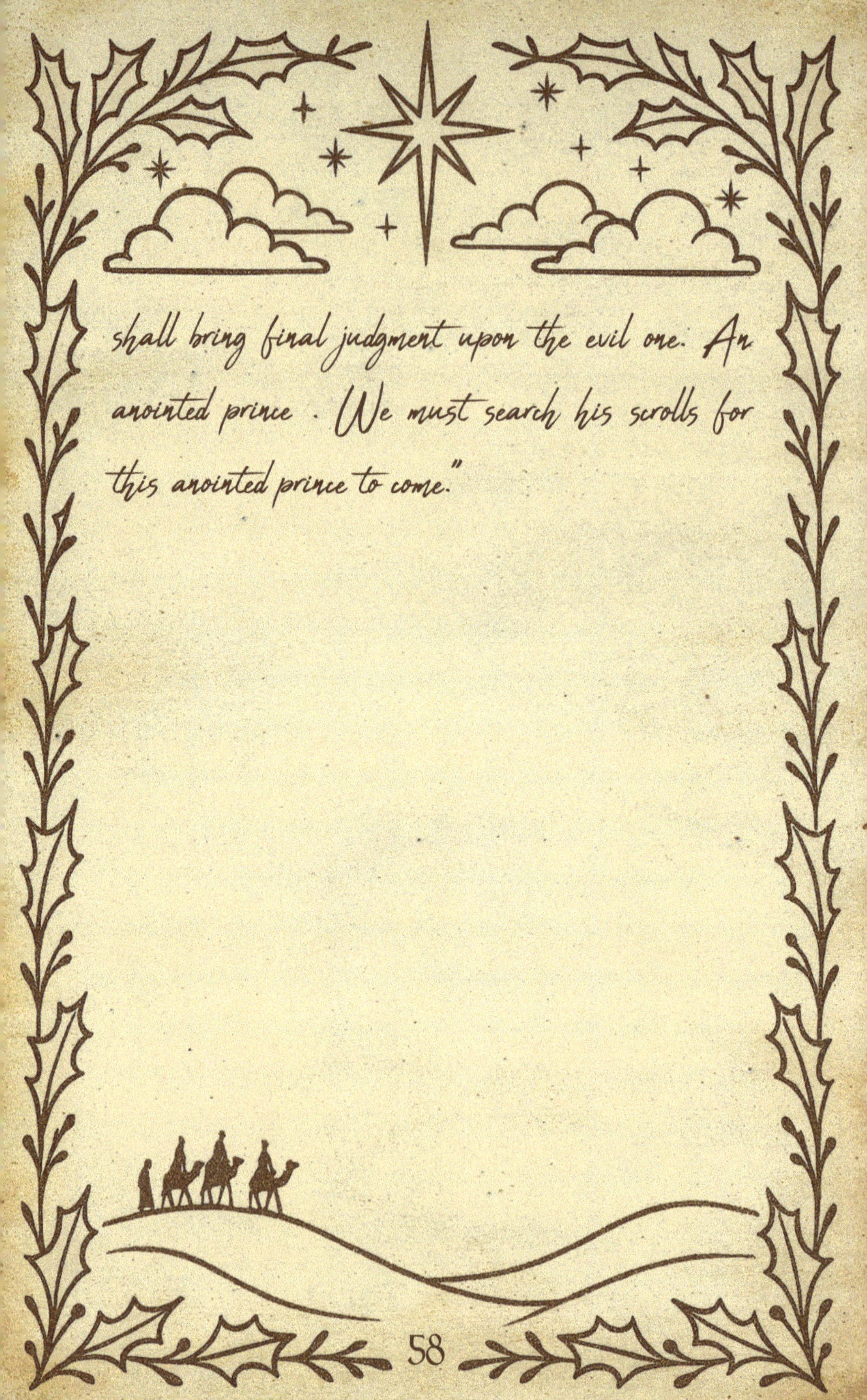

shall bring final judgment upon the evil one. An anointed prince . We must search his scrolls for this anointed prince to come."

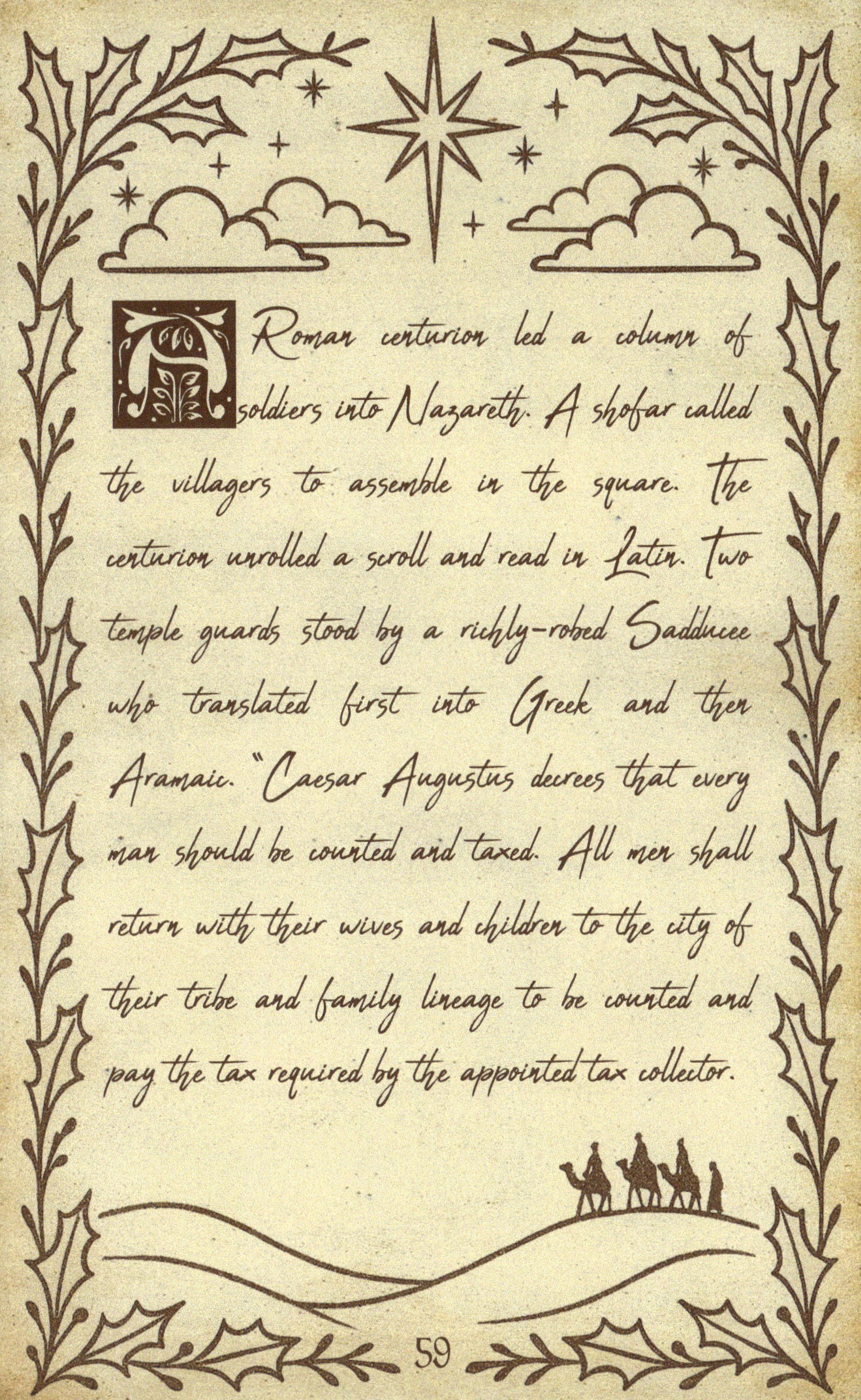

Roman centurion led a column of soldiers into Nazareth. A shofar called the villagers to assemble in the square. The centurion unrolled a scroll and read in Latin. Two temple guards stood by a richly-robed Sadducee who translated first into Greek and then Aramaic. "Caesar Augustus decrees that every man should be counted and taxed. All men shall return with their wives and children to the city of their tribe and family lineage to be counted and pay the tax required by the appointed tax collector.

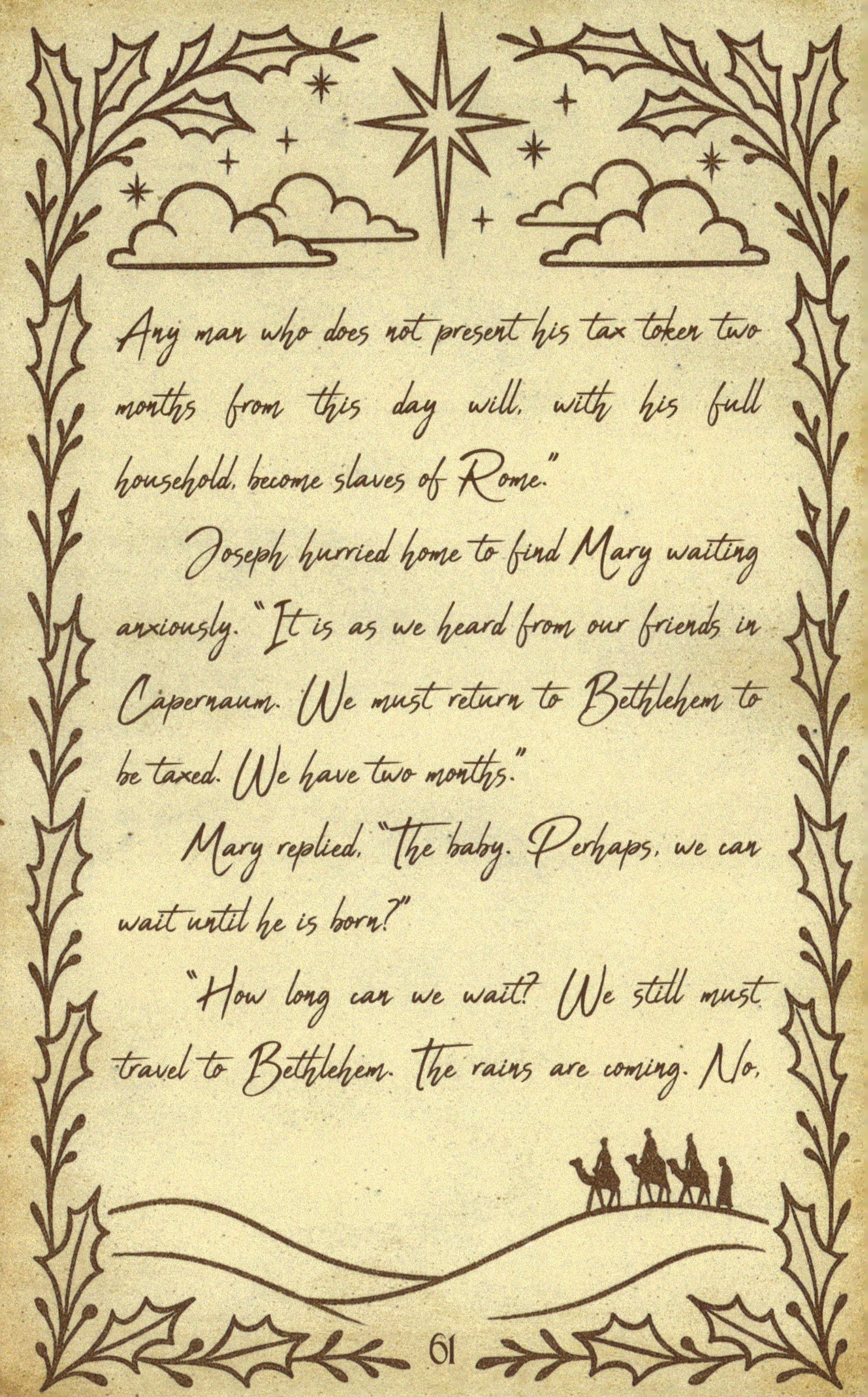

Any man who does not present his tax token two months from this day will, with his full household, become slaves of Rome."

Joseph hurried home to find Mary waiting anxiously. "It is as we heard from our friends in Capernaum. We must return to Bethlehem to be taxed. We have two months."

Mary replied, "The baby. Perhaps, we can wait until he is born?"

"How long can we wait? We still must travel to Bethlehem. The rains are coming. No,

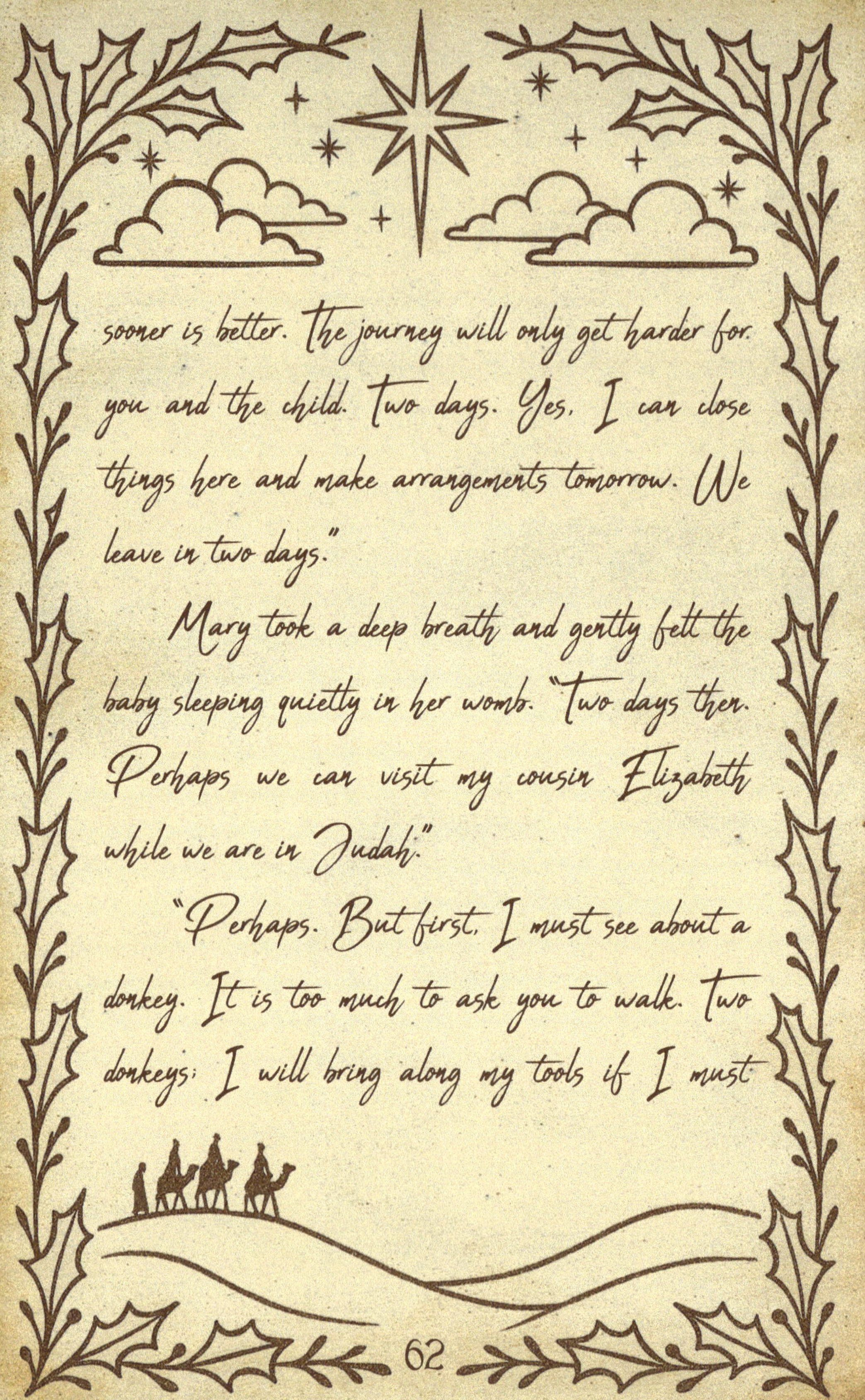

sooner is better. The journey will only get harder for you and the child. Two days. Yes. I can close things here and make arrangements tomorrow. We leave in two days."

Mary took a deep breath and gently felt the baby sleeping quietly in her womb. "Two days then. Perhaps we can visit my cousin Elizabeth while we are in Judah."

"Perhaps. But first, I must see about a donkey. It is too much to ask you to walk. Two donkeys; I will bring along my tools if I must

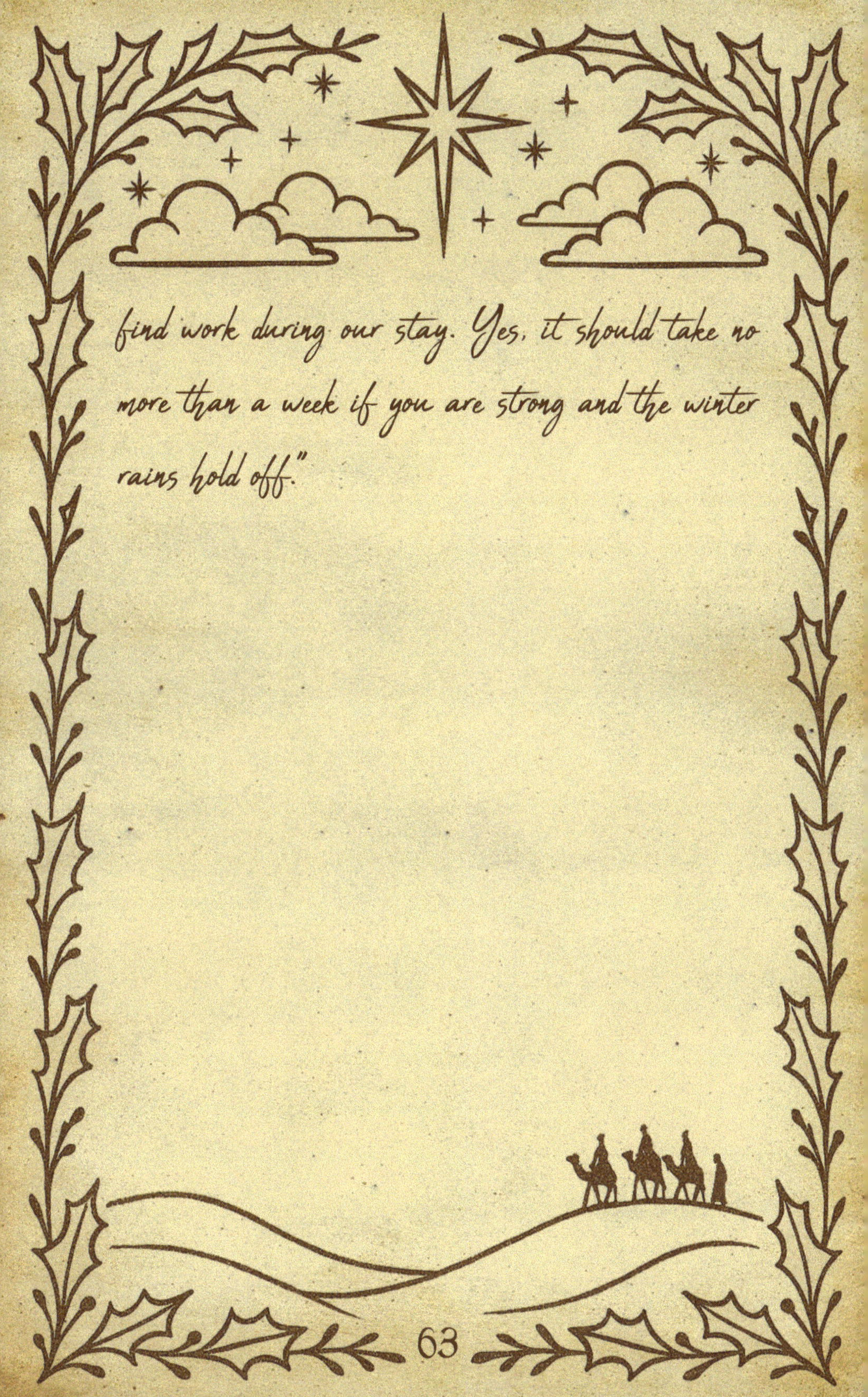

find work during our stay. Yes, it should take no more than a week if you are strong and the winter rains hold off."

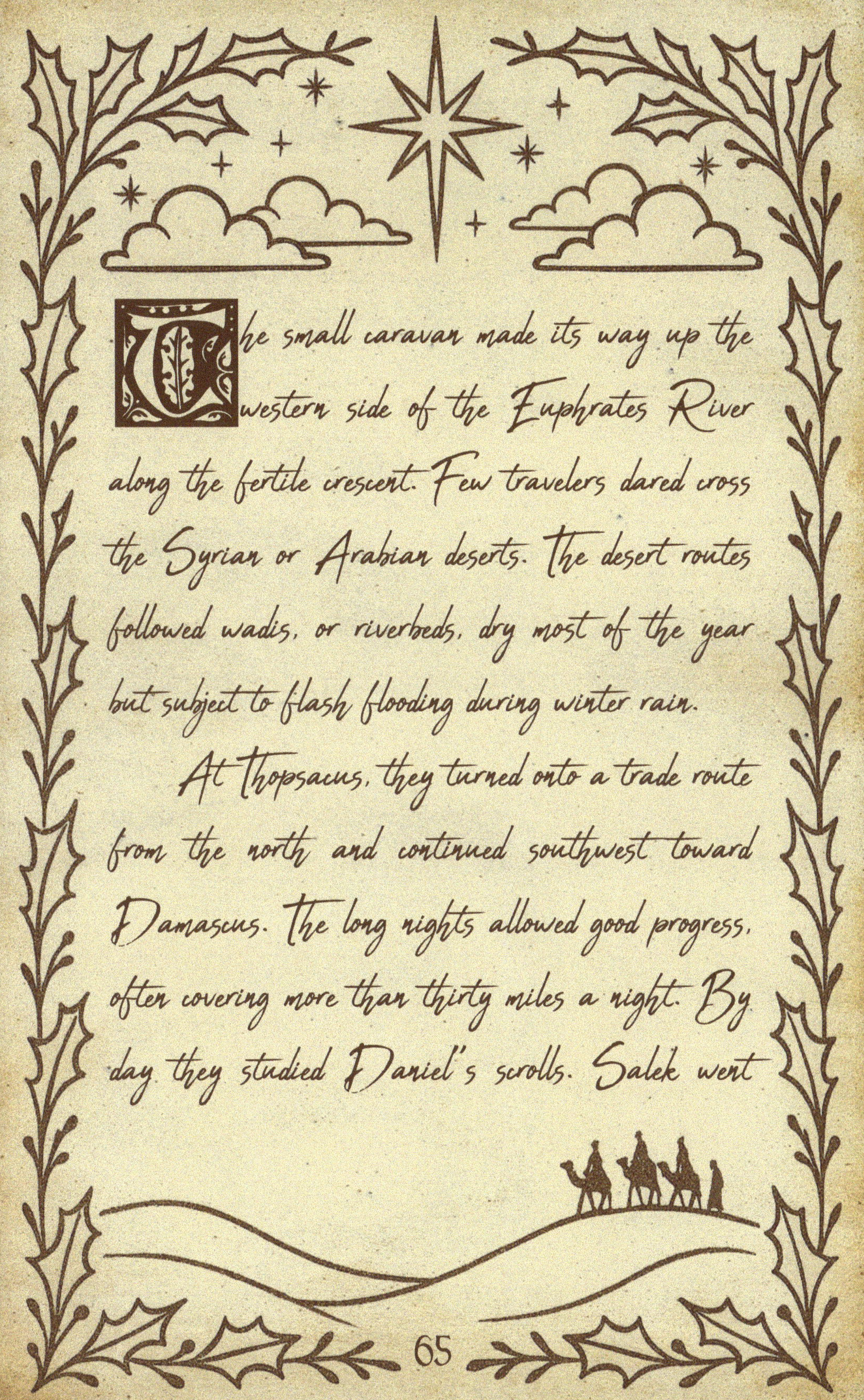

The small caravan made its way up the western side of the Euphrates River along the fertile crescent. Few travelers dared cross the Syrian or Arabian deserts. The desert routes followed wadis, or riverbeds, dry most of the year but subject to flash flooding during winter rain.

At Thopsacus, they turned onto a trade route from the north and continued southwest toward Damascus. The long nights allowed good progress, often covering more than thirty miles a night. By day they studied Daniel's scrolls. Salek went

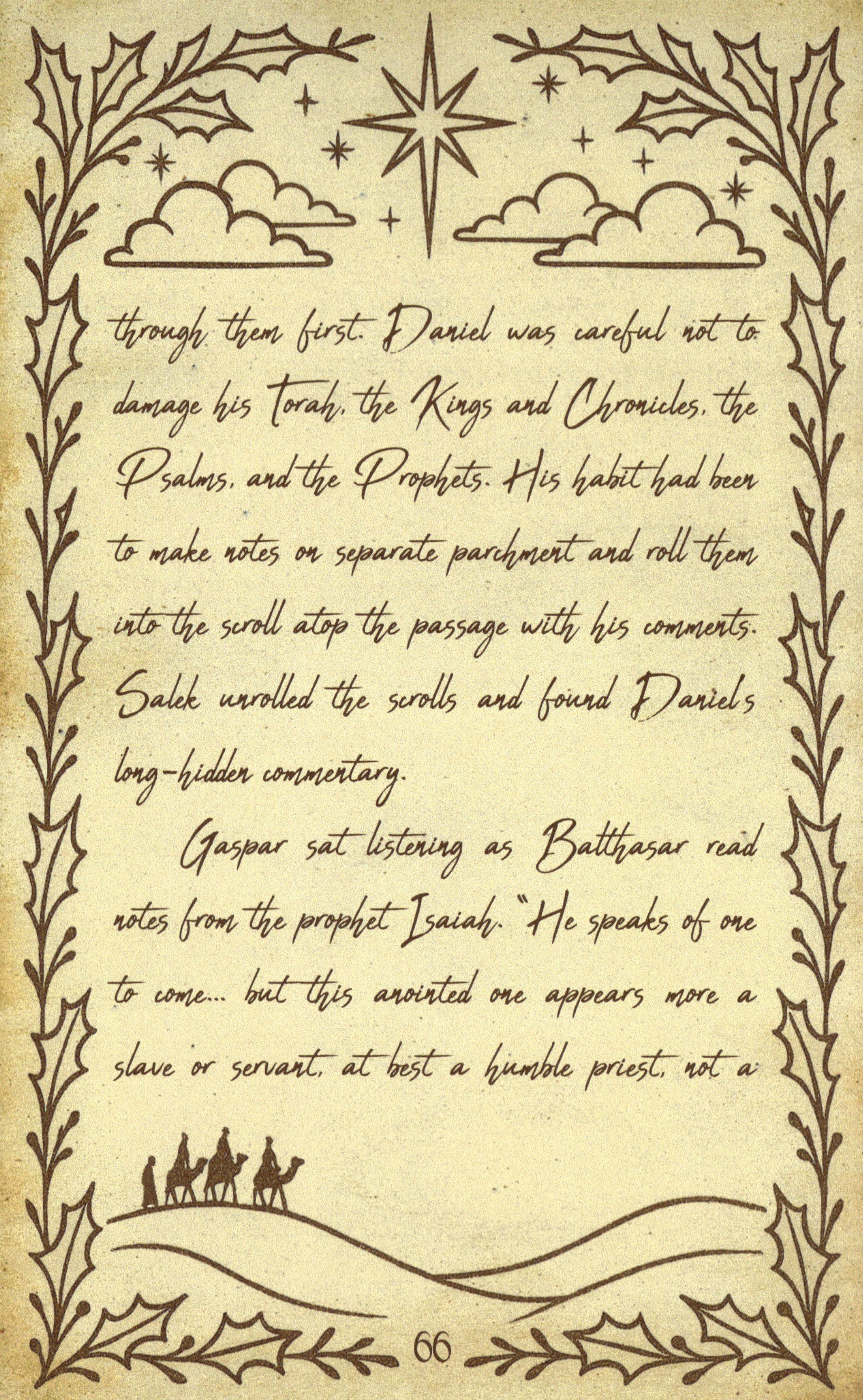

through them first. Daniel was careful not to damage his Torah, the Kings and Chronicles, the Psalms, and the Prophets. His habit had been to make notes on separate parchment and roll them into the scroll atop the passage with his comments. Salek unrolled the scrolls and found Daniel's long-hidden commentary.

Gaspar sat listening as Balthasar read notes from the prophet Isaiah. "He speaks of one to come... but this anointed one appears more a slave or servant, at best a humble priest, not a

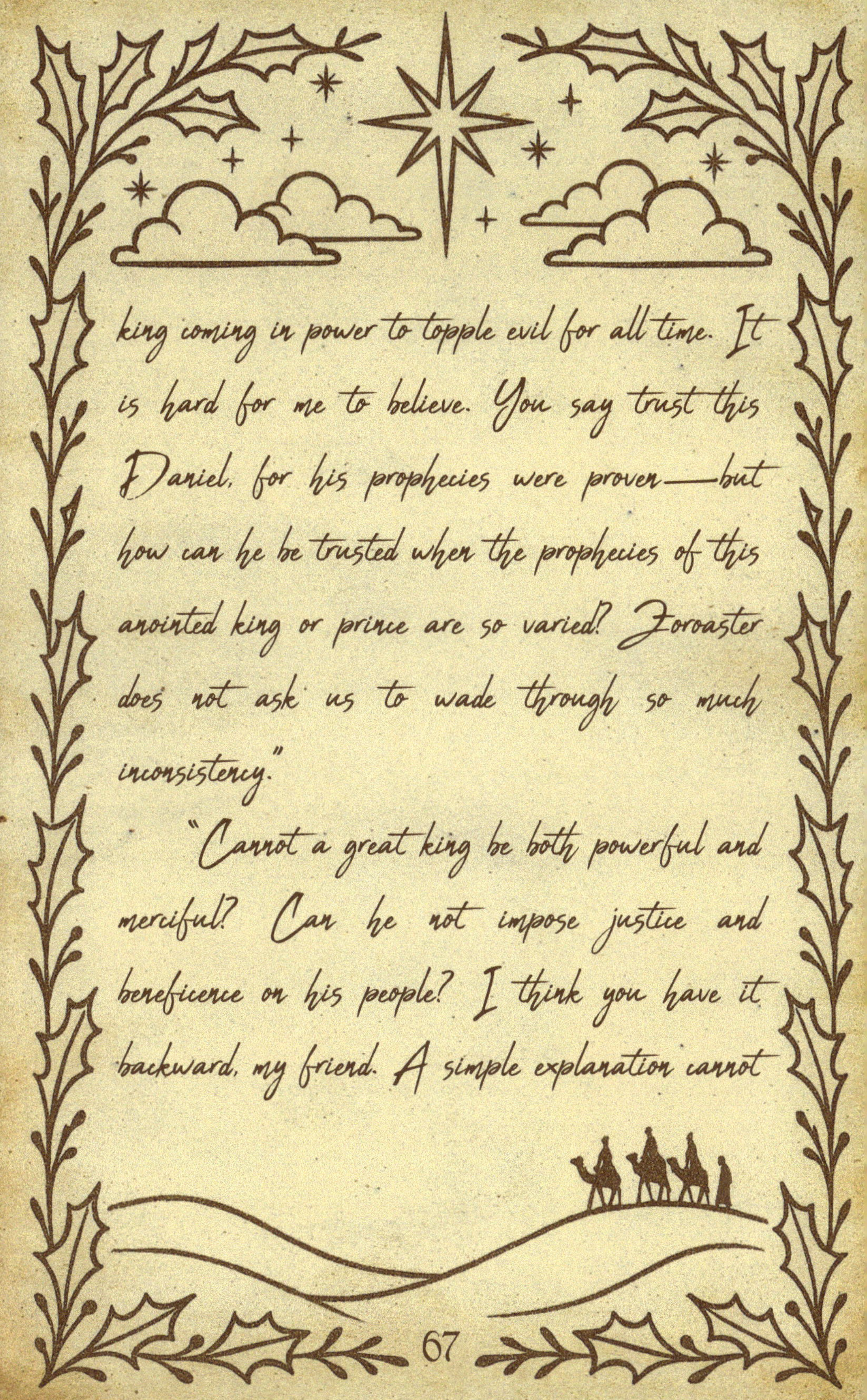

king coming in power to topple evil for all time. It is hard for me to believe. You say trust this Daniel, for his prophecies were proven—but how can he be trusted when the prophecies of this anointed king or prince are so varied? Zoroaster does not ask us to wade through so much inconsistency."

"Cannot a great king be both powerful and merciful? Can he not impose justice and beneficence on his people? I think you have it backward, my friend. A simple explanation cannot

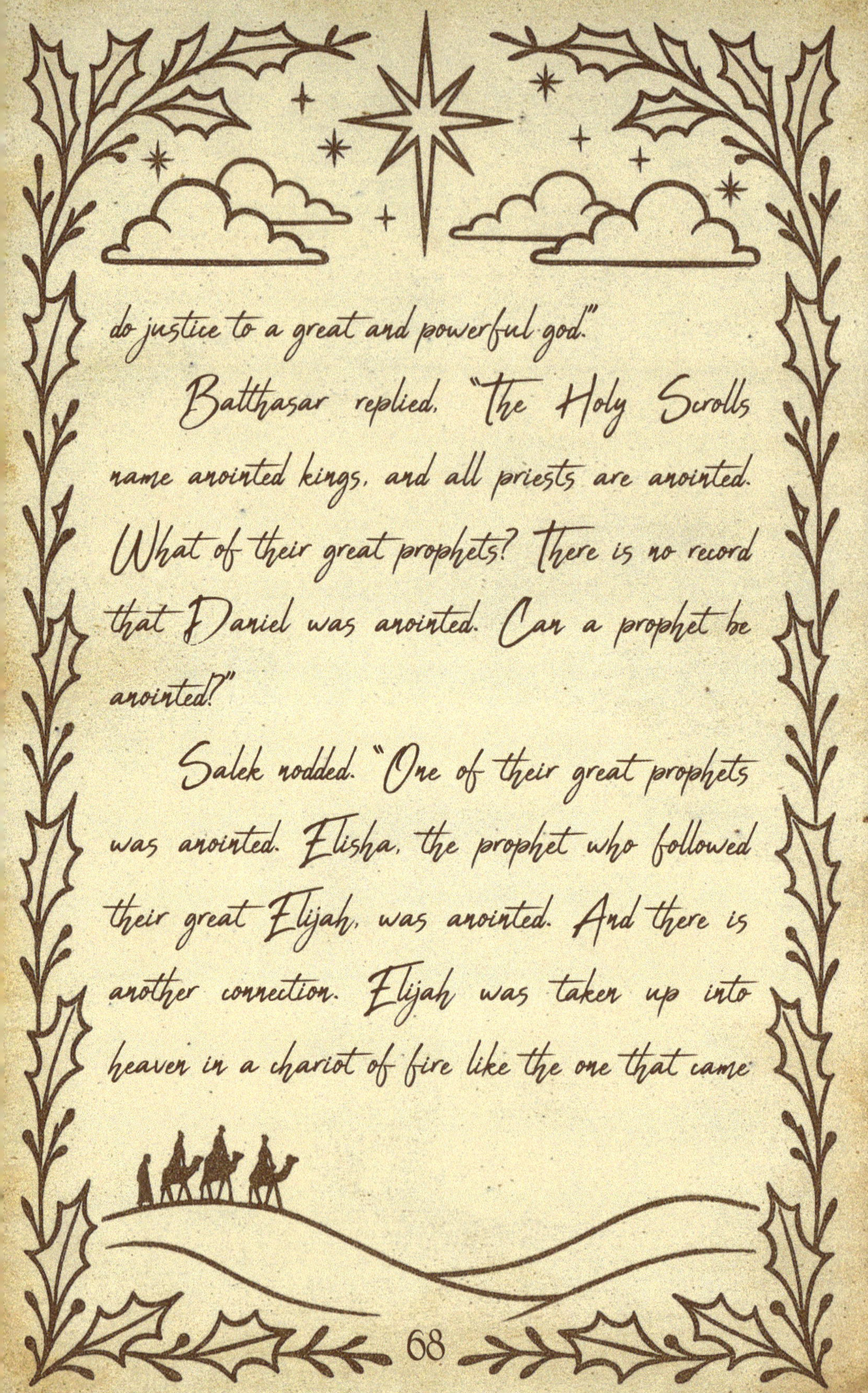

do justice to a great and powerful god."

Balthasar replied, "The Holy Scrolls name anointed kings, and all priests are anointed. What of their great prophets? There is no record that Daniel was anointed. Can a prophet be anointed?"

Salek nodded. "One of their great prophets was anointed. Elisha, the prophet who followed their great Elijah, was anointed. And there is another connection. Elijah was taken up into heaven in a chariot of fire like the one that came

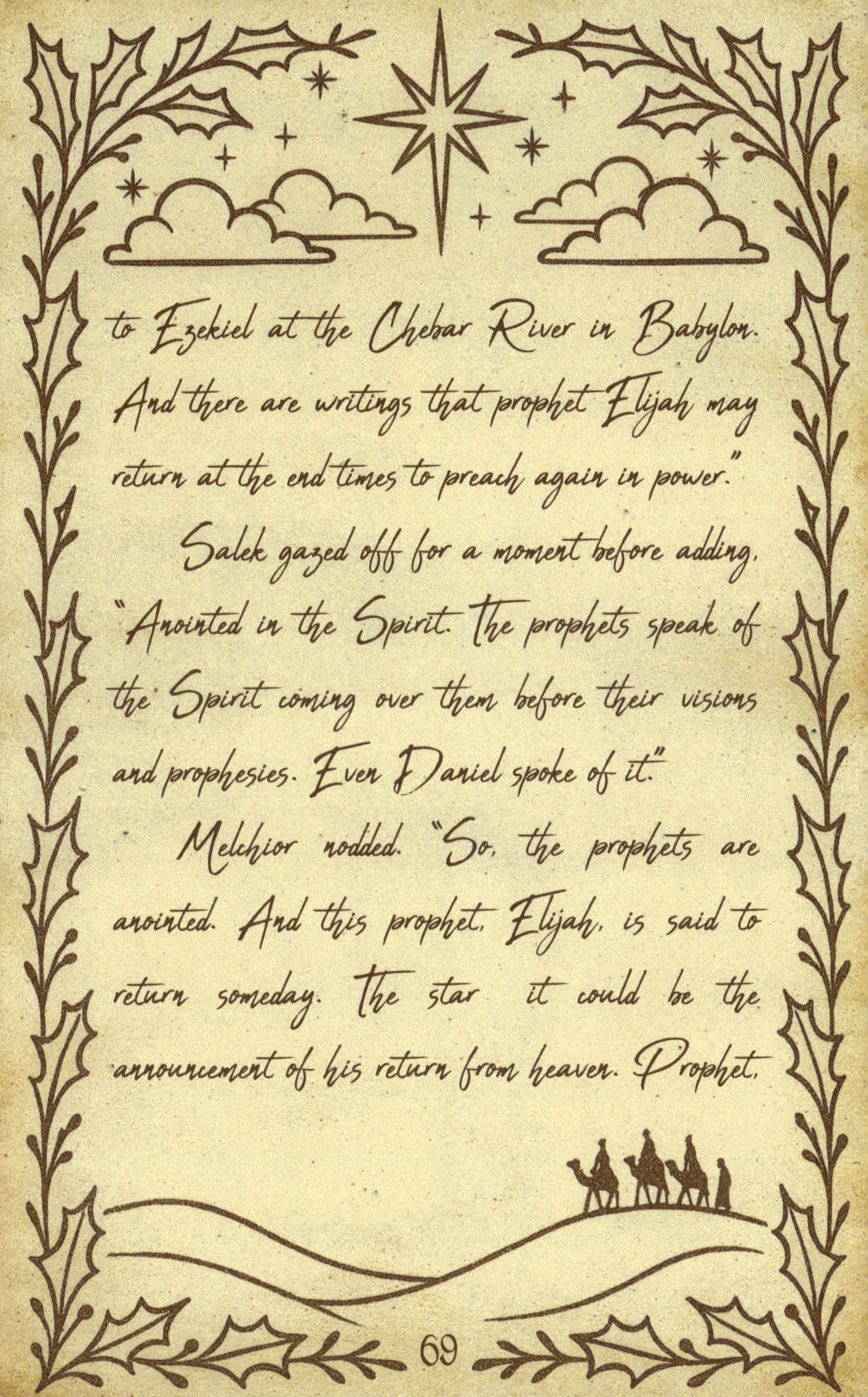

to Ezekiel at the Chebar River in Babylon. And there are writings that prophet Elijah may return at the end times to preach again in power."

Salek gazed off for a moment before adding, "Anointed in the Spirit. The prophets speak of the Spirit coming over them before their visions and prophesies. Even Daniel spoke of it."

Melchior nodded. "So, the prophets are anointed. And this prophet, Elijah, is said to return someday. The star it could be the announcement of his return from heaven. Prophet,

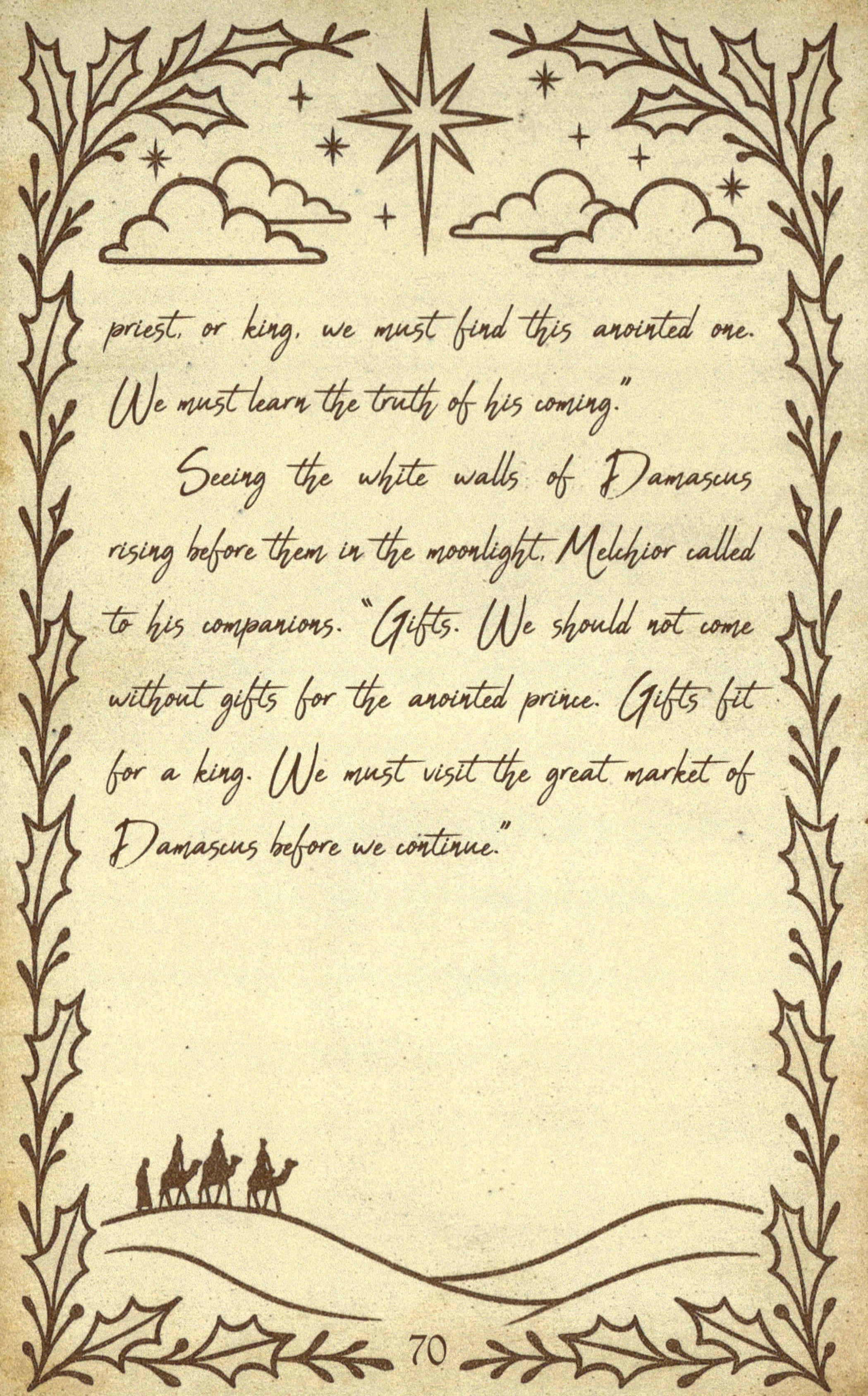

priest, or king, we must find this anointed one. We must learn the truth of his coming."

Seeing the white walls of Damascus rising before them in the moonlight, Melchior called to his companions. "Gifts. We should not come without gifts for the anointed prince. Gifts fit for a king. We must visit the great market of Damascus before we continue."

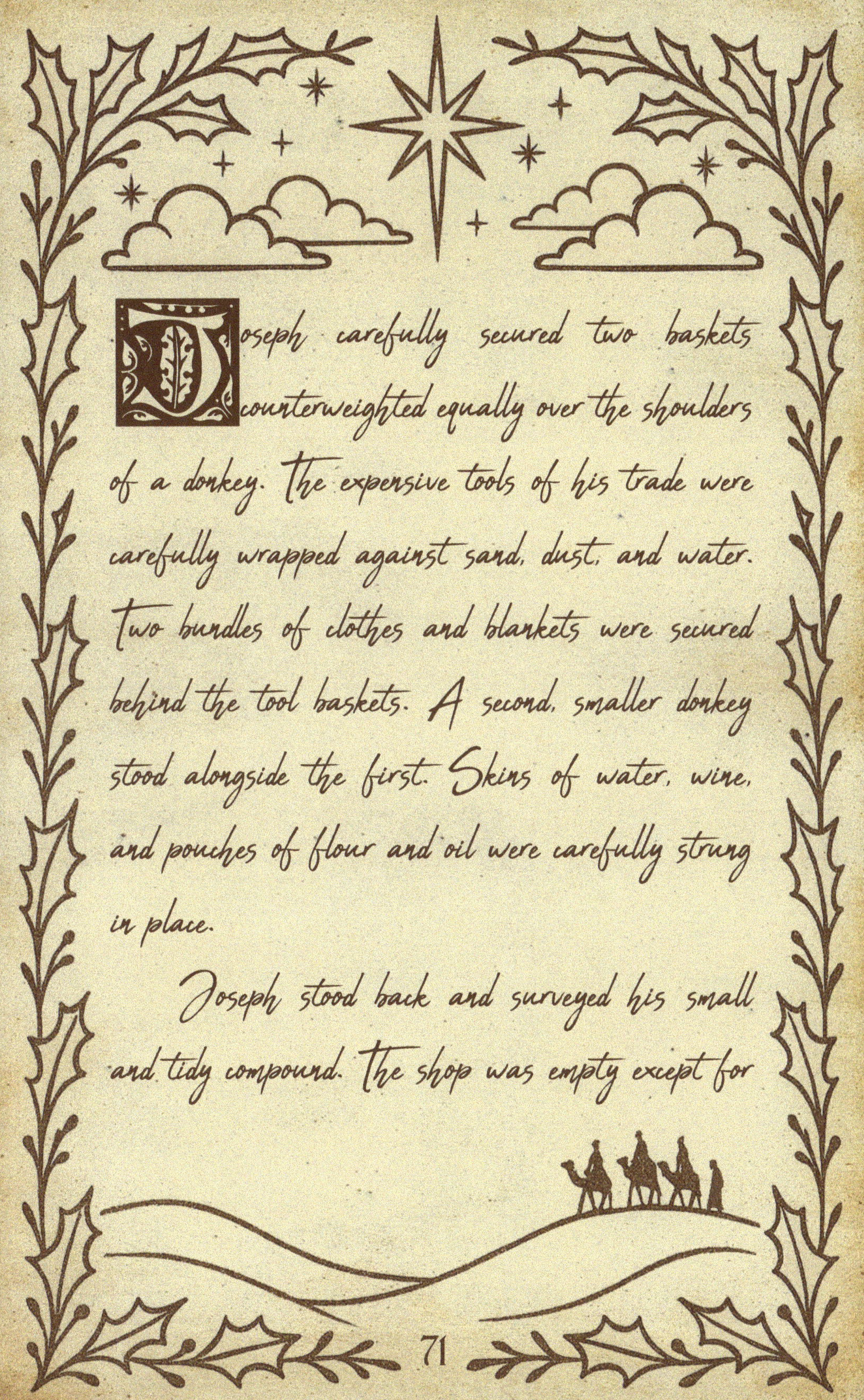

Joseph carefully secured two baskets counterweighted equally over the shoulders of a donkey. The expensive tools of his trade were carefully wrapped against sand, dust, and water. Two bundles of clothes and blankets were secured behind the tool baskets. A second, smaller donkey stood alongside the first. Skins of water, wine, and pouches of flour and oil were carefully strung in place.

Joseph stood back and surveyed his small and tidy compound. The shop was empty except for

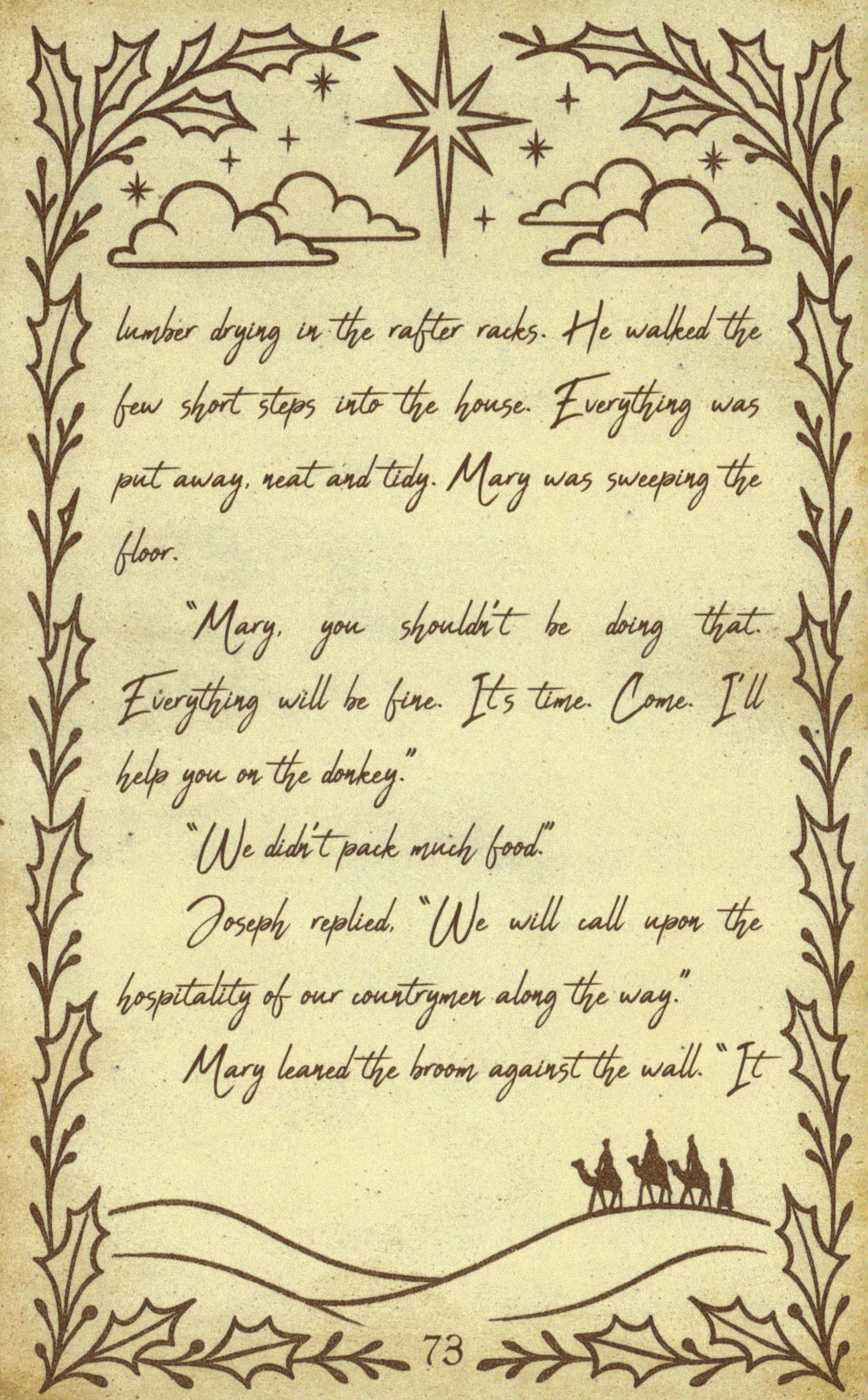

lumber drying in the rafter racks. He walked the few short steps into the house. Everything was put away, neat and tidy. Mary was sweeping the floor.

"Mary, you shouldn't be doing that. Everything will be fine. It's time. Come. I'll help you on the donkey."

"We didn't pack much food."

Joseph replied, "We will call upon the hospitality of our countrymen along the way."

Mary leaned the broom against the wall. "It

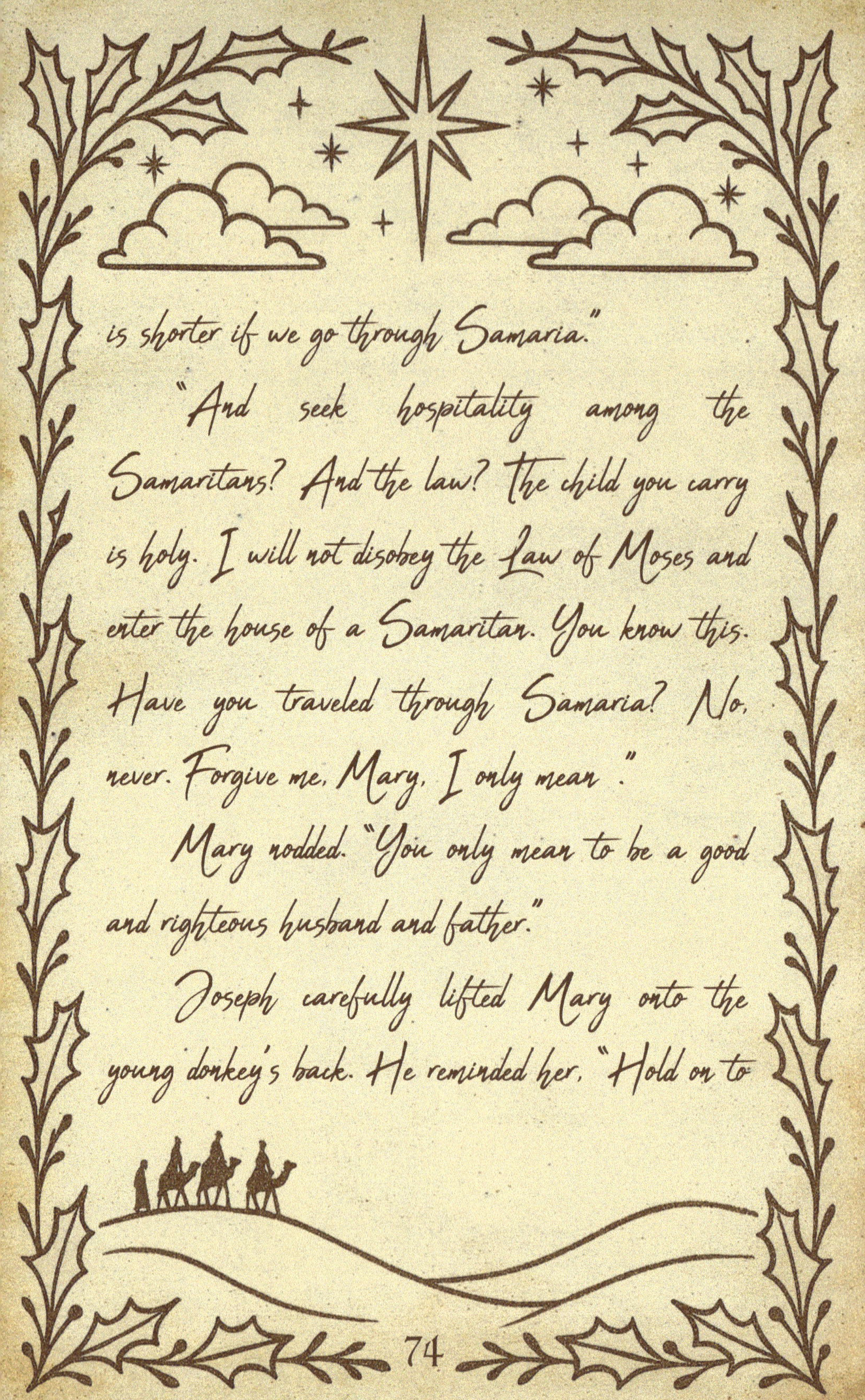

is shorter if we go through Samaria."

"And seek hospitality among the Samaritans? And the law? The child you carry is holy. I will not disobey the Law of Moses and enter the house of a Samaritan. You know this. Have you traveled through Samaria? No, never. Forgive me, Mary, I only mean ."

Mary nodded. "You only mean to be a good and righteous husband and father."

Joseph carefully lifted Mary onto the young donkey's back. He reminded her, "Hold on to

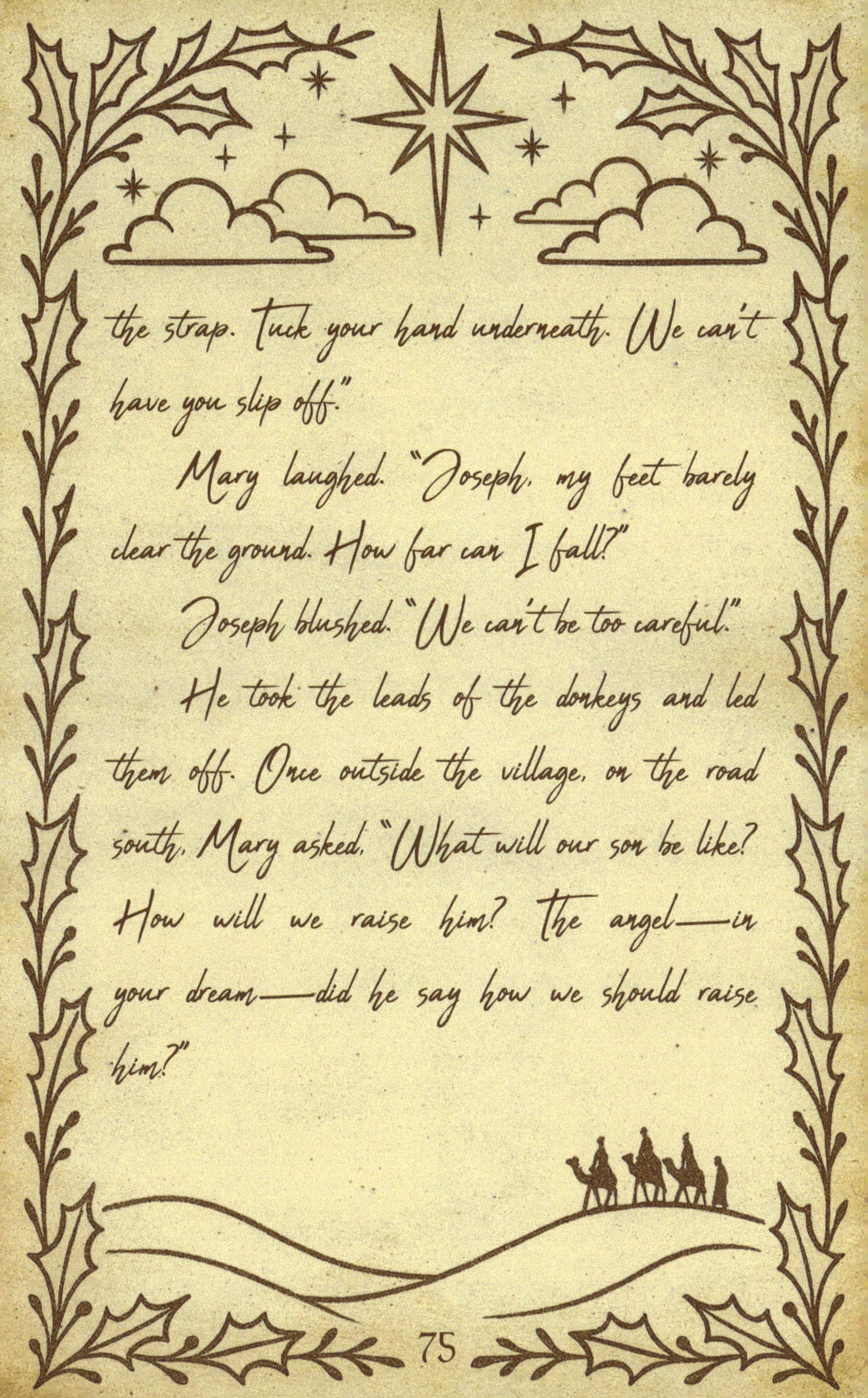

the strap. Tuck your hand underneath. We can't have you slip off."

Mary laughed. "Joseph, my feet barely clear the ground. How far can I fall?"

Joseph blushed. "We can't be too careful."

He took the leads of the donkeys and led them off. Once outside the village, on the road south, Mary asked, "What will our son be like? How will we raise him? The angel—in your dream—did he say how we should raise him?"

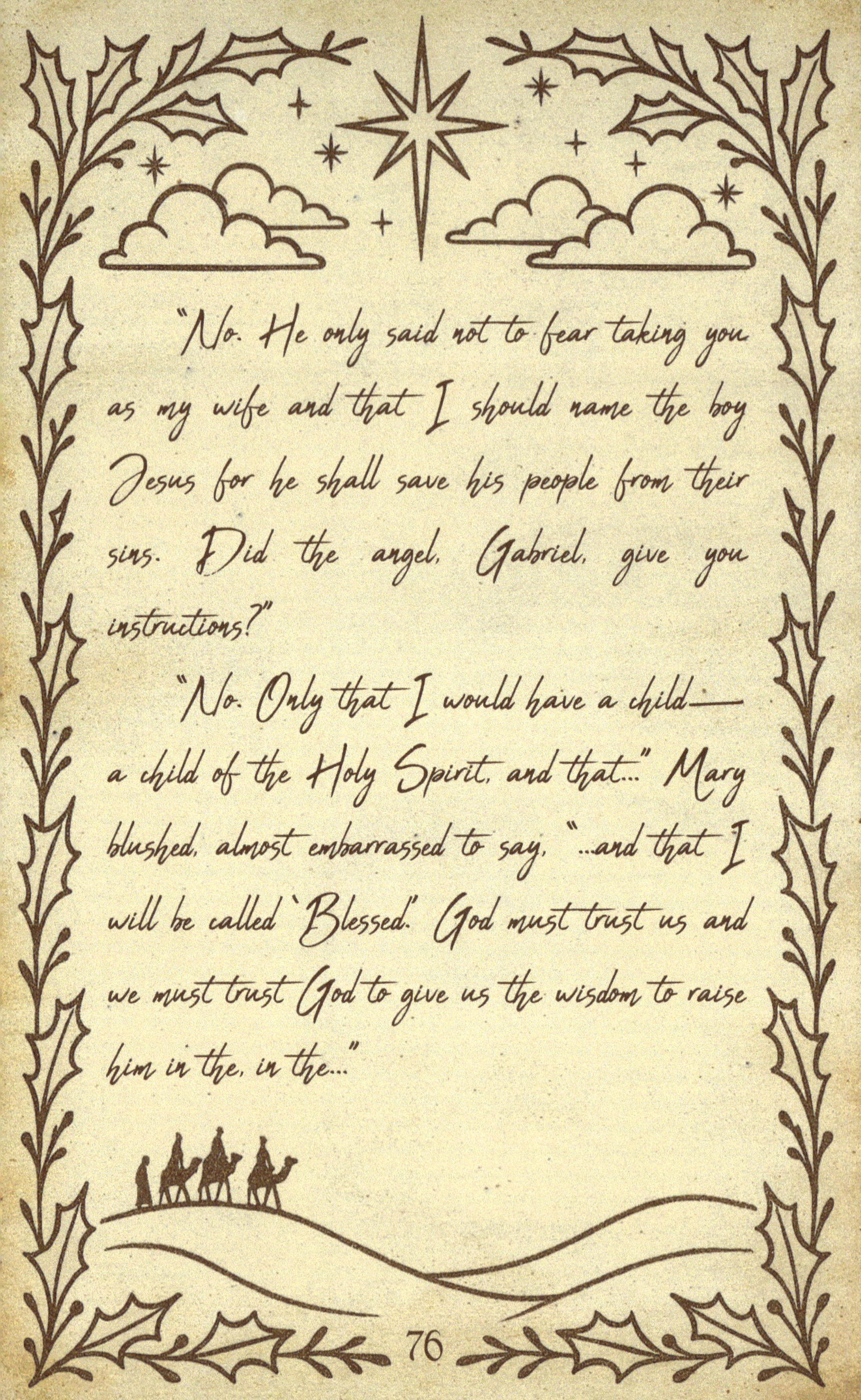

"No. He only said not to fear taking you as my wife and that I should name the boy Jesus for he shall save his people from their sins. Did the angel, Gabriel, give you instructions?"

"No. Only that I would have a child—a child of the Holy Spirit, and that..." Mary blushed, almost embarrassed to say, "...and that I will be called `Blessed'. God must trust us and we must trust God to give us the wisdom to raise him in the, in the..."

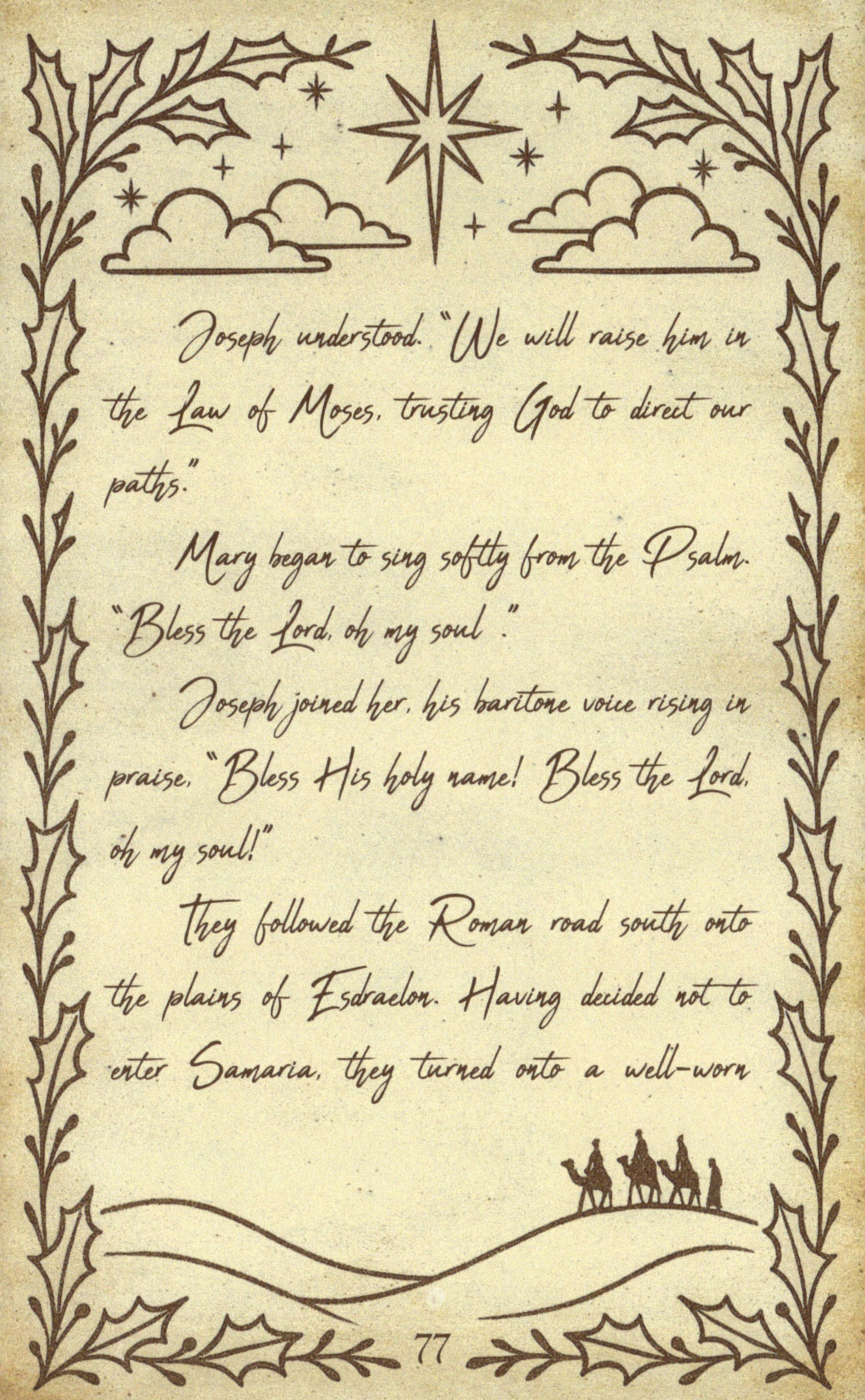

Joseph understood. "We will raise him in the Law of Moses, trusting God to direct our paths."

Mary began to sing softly from the Psalm. "Bless the Lord, oh my soul."

Joseph joined her, his baritone voice rising in praise. "Bless His holy name! Bless the Lord, oh my soul!"

They followed the Roman road south onto the plains of Esdraelon. Having decided not to enter Samaria, they turned onto a well-worn

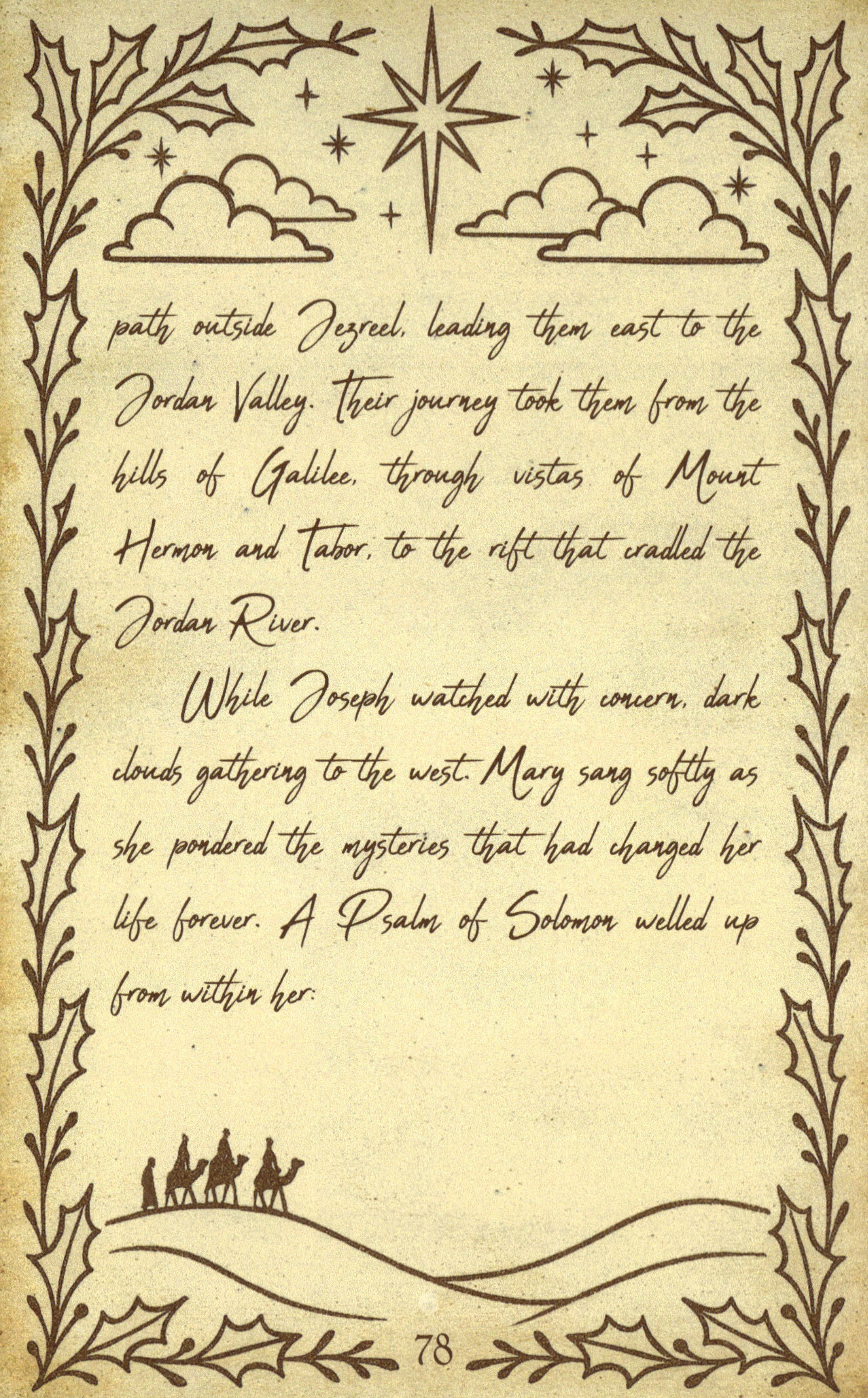

path outside Jezreel, leading them east to the Jordan Valley. Their journey took them from the hills of Galilee, through vistas of Mount Hermon and Tabor, to the rift that cradled the Jordan River.

While Joseph watched with concern, dark clouds gathering to the west, Mary sang softly as she pondered the mysteries that had changed her life forever. A Psalm of Solomon welled up from within her:

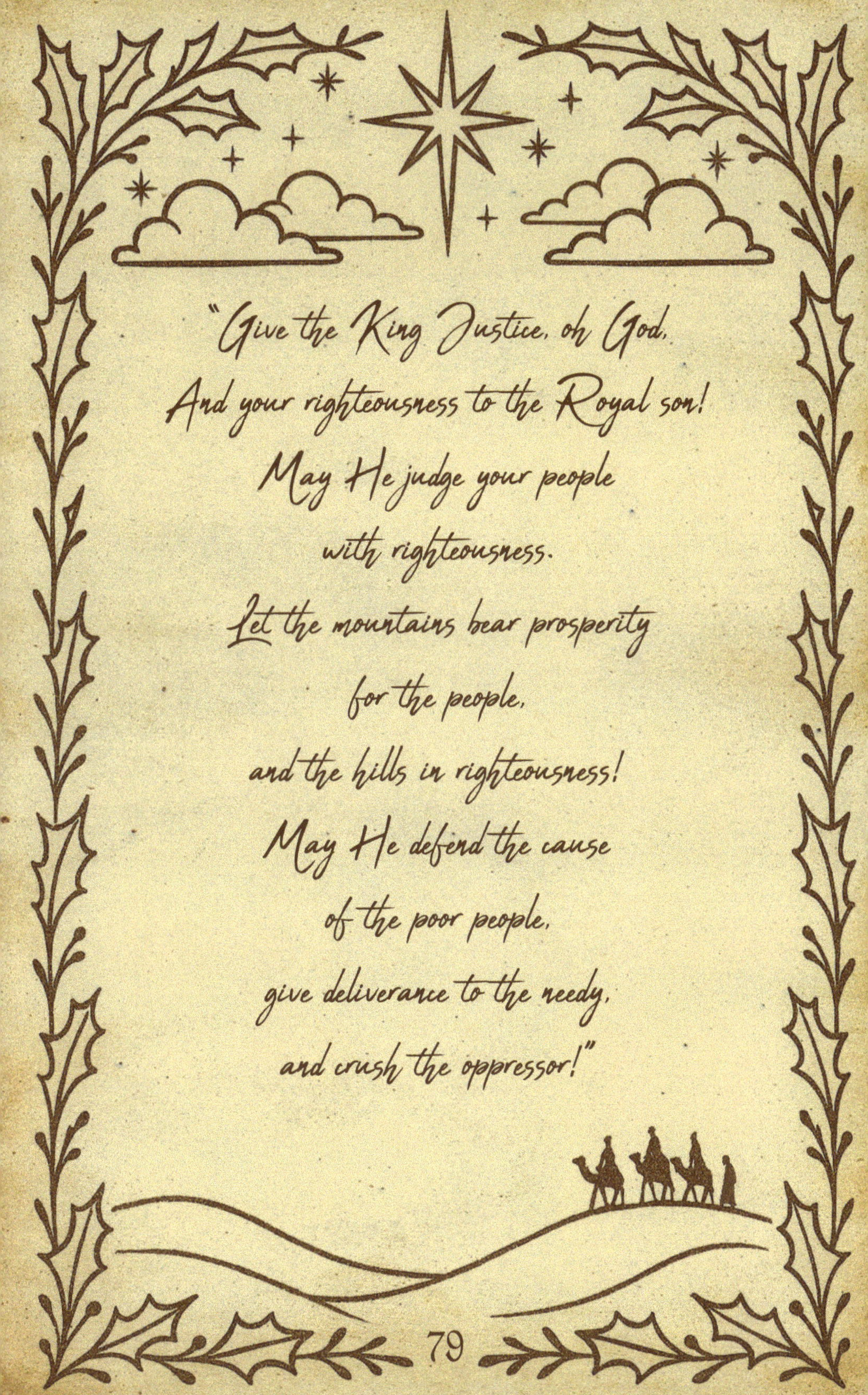

"Give the King Justice, oh God,

And your righteousness to the Royal son!

May He judge your people

with righteousness.

Let the mountains bear prosperity

for the people,

and the hills in righteousness!

May He defend the cause

of the poor people,

give deliverance to the needy,

and crush the oppressor!"

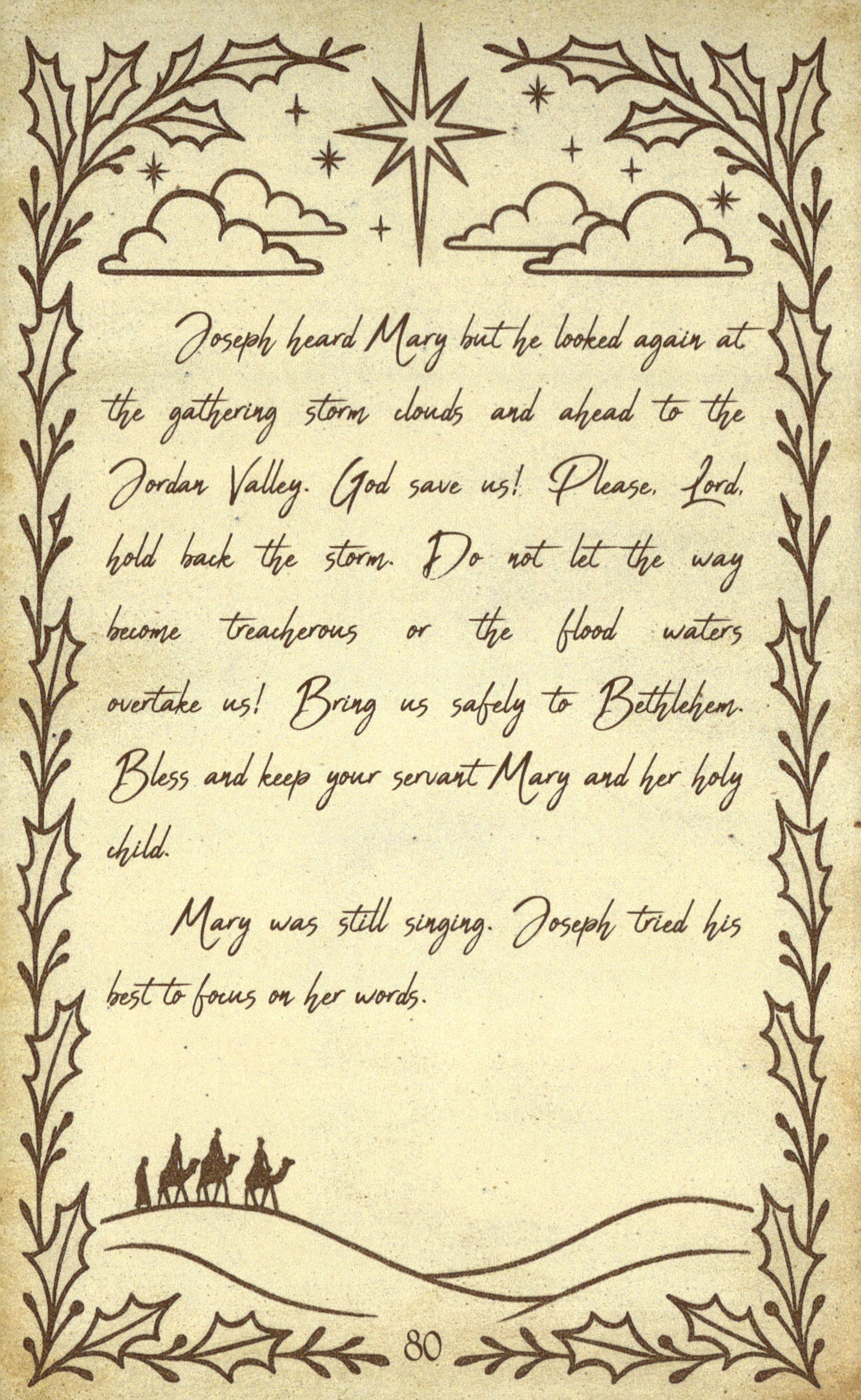

Joseph heard Mary but he looked again at the gathering storm clouds and ahead to the Jordan Valley. God save us! Please, Lord, hold back the storm. Do not let the way become treacherous or the flood waters overtake us! Bring us safely to Bethlehem. Bless and keep your servant Mary and her holy child.

Mary was still singing. Joseph tried his best to focus on her words.

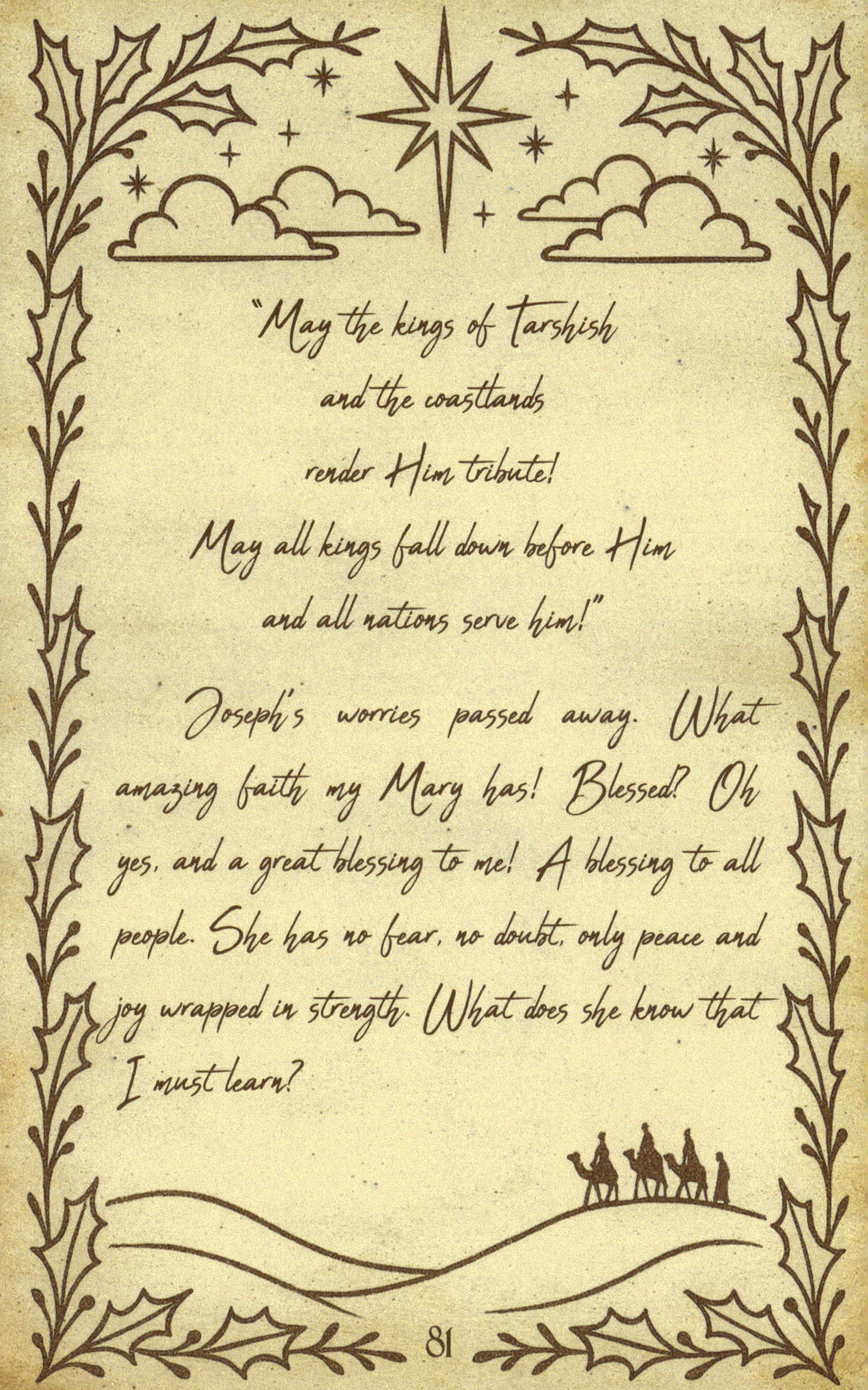

"May the kings of Tarshish
and the coastlands
render Him tribute!
May all kings fall down before Him
and all nations serve him!"

Joseph's worries passed away. What amazing faith my Mary has! Blessed? Oh yes, and a great blessing to me! A blessing to all people. She has no fear, no doubt, only peace and joy wrapped in strength. What does she know that I must learn?

Mary was finishing the Psalm:

"May His name endure forever,

his fame continue as long as the sun!

May people be blessed in Him,

and all nations call Him blessed!

Blessed be the Lord, the God of Israel,

who alone does wondrous things.

Blessed be His glorious name forever!

May the whole earth be filled

with His glory!"

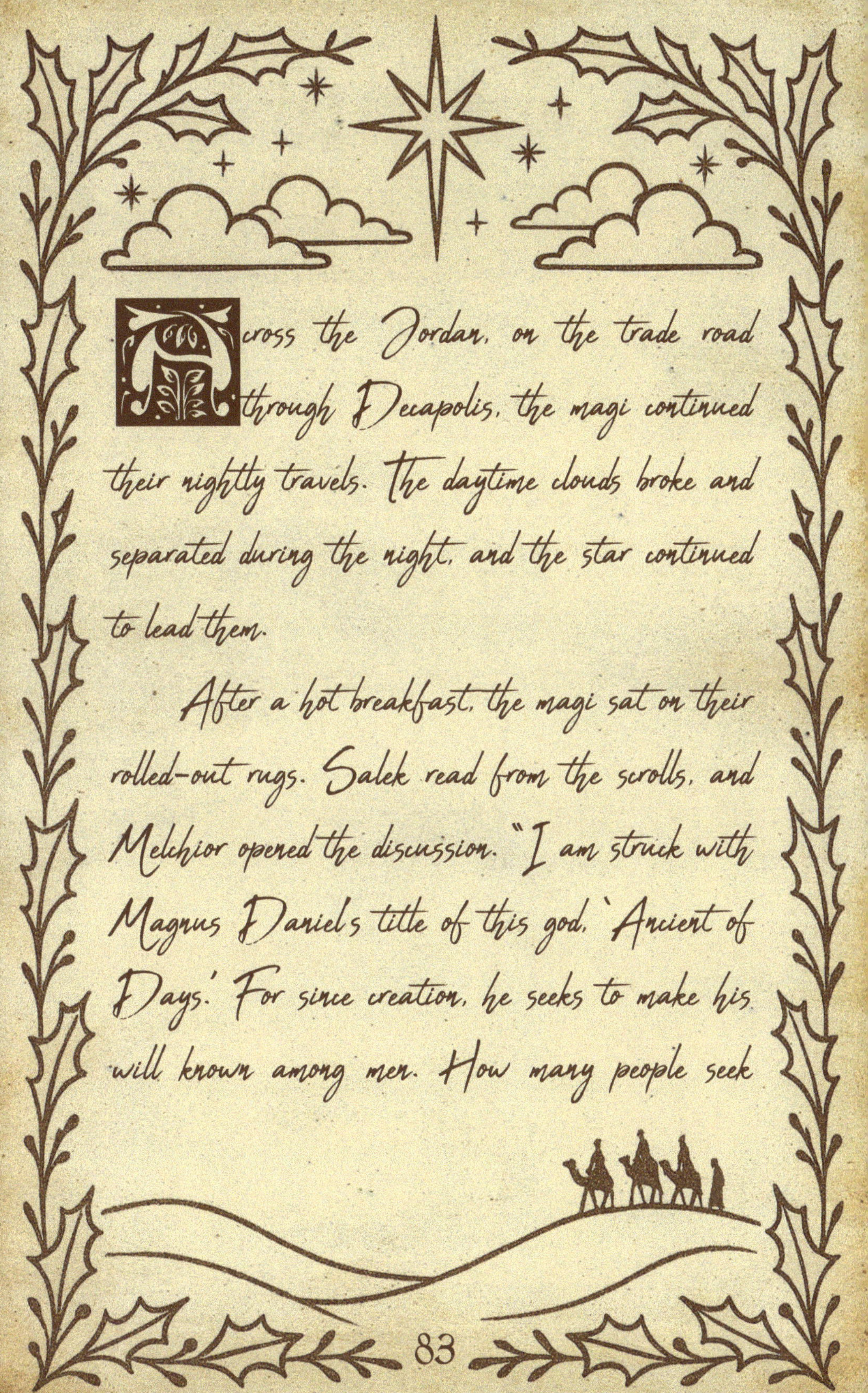

Across the Jordan, on the trade road through Decapolis, the magi continued their nightly travels. The daytime clouds broke and separated during the night, and the star continued to lead them.

After a hot breakfast, the magi sat on their rolled-out rugs. Salek read from the scrolls, and Melchior opened the discussion. "I am struck with Magnus Daniel's title of this god, 'Ancient of Days.' For since creation, he seeks to make his will known among men. How many people seek

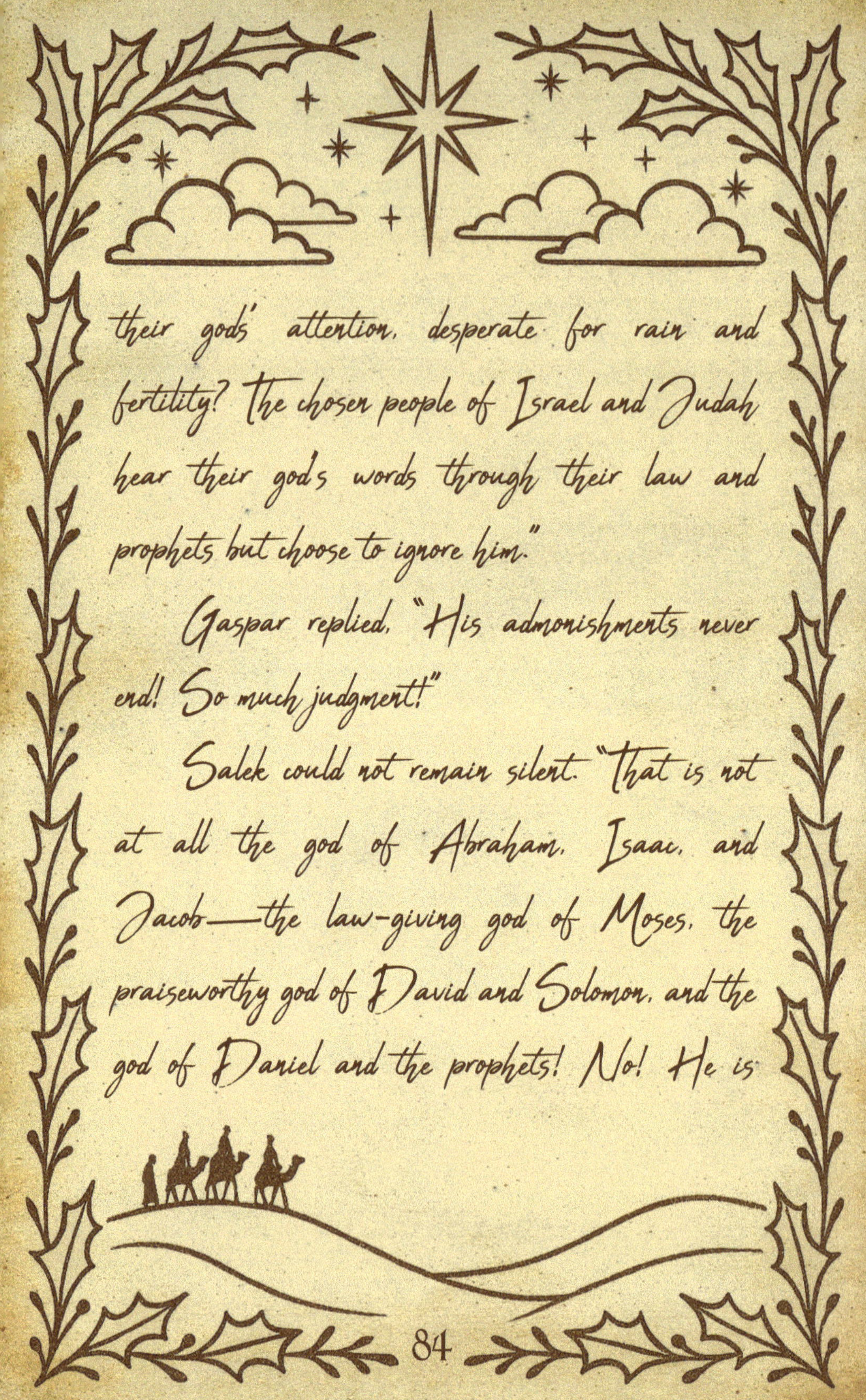

their gods' attention, desperate for rain and fertility? The chosen people of Israel and Judah hear their god's words through their law and prophets but choose to ignore him."

Gaspar replied, "His admonishments never end! So much judgment!"

Salek could not remain silent. "That is not at all the god of Abraham, Isaac, and Jacob—the law-giving god of Moses, the praiseworthy god of David and Solomon, and the god of Daniel and the prophets! No! He is

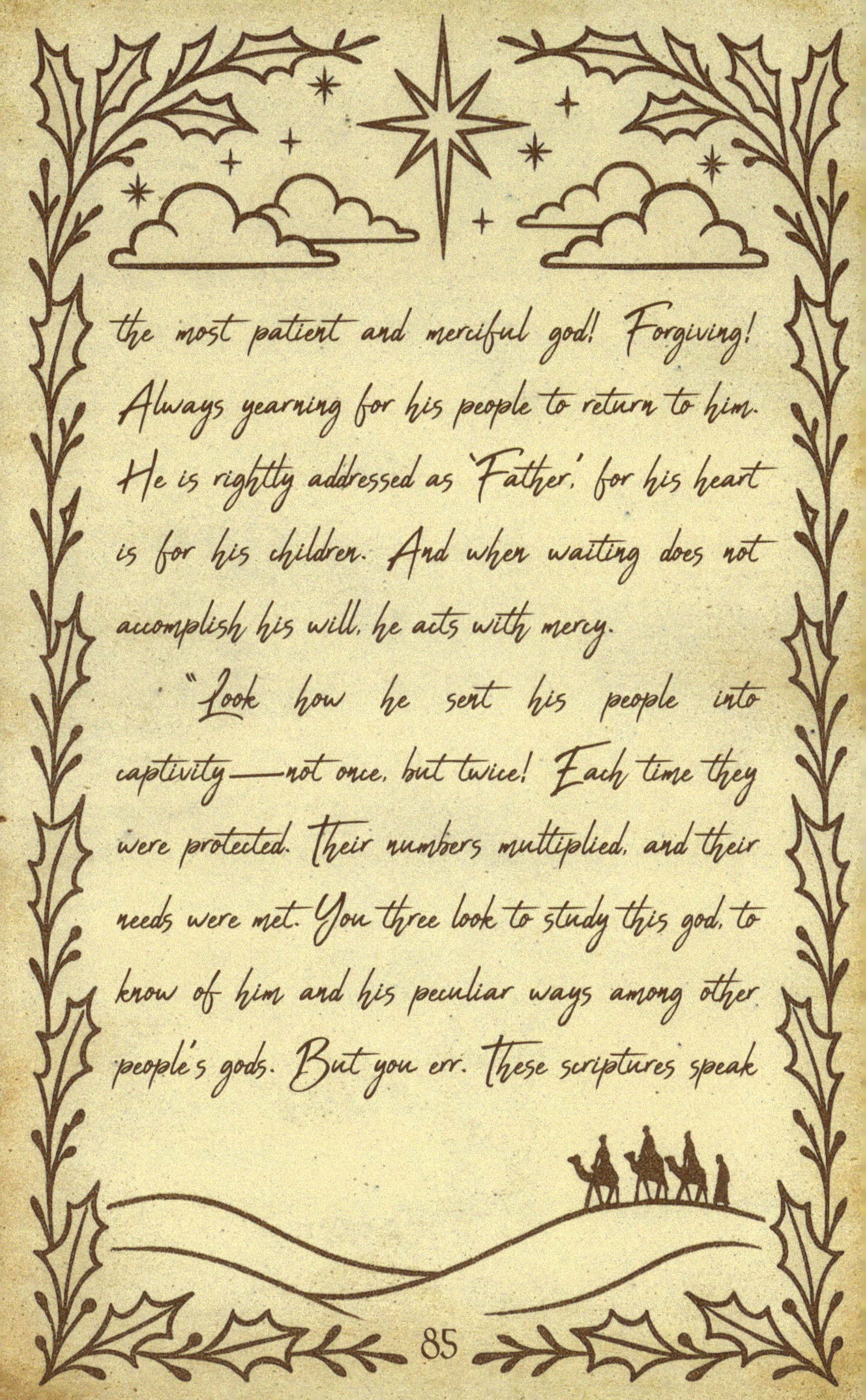

the most patient and merciful god! Forgiving! Always yearning for his people to return to him. He is rightly addressed as 'Father,' for his heart is for his children. And when waiting does not accomplish his will, he acts with mercy.

"Look how he sent his people into captivity—not once, but twice! Each time they were protected. Their numbers multiplied, and their needs were met. You three look to study this god, to know of him and his peculiar ways among other people's gods. But you err. These scriptures speak to me of a god who asks for my love and for me to love others. That is his law. That is what I hope to find beneath the star——a gift of love from surely an Almighty God."

The three magi sat silently. At last, Melchior replied: "I have rightly named you Salek or 'Seeker.' Wisdom is better than knowledge. I pray you have found what you seek. You have opened my eyes to my error."

Salek mumbled. "Forgive me for my impatience. You have treated me with respect and

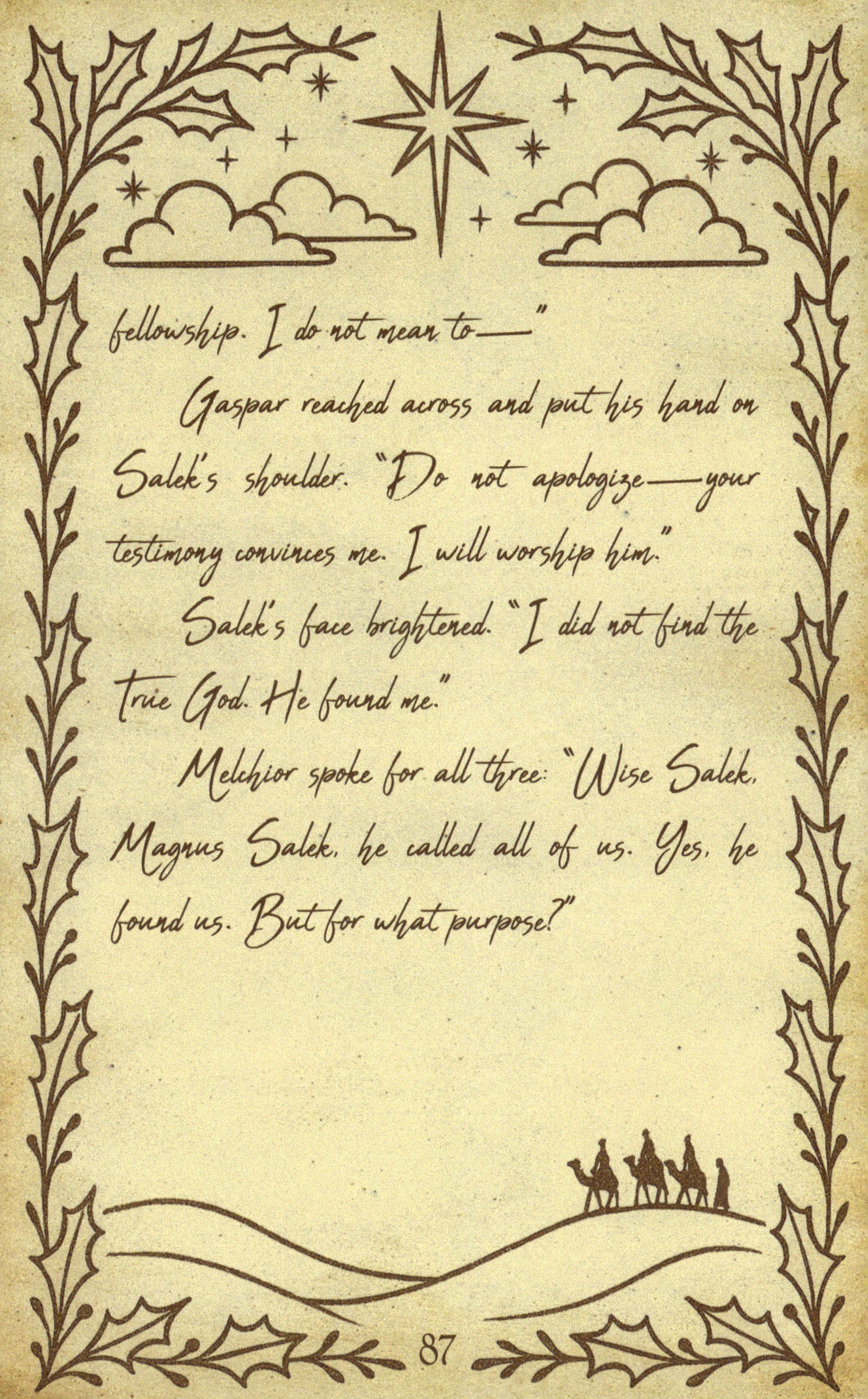

fellowship. I do not mean to——"

Gaspar reached across and put his hand on Salek's shoulder. "Do not apologize——your testimony convinces me. I will worship him."

Salek's face brightened. "I did not find the true God. He found me."

Melchior spoke for all three: "Wise Salek, Magnus Salek, he called all of us. Yes, he found us. But for what purpose?"

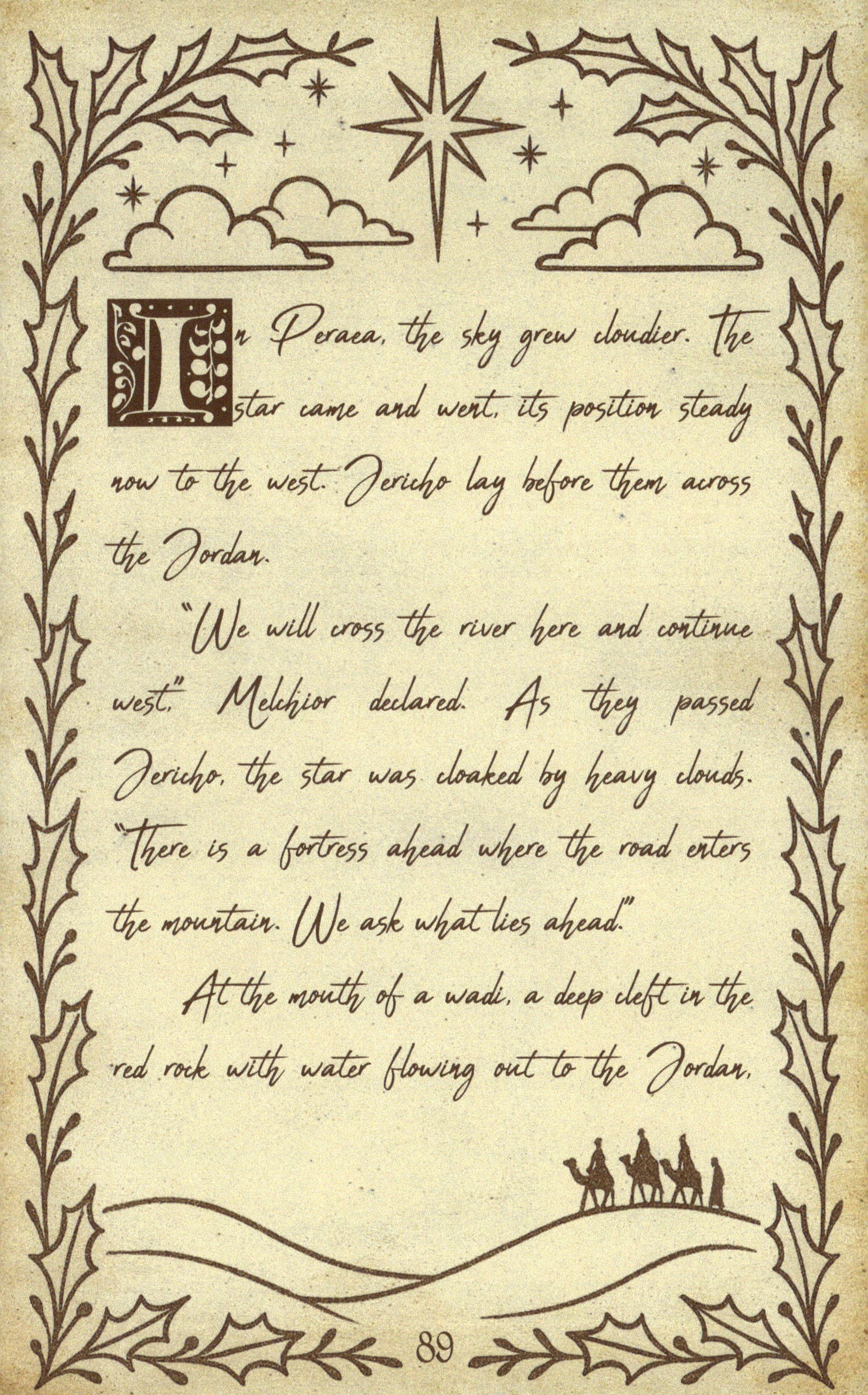

In Peraea, the sky grew cloudier. The star came and went, its position steady now to the west. Jericho lay before them across the Jordan.

"We will cross the river here and continue west." Melchior declared. As they passed Jericho, the star was cloaked by heavy clouds. "There is a fortress ahead where the road enters the mountain. We ask what lies ahead."

At the mouth of a wadi, a deep cleft in the red rock with water flowing out to the Jordan,

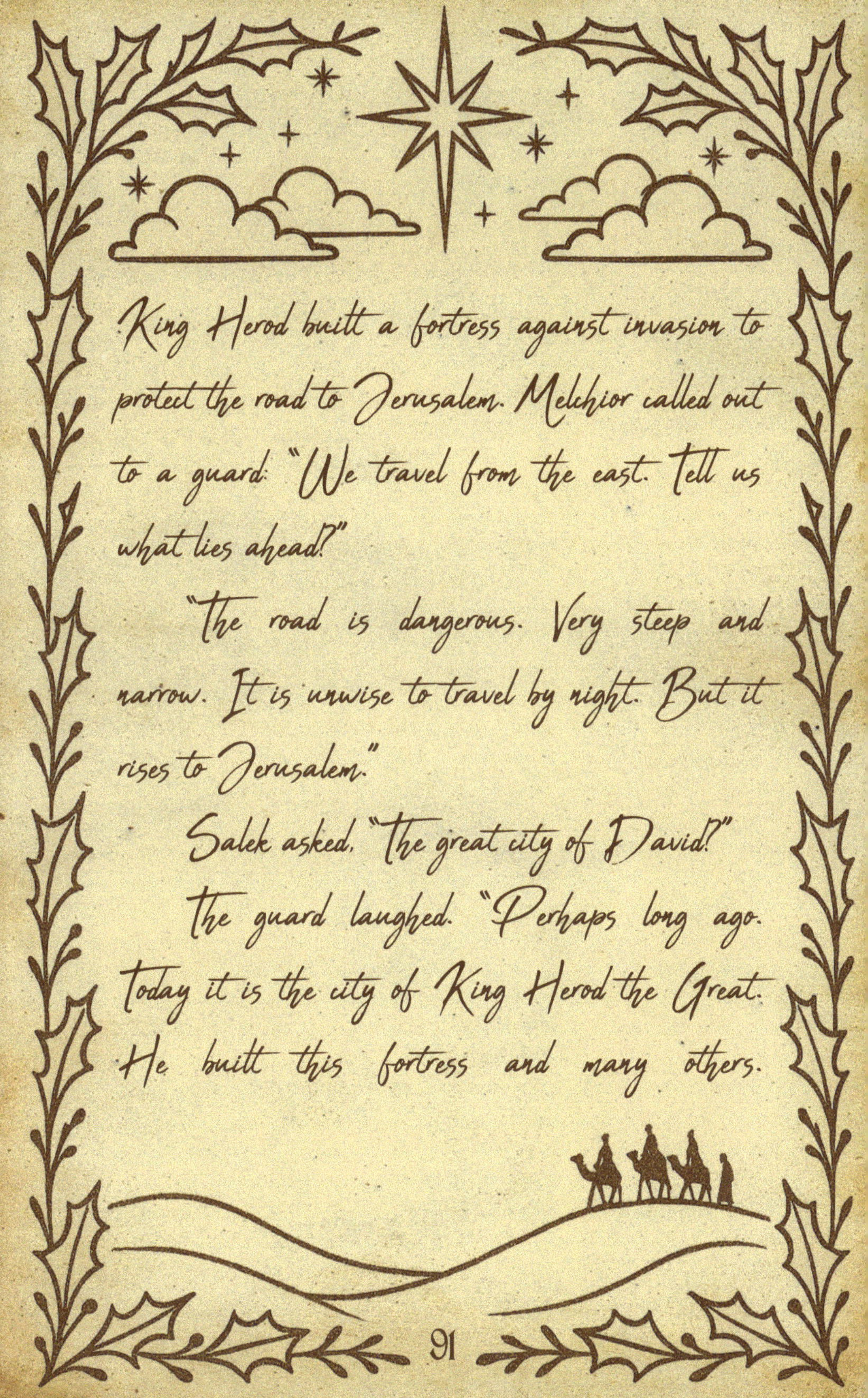

King Herod built a fortress against invasion to protect the road to Jerusalem. Melchior called out to a guard: "We travel from the east. Tell us what lies ahead?"

"The road is dangerous. Very steep and narrow. It is unwise to travel by night. But it rises to Jerusalem."

Salek asked, "The great city of David?"

The guard laughed. "Perhaps long ago. Today it is the city of King Herod the Great. He built this fortress and many others.

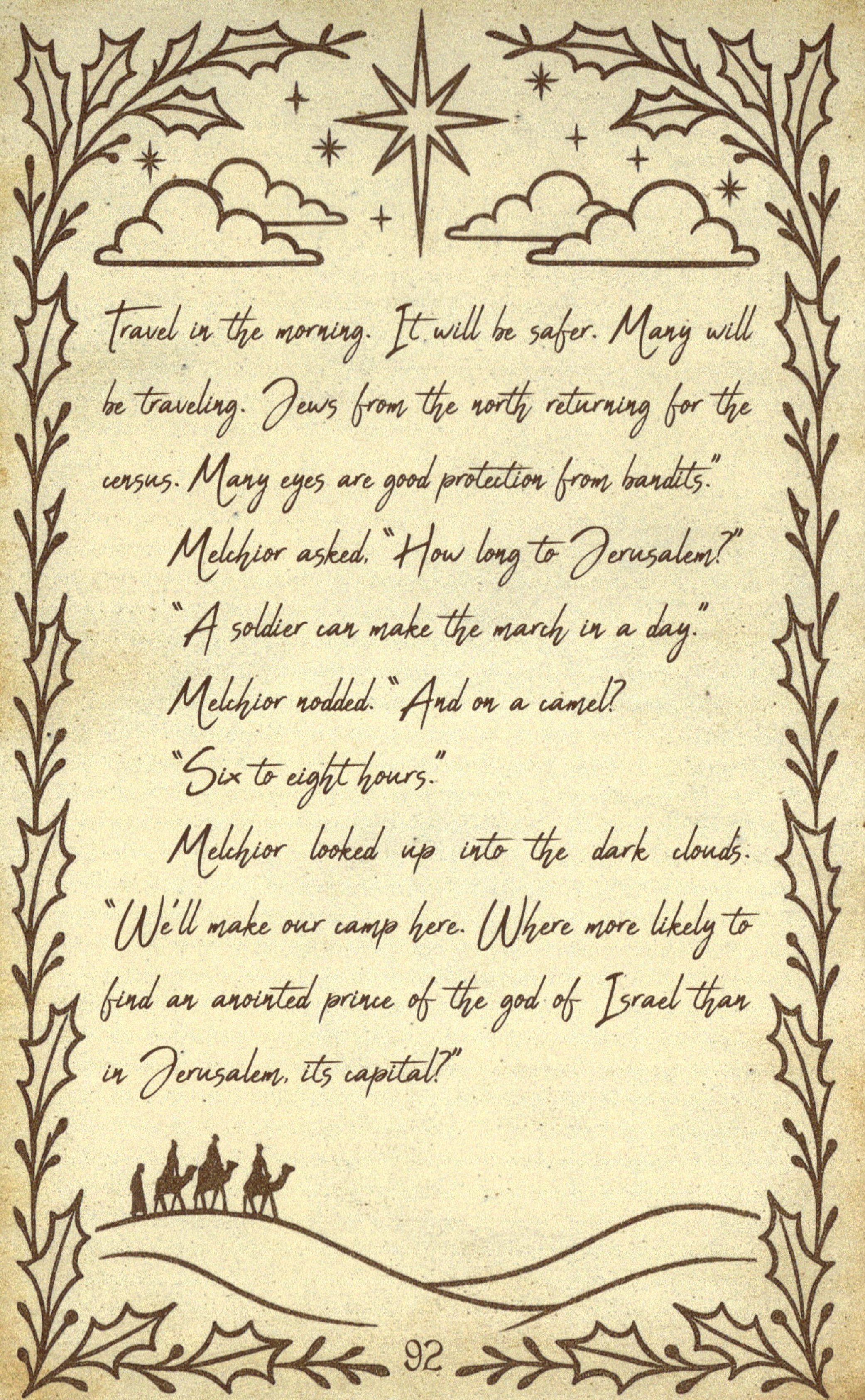

Travel in the morning. It will be safer. Many will be traveling. Jews from the north returning for the census. Many eyes are good protection from bandits."

Melchior asked, "How long to Jerusalem?"

"A soldier can make the march in a day."

Melchior nodded. "And on a camel?

"Six to eight hours."

Melchior looked up into the dark clouds. "We'll make our camp here. Where more likely to find an anointed prince of the god of Israel than in Jerusalem, its capital?"

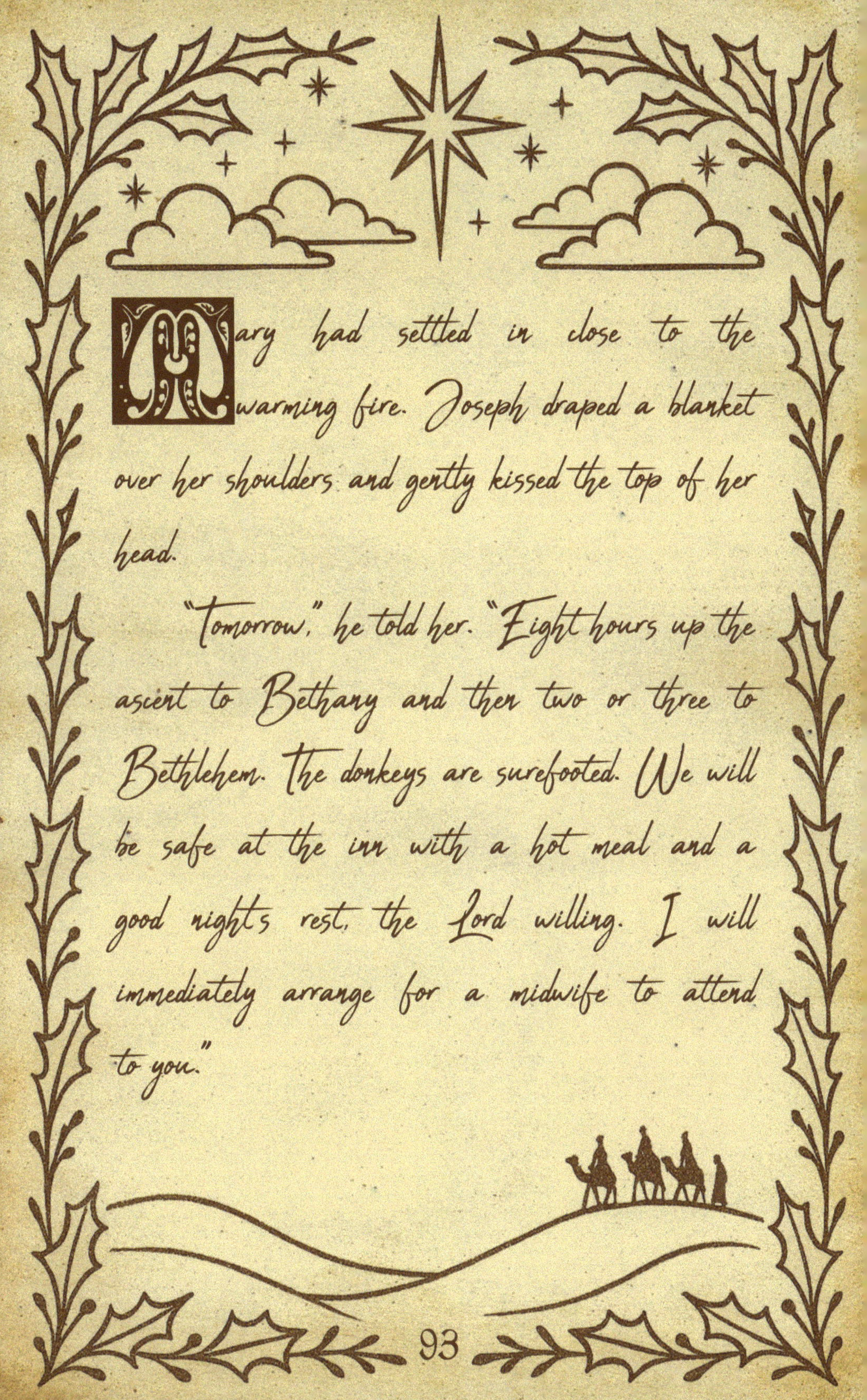

ary had settled in close to the warming fire. Joseph draped a blanket over her shoulders and gently kissed the top of her head.

"Tomorrow," he told her. "Eight hours up the ascent to Bethany and then two or three to Bethlehem. The donkeys are surefooted. We will be safe at the inn with a hot meal and a good night's rest, the Lord willing. I will immediately arrange for a midwife to attend to you."

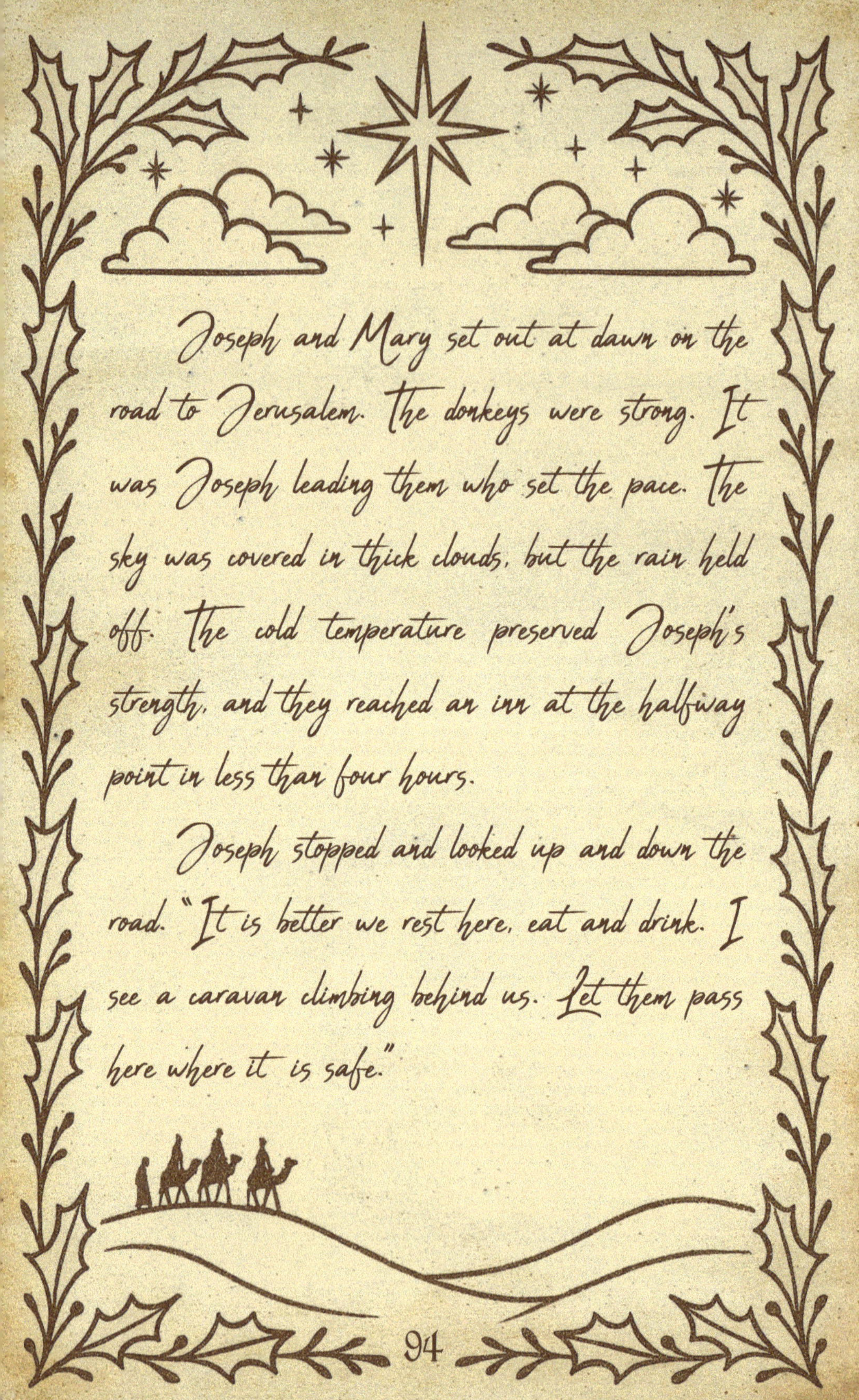

Joseph and Mary set out at dawn on the road to Jerusalem. The donkeys were strong. It was Joseph leading them who set the pace. The sky was covered in thick clouds, but the rain held off. The cold temperature preserved Joseph's strength, and they reached an inn at the halfway point in less than four hours.

Joseph stopped and looked up and down the road. "It is better we rest here, eat and drink. I see a caravan climbing behind us. Let them pass here where it is safe."

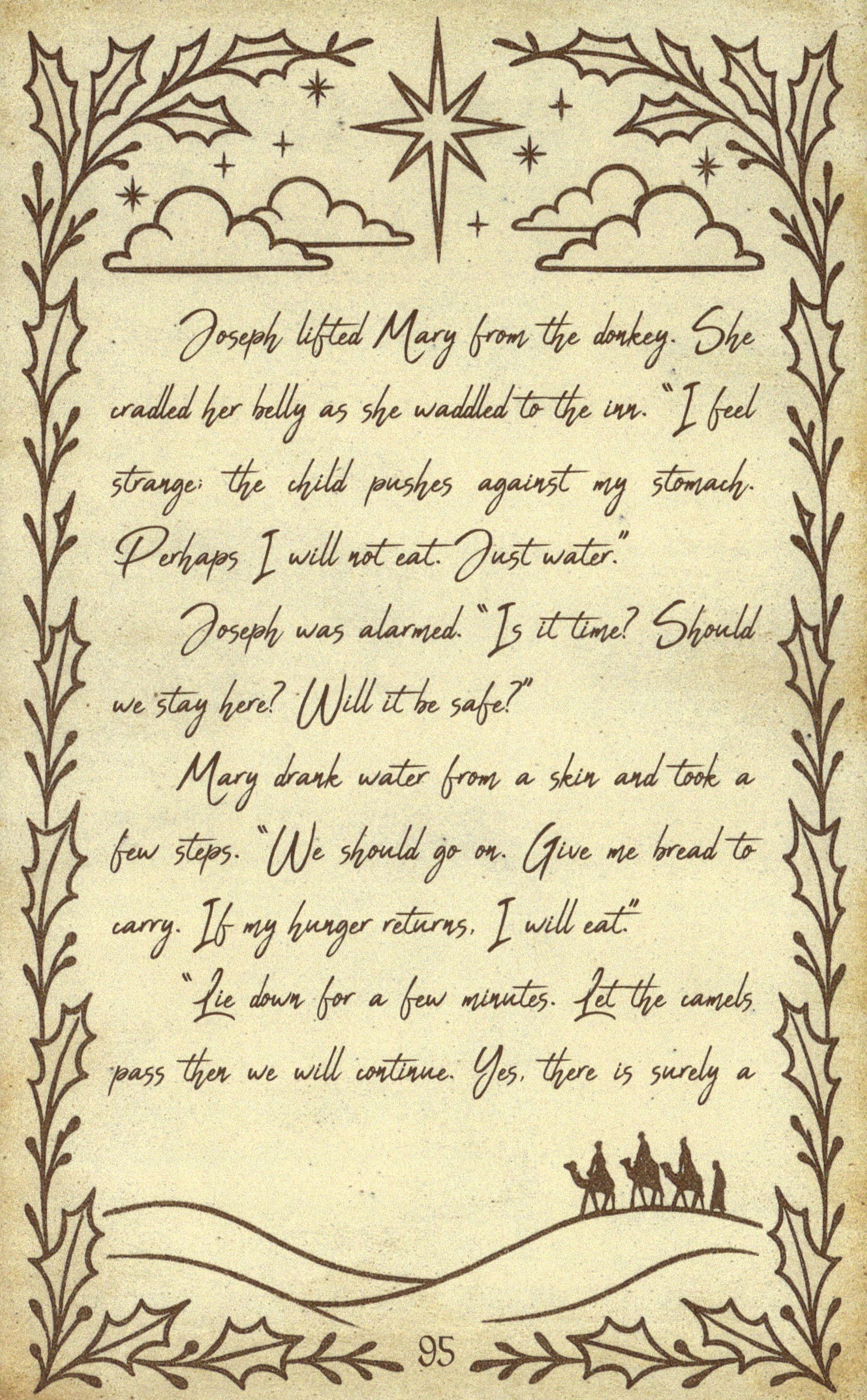

Joseph lifted Mary from the donkey. She cradled her belly as she waddled to the inn. "I feel strange; the child pushes against my stomach. Perhaps I will not eat. Just water."

Joseph was alarmed. "Is it time? Should we stay here? Will it be safe?"

Mary drank water from a skin and took a few steps. "We should go on. Give me bread to carry. If my hunger returns, I will eat."

"Lie down for a few minutes. Let the camels pass then we will continue. Yes, there is surely a

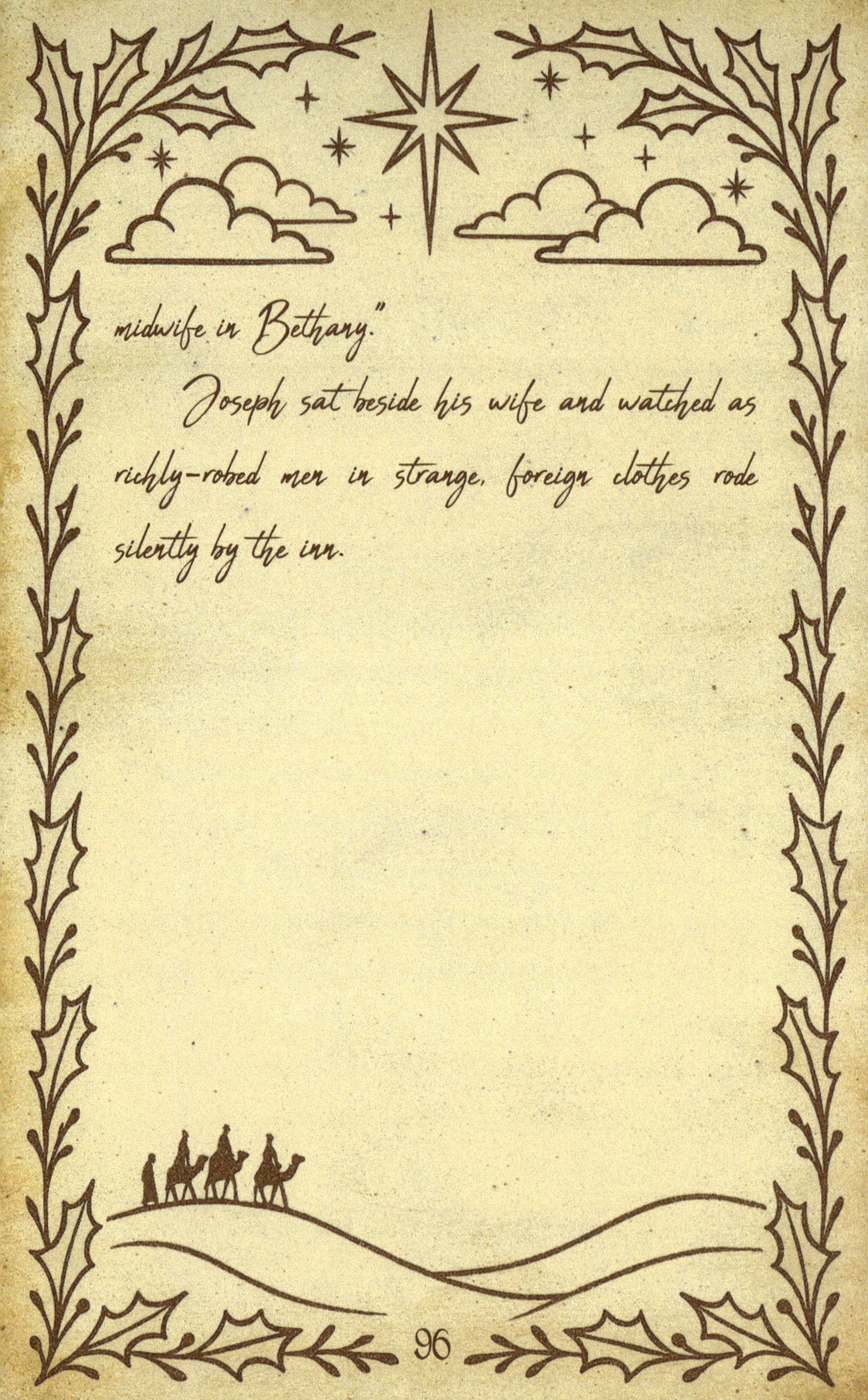

midwife in Bethany."

Joseph sat beside his wife and watched as richly-robed men in strange, foreign clothes rode silently by the inn.

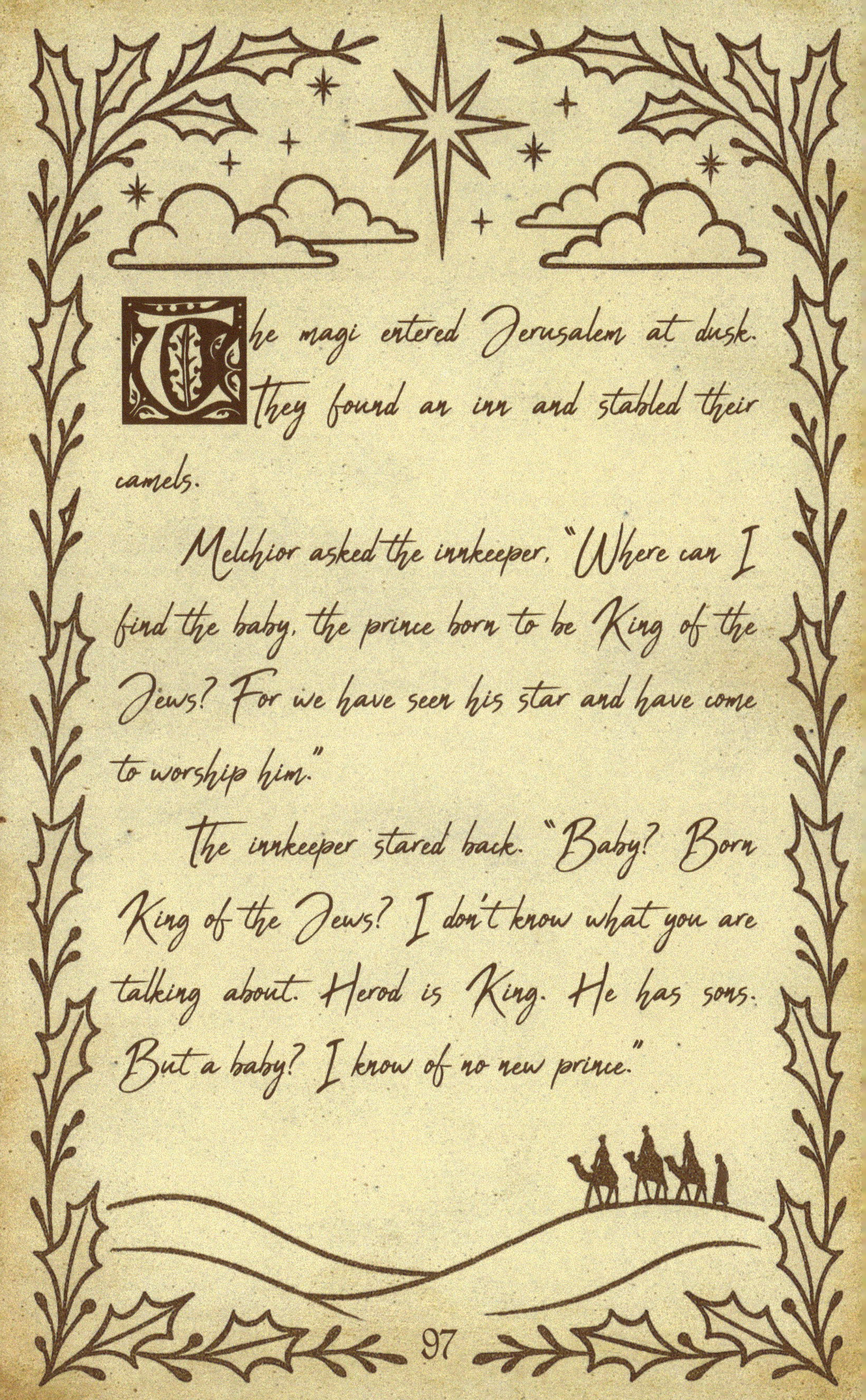

The magi entered Jerusalem at dusk. They found an inn and stabled their camels.

Melchior asked the innkeeper, "Where can I find the baby, the prince born to be King of the Jews? For we have seen his star and have come to worship him."

The innkeeper stared back. "Baby? Born King of the Jews? I don't know what you are talking about. Herod is King. He has sons. But a baby? I know of no new prince."

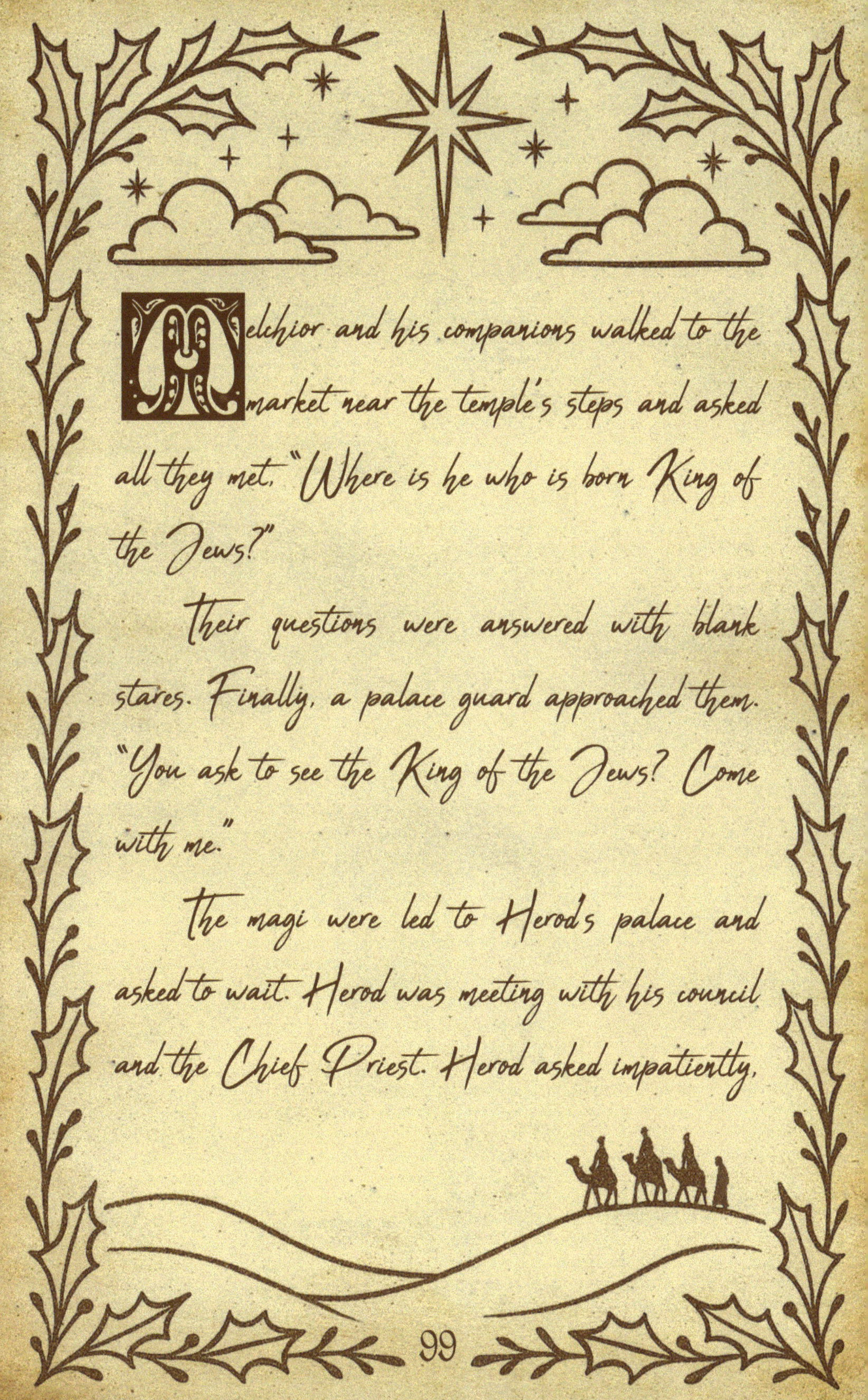

elchior and his companions walked to the market near the temple's steps and asked all they met, "Where is he who is born King of the Jews?"

Their questions were answered with blank stares. Finally, a palace guard approached them. "You ask to see the King of the Jews? Come with me."

The magi were led to Herod's palace and asked to wait. Herod was meeting with his council and the Chief Priest. Herod asked impatiently,

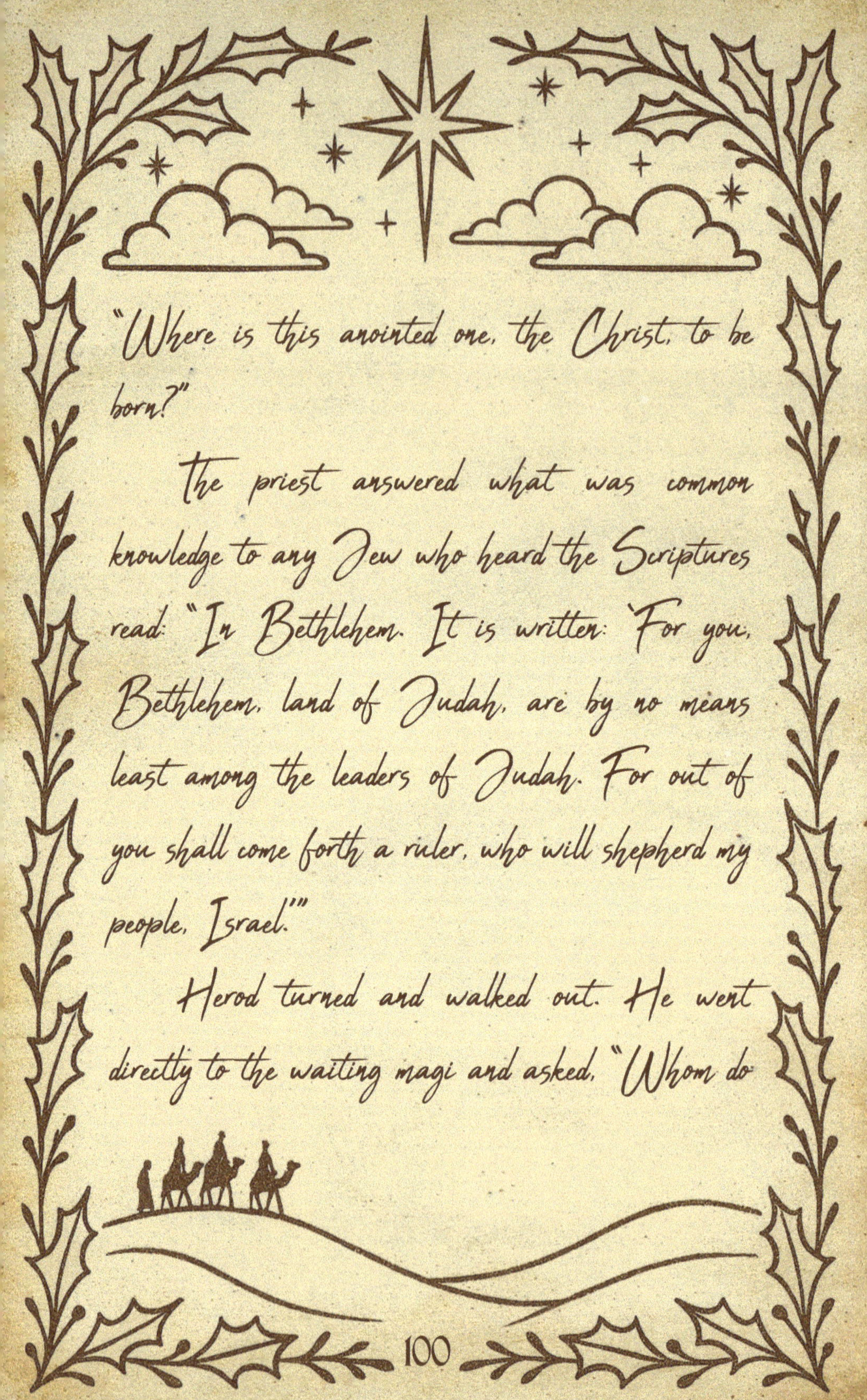

"Where is this anointed one, the Christ, to be born?"

The priest answered what was common knowledge to any Jew who heard the Scriptures read: "In Bethlehem. It is written: For you, Bethlehem, land of Judah, are by no means least among the leaders of Judah. For out of you shall come forth a ruler, who will shepherd my people, Israel.'"

Herod turned and walked out. He went directly to the waiting magi and asked, "Whom do

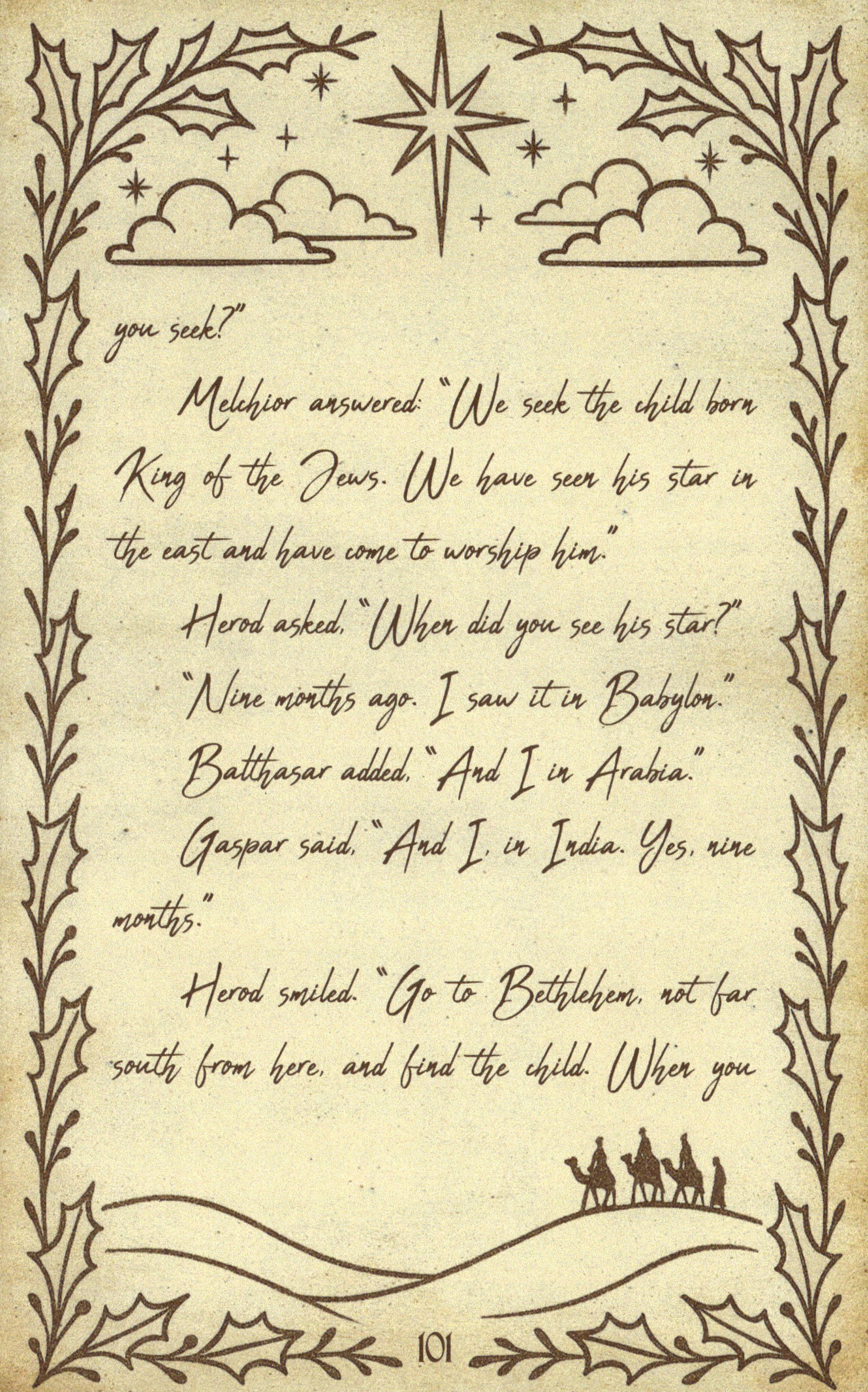

you seek?"

Melchior answered: "We seek the child born King of the Jews. We have seen his star in the east and have come to worship him."

Herod asked, "When did you see his star?"

"Nine months ago. I saw it in Babylon."

Balthasar added, "And I in Arabia."

Gaspar said, "And I, in India. Yes, nine months."

Herod smiled. "Go to Bethlehem, not far south from here, and find the child. When you

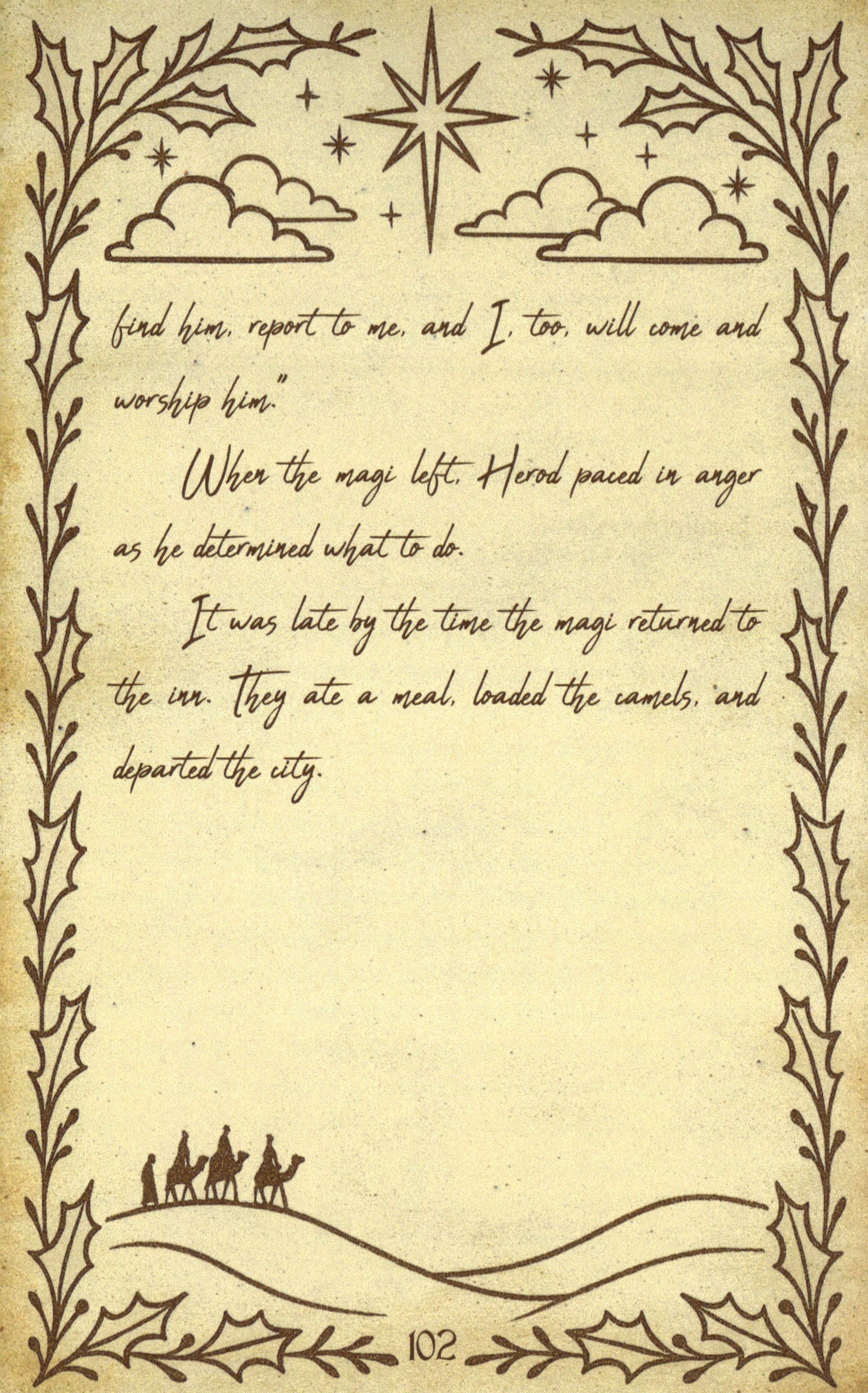

find him, report to me, and I, too, will come and worship him."

When the magi left, Herod paced in anger as he determined what to do.

It was late by the time the magi returned to the inn. They ate a meal, loaded the camels, and departed the city.

Jerusalem
Bethany
Bethlehem

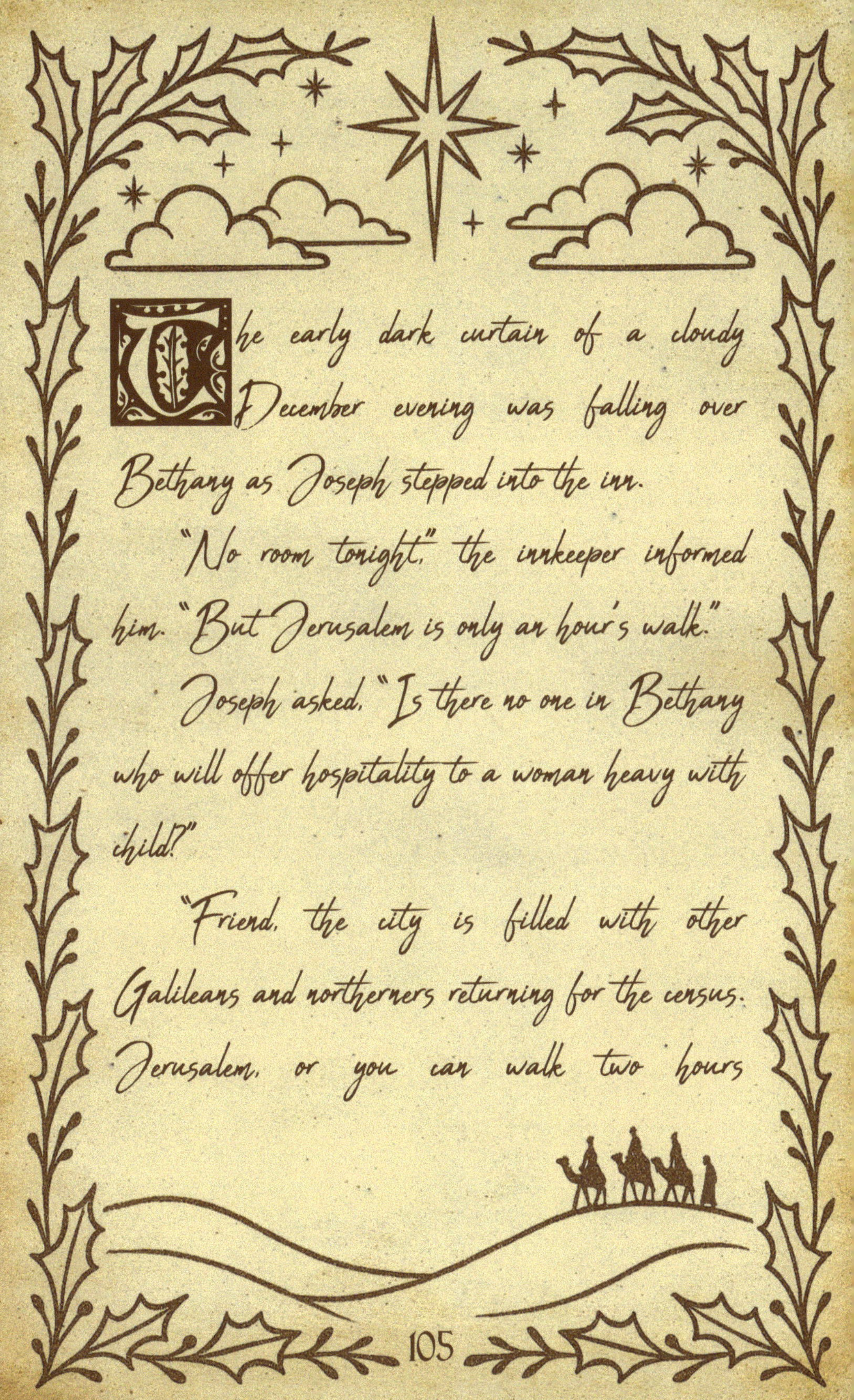

The early dark curtain of a cloudy December evening was falling over Bethany as Joseph stepped into the inn.

"No room tonight," the innkeeper informed him. "But Jerusalem is only an hour's walk."

Joseph asked, "Is there no one in Bethany who will offer hospitality to a woman heavy with child?"

"Friend, the city is filled with other Galileans and northerners returning for the census. Jerusalem, or you can walk two hours

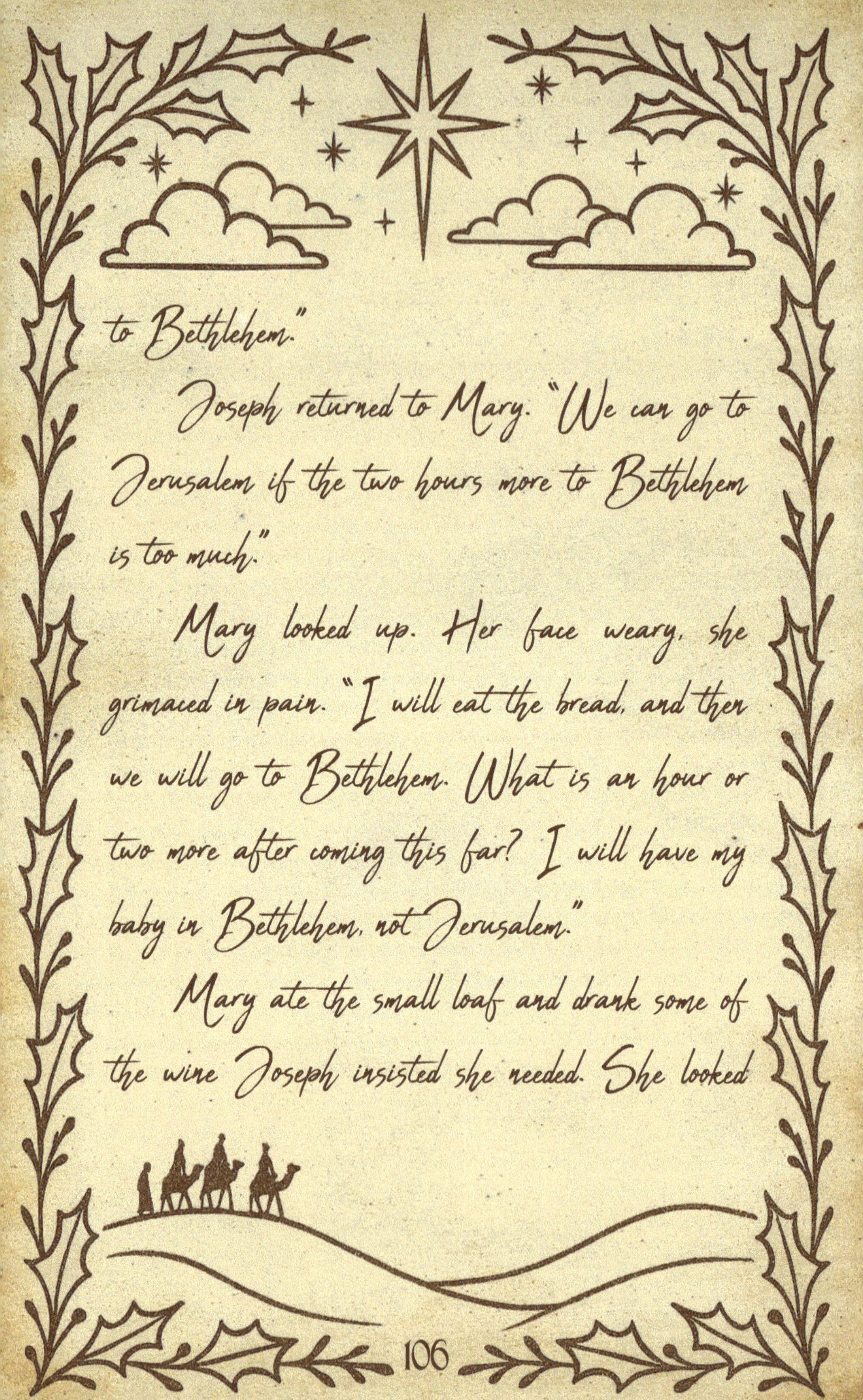

to Bethlehem."

Joseph returned to Mary. "We can go to Jerusalem if the two hours more to Bethlehem is too much."

Mary looked up. Her face weary, she grimaced in pain. "I will eat the bread, and then we will go to Bethlehem. What is an hour or two more after coming this far? I will have my baby in Bethlehem, not Jerusalem."

Mary ate the small loaf and drank some of the wine Joseph insisted she needed. She looked

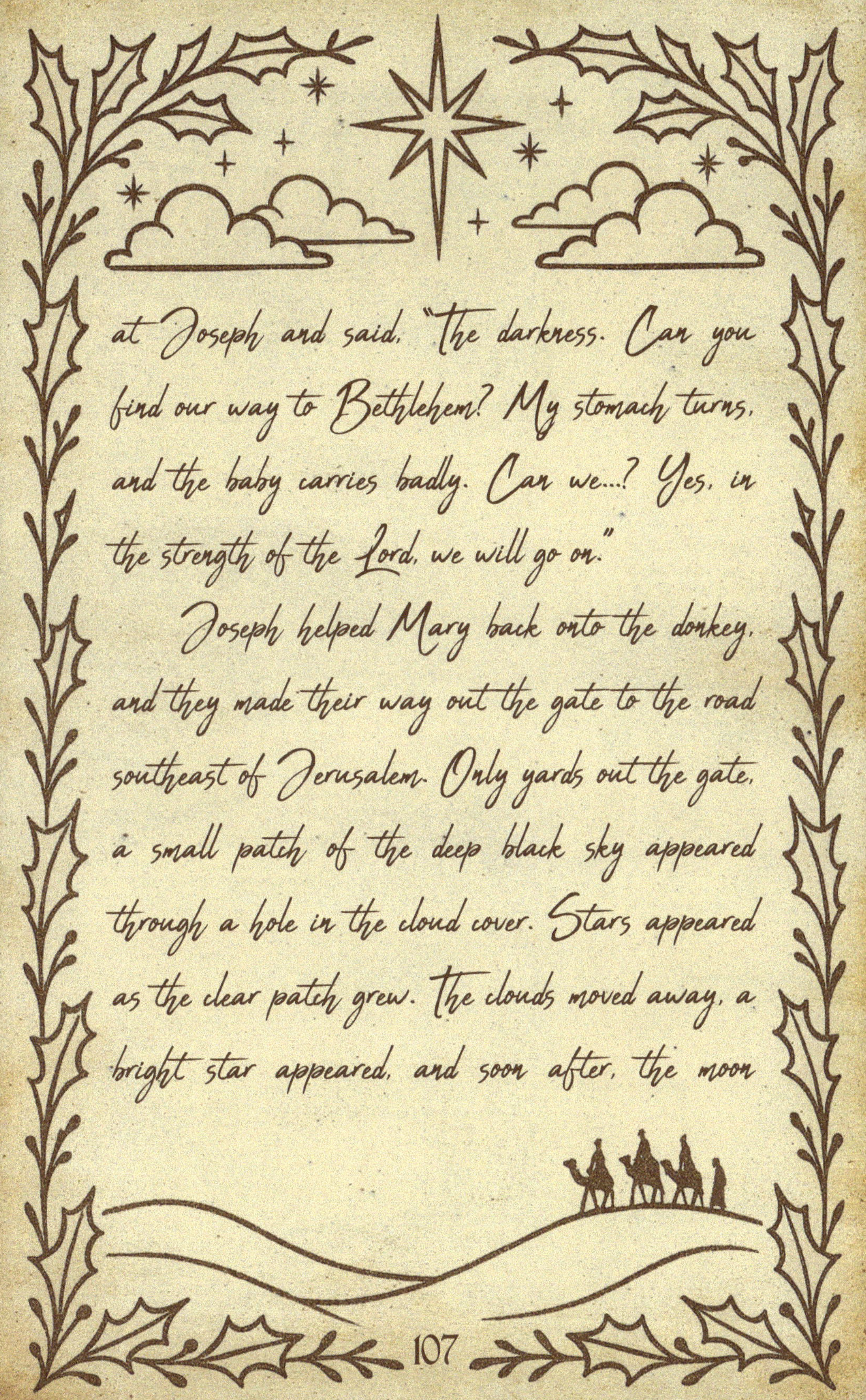

at Joseph and said, "The darkness. Can you find our way to Bethlehem? My stomach turns, and the baby carries badly. Can we...? Yes, in the strength of the Lord, we will go on."

Joseph helped Mary back onto the donkey, and they made their way out the gate to the road southeast of Jerusalem. Only yards out the gate, a small patch of the deep black sky appeared through a hole in the cloud cover. Stars appeared as the clear patch grew. The clouds moved away, a bright star appeared, and soon after, the moon

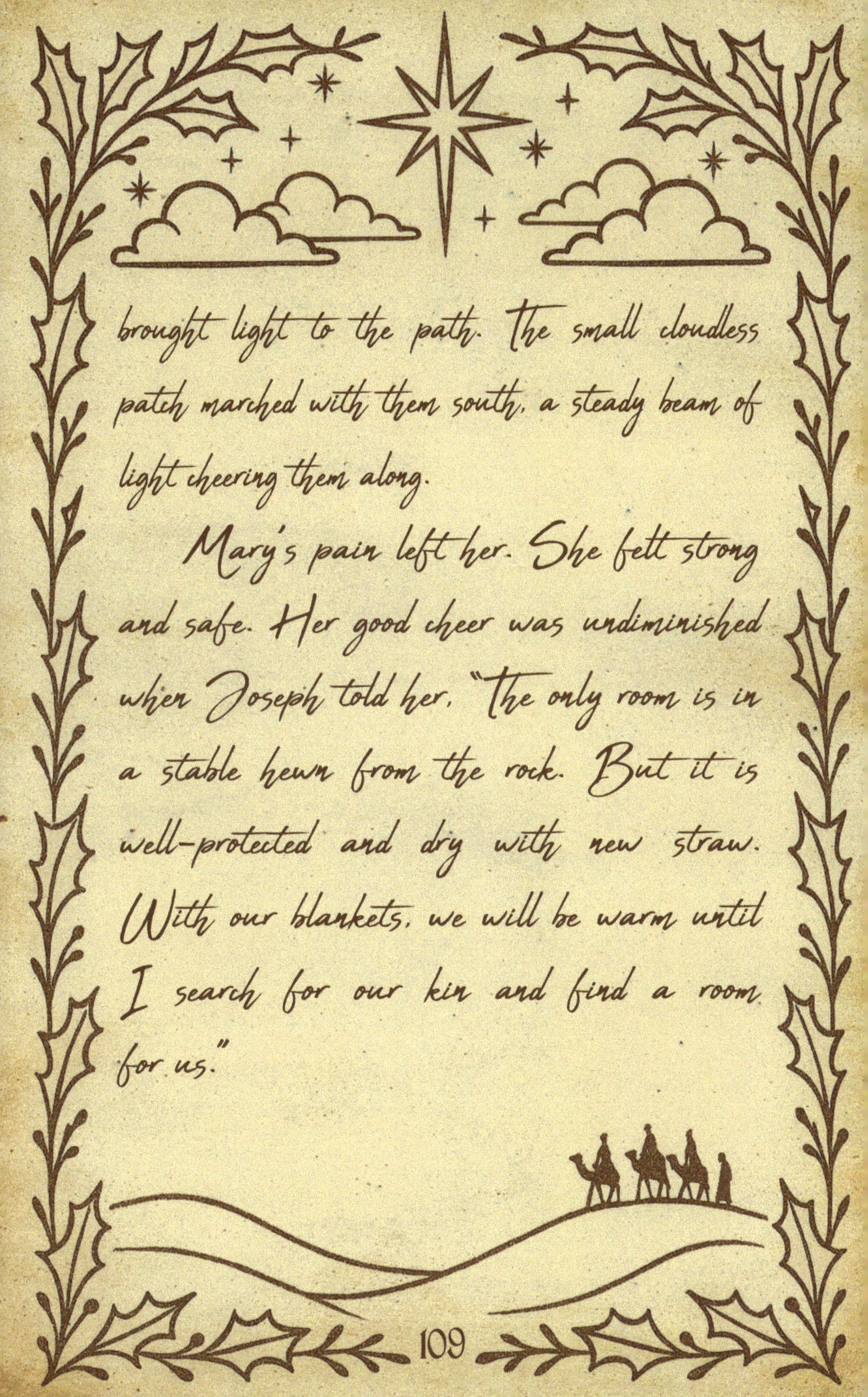

brought light to the path. The small cloudless patch marched with them south, a steady beam of light cheering them along.

Mary's pain left her. She felt strong and safe. Her good cheer was undiminished when Joseph told her, "The only room is in a stable hewn from the rock. But it is well-protected and dry with new straw. With our blankets, we will be warm until I search for our kin and find a room for us."

Mary smiled then looked up at the star. "It seems right to me. Our Father has sent us to this very place."

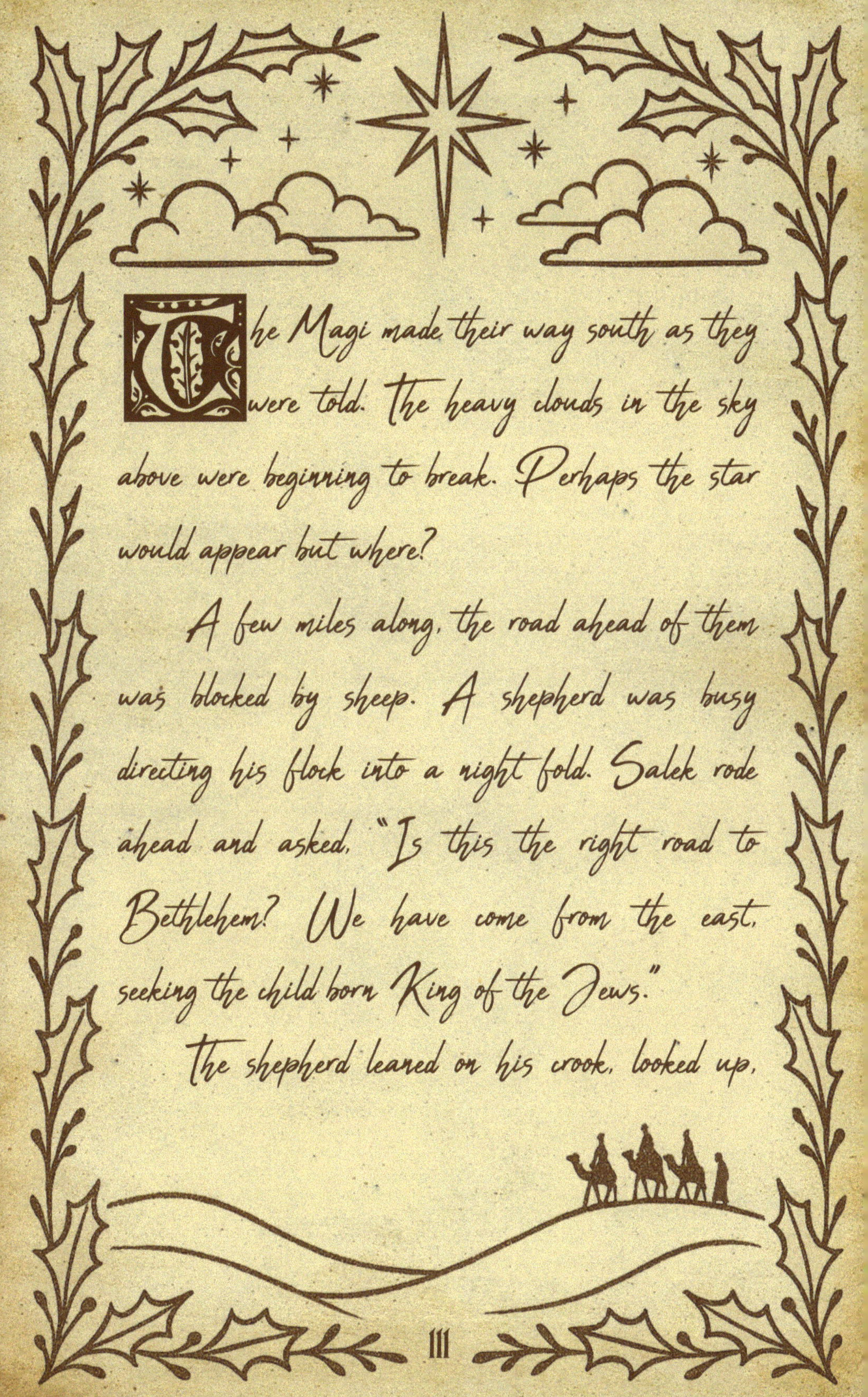

The Magi made their way south as they were told. The heavy clouds in the sky above were beginning to break. Perhaps the star would appear but where?

A few miles along, the road ahead of them was blocked by sheep. A shepherd was busy directing his flock into a night fold. Salek rode ahead and asked, "Is this the right road to Bethlehem? We have come from the east, seeking the child born *King of the Jews.*"

The shepherd leaned on his crook, looked up,

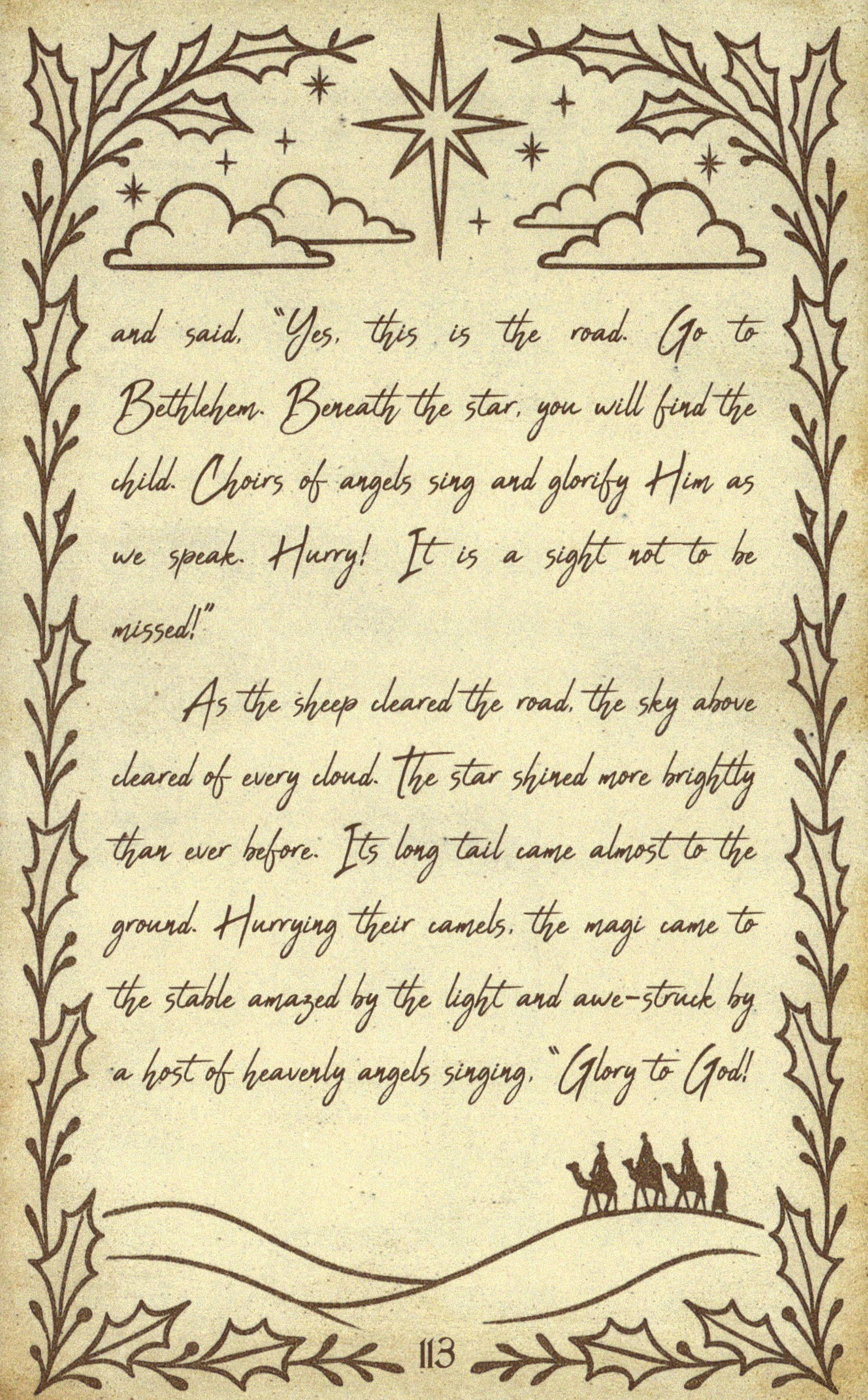

and said, "Yes, this is the road. Go to Bethlehem. Beneath the star, you will find the child. Choirs of angels sing and glorify Him as we speak. Hurry! It is a sight not to be missed!"

As the sheep cleared the road, the sky above cleared of every cloud. The star shined more brightly than ever before. Its long tail came almost to the ground. Hurrying their camels, the magi came to the stable amazed by the light and awe-struck by a host of heavenly angels singing, "Glory to God!

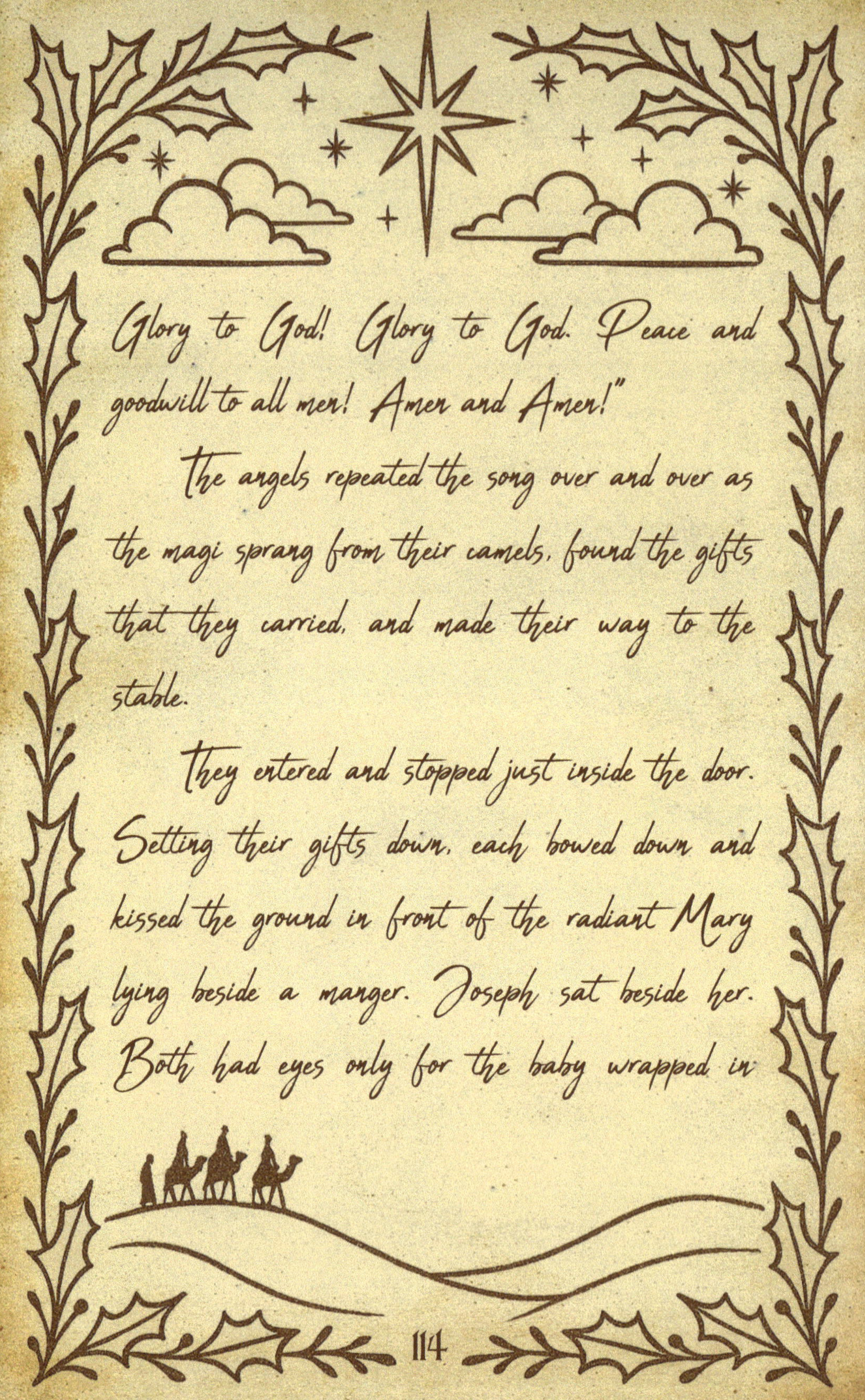

Glory to God! Glory to God. Peace and goodwill to all men! Amen and Amen!"

The angels repeated the song over and over as the magi sprang from their camels, found the gifts that they carried, and made their way to the stable.

They entered and stopped just inside the door. Setting their gifts down, each bowed down and kissed the ground in front of the radiant Mary lying beside a manger. Joseph sat beside her. Both had eyes only for the baby wrapped in

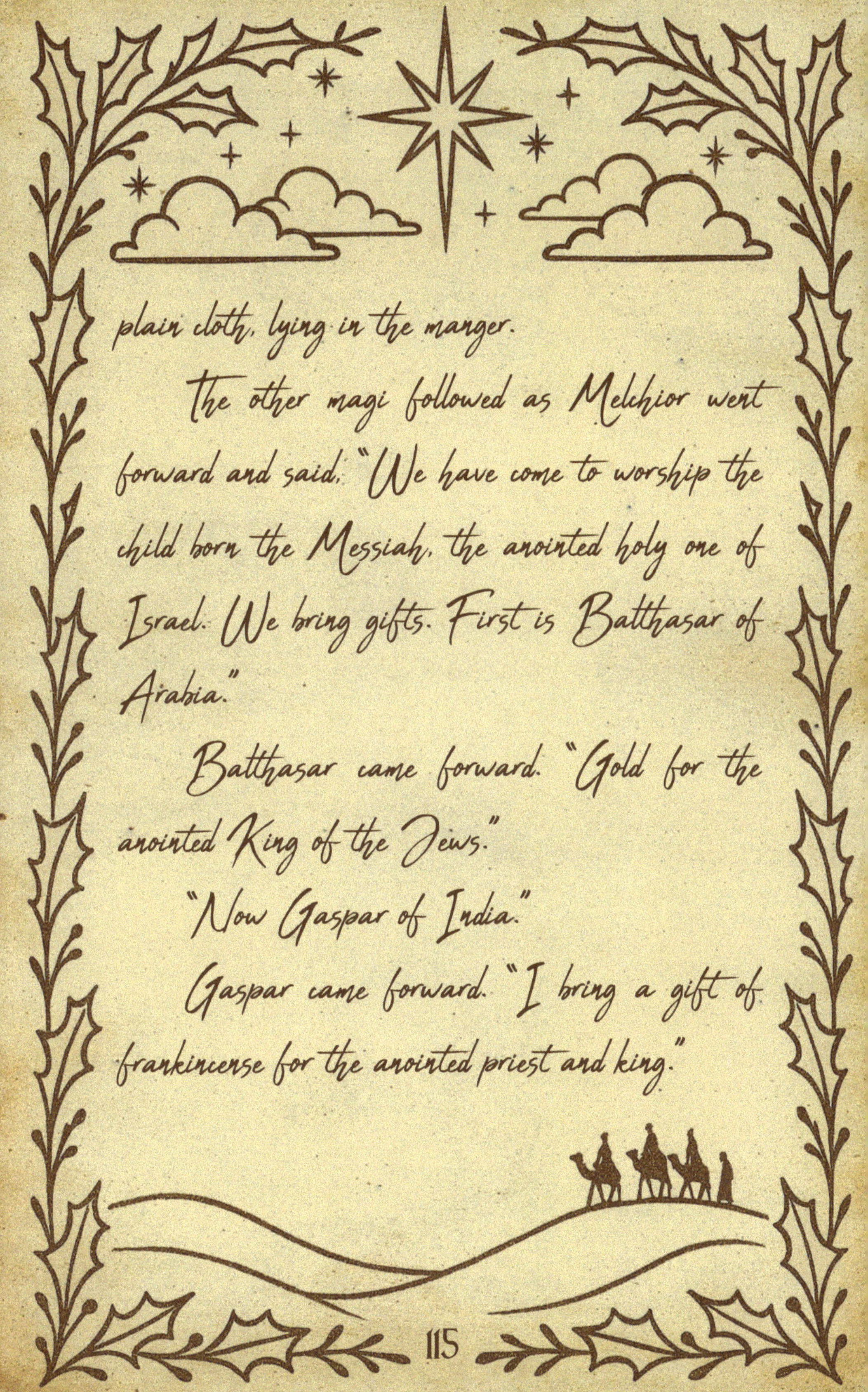

plain cloth, lying in the manger.

The other magi followed as Melchior went forward and said, "We have come to worship the child born the Messiah, the anointed holy one of Israel. We bring gifts. First is Balthasar of Arabia."

Balthasar came forward. "Gold for the anointed King of the Jews."

"Now Gaspar of India."

Gaspar came forward. "I bring a gift of frankincense for the anointed priest and king."

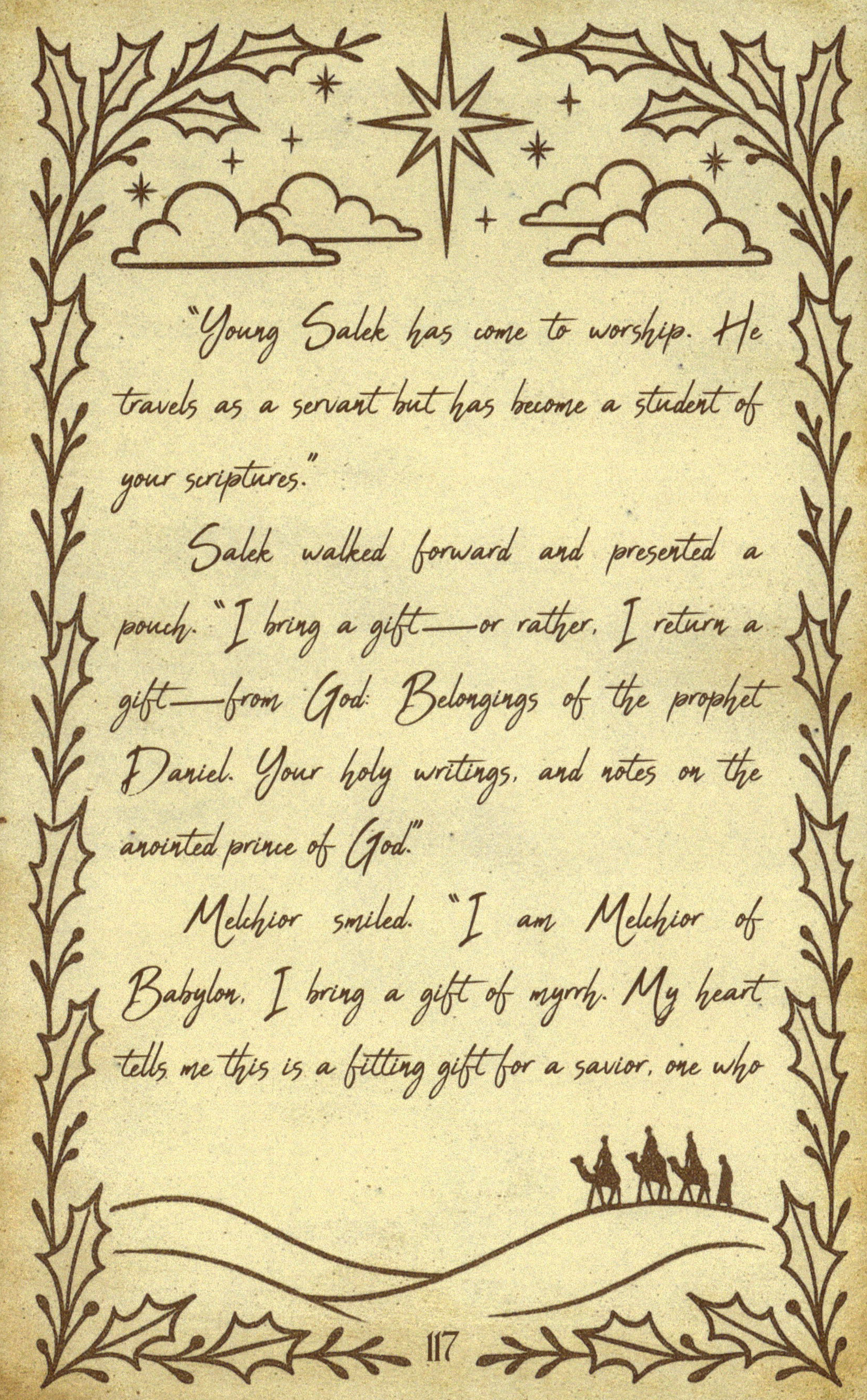

"Young Salek has come to worship. He travels as a servant but has become a student of your scriptures."

Salek walked forward and presented a pouch. "I bring a gift——or rather, I return a gift——from God: Belongings of the prophet Daniel. Your holy writings, and notes on the anointed prince of God."

Melchior smiled. "I am Melchior of Babylon. I bring a gift of myrrh. My heart tells me this is a fitting gift for a savior, one who

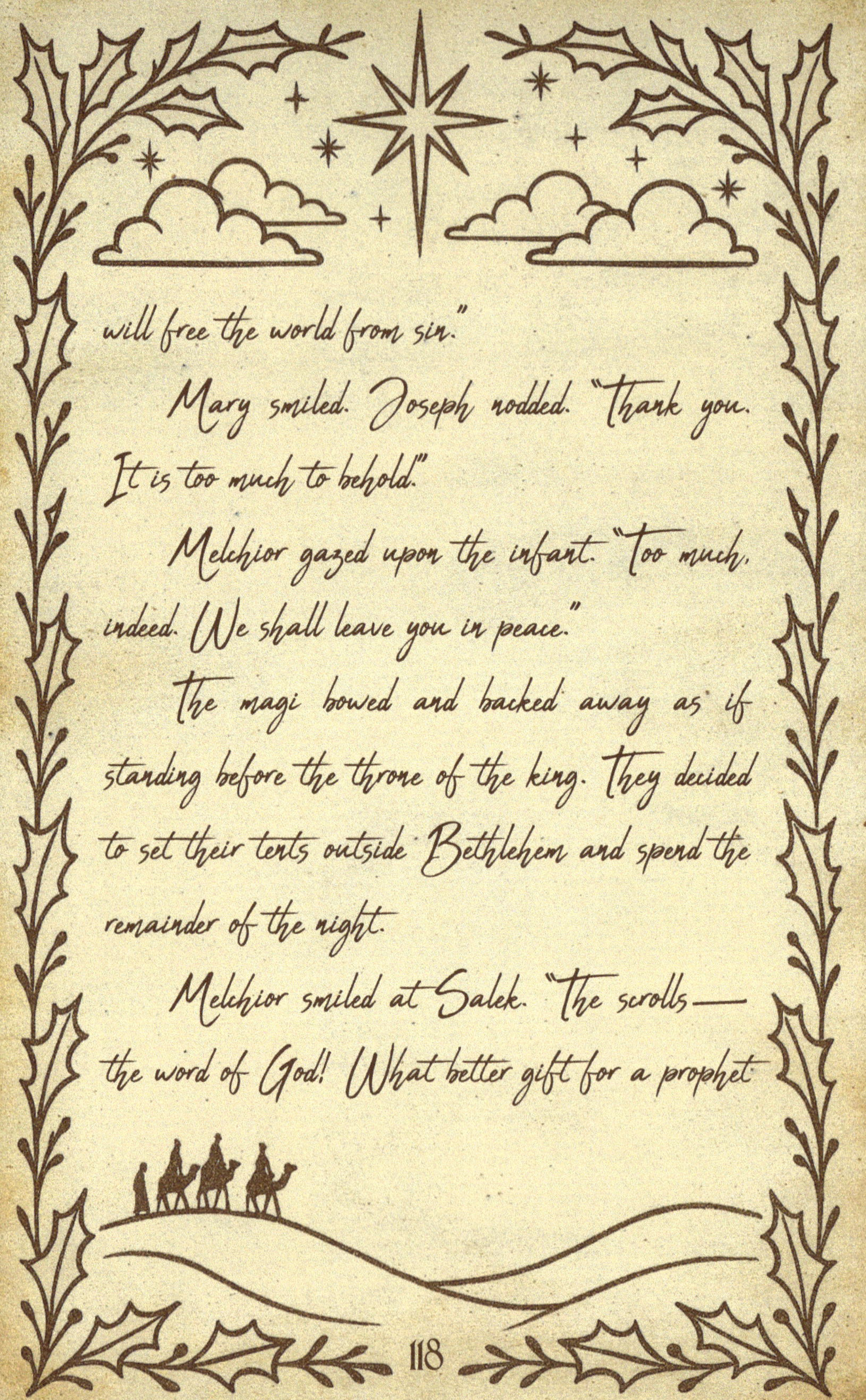

will free the world from sin."

Mary smiled. Joseph nodded. "Thank you. It is too much to behold."

Melchior gazed upon the infant. "Too much, indeed. We shall leave you in peace."

The magi bowed and backed away as if standing before the throne of the king. They decided to set their tents outside Bethlehem and spend the remainder of the night.

Melchior smiled at Salek. "The scrolls—the word of God! What better gift for a prophet

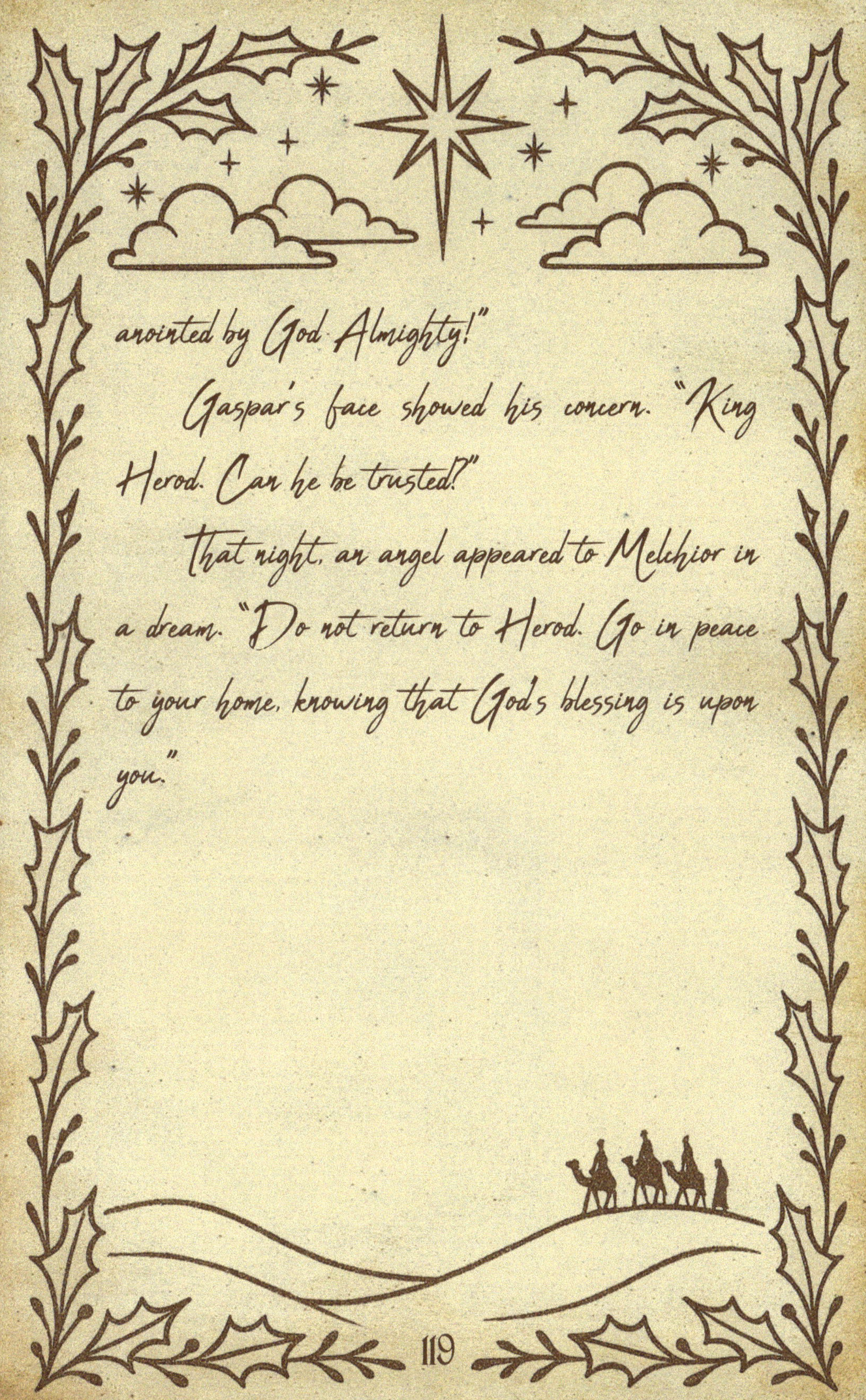

anointed by God Almighty!"

Gaspar's face showed his concern. "King Herod. Can he be trusted?"

That night, an angel appeared to Melchior in a dream. "Do not return to Herod. Go in peace to your home, knowing that God's blessing is upon you."

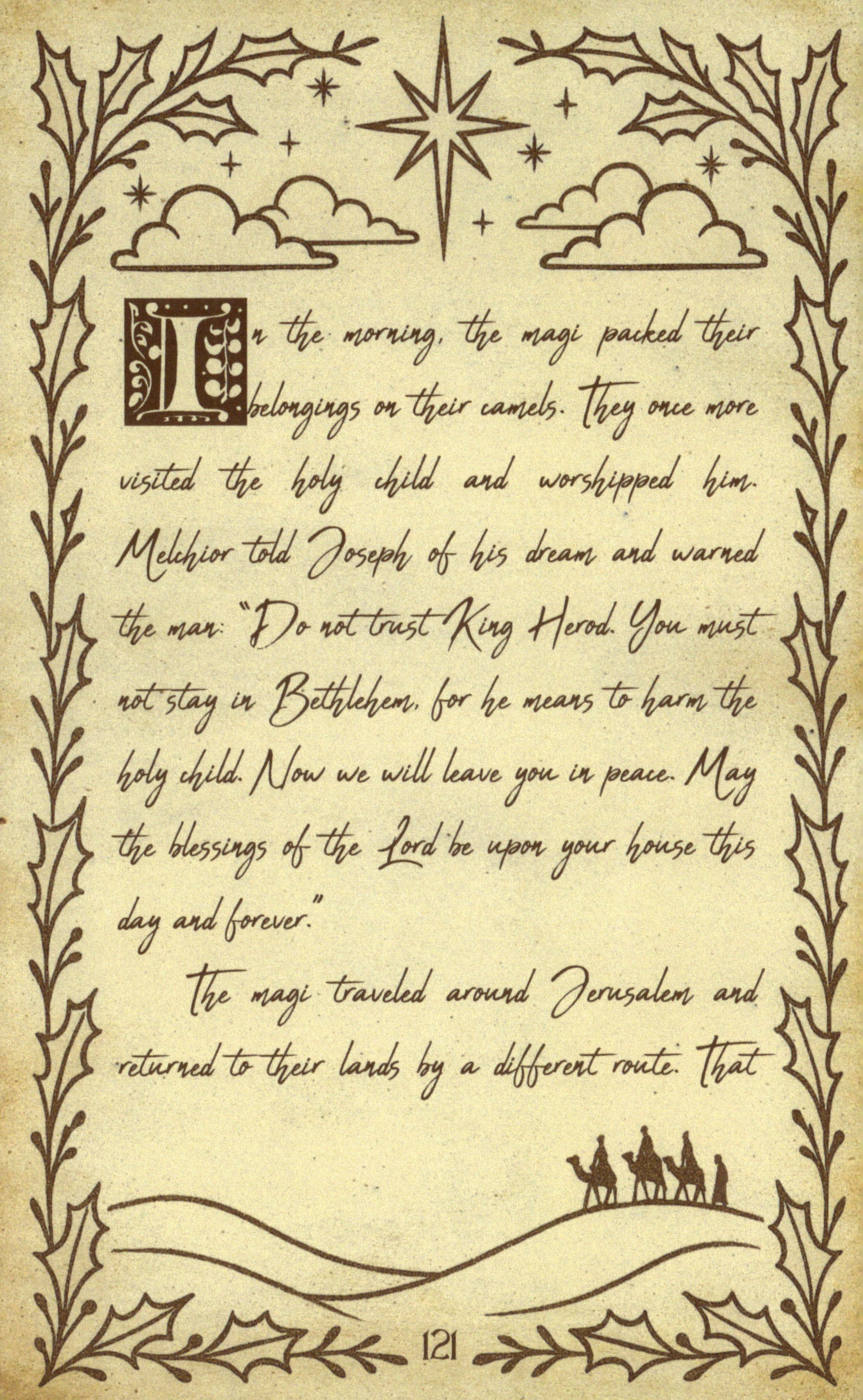

In the morning, the magi packed their belongings on their camels. They once more visited the holy child and worshipped him. Melchior told Joseph of his dream and warned the man: "Do not trust King Herod. You must not stay in Bethlehem, for he means to harm the holy child. Now we will leave you in peace. May the blessings of the Lord be upon your house this day and forever."

The magi traveled around Jerusalem and returned to their lands by a different route. That

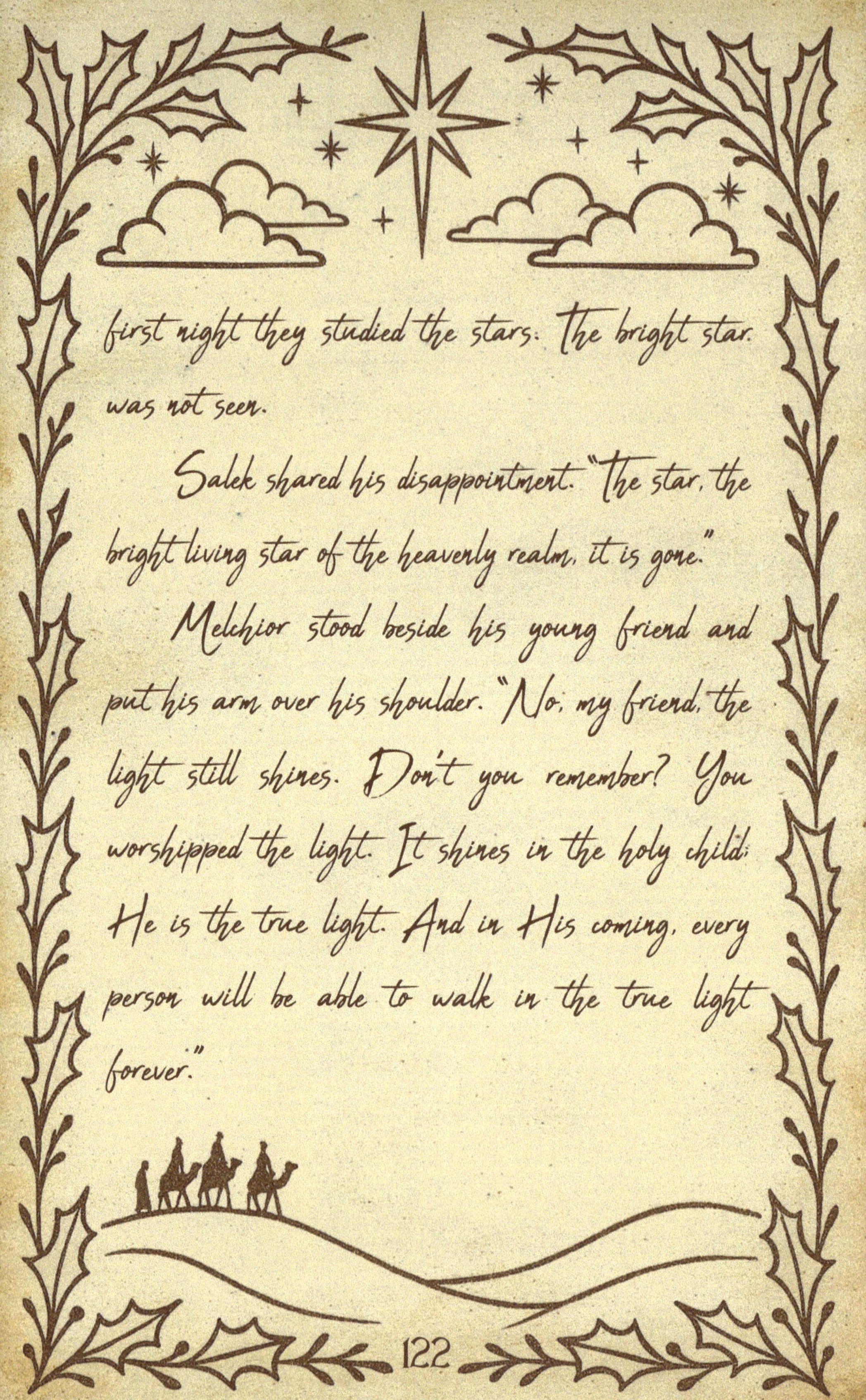

first night they studied the stars. The bright star was not seen.

Salek shared his disappointment. "The star, the bright living star of the heavenly realm, it is gone."

Melchior stood beside his young friend and put his arm over his shoulder. "No, my friend, the light still shines. Don't you remember? You worshipped the light. It shines in the holy child. He is the true light. And in His coming, every person will be able to walk in the true light forever."

ABOUT THE AUTHOR

David Martyn retired from a career in the Maritime industry and lives in Gig Harbor, Washington (nicknamed the Maritime City) with his wife Karen. David writes Christian fiction.